Praise for
The Liar Society

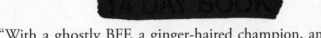

"With a ghostly BFF, a ginger-haired champion, and a super-hot boy, *The Liar Society* is a page-turning, pearl-clutching mystery!"

—Kimberly Derting, author of *The Body Finder*
and *Desires of the Dead*

"Who doesn't think their high school is conspiring against them? Toss in an unsolved murder, unstoppable heroine, ancient puzzles, and a hot guy and you've got one killer novel."

—Lee Nichols, author of the Haunting Emma series

"A masterful blend of suspense and danger—from the first page to the nail-biting conclusion, *The Liar Society* takes hold and never lets go."

—Mandy Hubbard, author of *Prada & Prejudice*
and *You Wish*

"A romantic mystery so suspenseful, so snort-out-loud funny, so disarmingly charming, that the moment you finish is when you'll want to start writing your fan letter, begging for more."

—Adele Griffin, National Book Award Finalist and author
of *The Julian Game* and *Picture the Dead*

DEMCO

THE LIAR SOCIETY

LISA & LAURA ROECKER

sourcebooks
fire

To Mike, for looking out for all of us

Published by Sourcebooks Fire, an imprint of Sourcebooks, Inc.
P.O. Box 4410, Naperville, Illinois 60567-4410
(630) 961-3900
Fax: (630) 961-2168
teenfire.sourcebooks.com

Library of Congress Cataloging-in-Publication data is on file with the publisher.

Printed and bound in the United States of America.
VP 10 9 8 7 6 5 4 3 2 1

Chapter 1

Her email didn't move or disappear or do any of the creepy things I'd expect an email from a ghost to do. It was just there.

Existing.

To: KateLowry@pemberlybrown.edu

Sent: Tues 11:59 PM

From: GraceLee@pemberlybrown.edu

Subject: (no subject)

Kate,

I'm here...

Sort of.

Find Cameron.

He knows.

I shouldn't be writing.

Don't tell.

They'll hurt you.

The words blurred on the screen, and my hands went limp. My phone clattered to the hardwood floor, the battery popping off and sliding beneath my bed.

Dead best friends didn't send emails.

I shook my head fiercely in an attempt to clear my thoughts. It was the anniversary of her death, and I missed Grace more than anything. Maybe my mind was just playing tricks on me. Maybe this wasn't really happening.

I took a deep breath, grabbed my laptop, and refreshed my mail. My hand flew to cover my mouth when I saw her name on the screen again. As much as I wanted to believe that the email was from Grace, my mind just couldn't make the leap.

Maybe this was some kind of joke, but that kind of cruelty didn't seem possible. Plus we guarded our email passwords with our lives, and there was no way anyone was capable of hacking into the school's database.

When I reread the words, something deep inside of me—buried beneath all the anger and guilt—woke up. It was as though I'd spent the last year living in a fog of grief and regret, and suddenly the atmosphere had cleared. My room looked the same, but the blue of the walls was more vibrant, the white of my duvet brighter.

I had sent Grace hundreds of emails over the past year. Trying to describe how much I missed her, how much my life sucked without her, and how much I needed my best friend back. I kept expecting our school, Pemberly Brown, to delete her account, kept waiting for the moment my emails would bounce back undeliverable. But that moment never came. Was it possible that after all this time, after all those emails, Grace had actually written me back?

I'm here...

She was where? In my room? A trickle of sweat rolled down the center of my chest, sending a fresh trail of goose bumps straight down my legs.

"Grace?" My voice cracked.

As soon as the sound left my lips, I regretted it. *Really, Kate? A ghost?* No wonder my parents sent me to a shrink.

My mind reeled. What if she wasn't a ghost? What if Grace was still alive? I remembered her funeral like one of those black-and-white silent movies. People's lips moved, but I couldn't make out the words. The memory was grainy and parts were missing, as though someone had forgotten to tape back together the pieces of a broken filmstrip. One image remained clear, though: the casket at the altar, its lid tightly closed, the box that looked way too small to hold my best friend.

Maybe there had been some terrible misunderstanding...maybe Grace was still out there somewhere.

I read her words again, and this time one word, one name stuck. *Cameron.*

I leaped up from my chair, misjudged the distance between knee and desk, and slammed into the wood.

I squeezed my eyes shut for a second. The humid September air hung heavy in the room, practically suffocating me as I tried to make sense of her words. The email was a clue, a clue I'd spent the last year trying to find. Someone or something was trying to tell me what I'd always known in my heart: Grace's death was more than just a horrible accident.

She needed my help.

The chair scraped against the floor as I pushed it in front of my closet, climbed on top, and pulled down the huge box that held the artifacts of our friendship. I ran my fingers over the word "Memories" written on the box. A fat tear landed on the *o* and magnified the letter. I hadn't even realized I was crying. As I pressed my palms against my eyes, I willed the tears to stop. I had to focus.

The ceiling fan rattled overhead, fighting a losing battle against the heat, and as soon as I lifted the box's lid, a bunch of the emails I'd sent to Grace over the past year scattered onto my bed. I shoved the ones still in the box aside impatiently, not completely sure why I printed them in the first place.

I guess maybe I needed my words to be real. Sometimes sending my thoughts out into cyberspace to Grace wasn't enough. The emails were proof that she had existed and proof that, for me, she was still out there somewhere. And as crazy as it sounds, part of me always hoped that somehow, somewhere, she could read them.

I picked up the pink-and-purple jewelry box Grace had given me for my seventh birthday. It used to be full of the half-heart charms that marked our friendship—bracelets, necklaces, even dangle earrings that Grace couldn't wear because her parents never let her get her ears pierced. But now there was only one piece of jewelry left—Grace's pearls. I hadn't touched them since her mother had tearfully wound them around my wrist like a rosary after the funeral.

I lifted the lock and opened the lid. The long strand of pearls filled the box, and I imagined Grace twisting the necklace around her finger like she always did when she was lost in thought or cooking up another one of her schemes. I looped the beads around my neck three times, just like Grace used to. Their weight was somehow reassuring, and it gave me the strength to finally unearth the picture frame.

And there she was.

Grace.

Actually, the picture was of the three of us—me, Maddie, and Grace. Best friends forever. It had been taken two summers ago—before everything and everyone changed.

None of us had been ready when Grace's mom snapped the shot. We begged her to take another as we huddled in front of the camera. I pointed to my eyes, squinty because I was laughing so hard; Maddie grumbled that her face looked fat, self-consciously pinching the skin beneath her chin; and Grace complained that we were too old for pictures, threatening to hit Delete. But Mrs. Lee pulled the camera out of our reach and waved her hand. She promised that the picture had captured everything we'd want to remember about that summer.

And she was right: the picture was perfect.

I picked up the frame and stared into Grace's eyes—her best feature. They were dark and almond shaped, and she always looked like she was wearing eyeliner, even though makeup was strictly forbidden in the Lee house.

Genuine smiles lit our faces, and I could almost hear the echo of our laughter. We were happy in that just-before-high-school way when it was still cool to ride your bike to the pool or eat box after box of Hot Tamales while playing truth or dare in a tent set up in your friend's backyard.

I missed that kind of happy.

A strand of my bright pink hair slipped from behind my ear, only one reminder of how much had changed. I put the picture aside and dug through the box until I found the small white notebook decorated with glitter, rhinestones, and puff paint. It looked like an entire craft store had thrown up on the cover.

I remembered the sleepover in seventh grade when Grace had decided we needed a slam book to hold our deepest and darkest secrets. Each page had a different question, and each of us had chosen a different color to write our "secret" answers. Grace had chosen orange, as usual.

My stomach lurched a little as I flipped through the book and scanned the pages for her loopy handwriting.

Favorite Outfit?

Dark jeans and anything orange.

Best Friends?

Kate and Maddie (of course).

Dream Vacation?

Anywhere with white sand and turquoise blue water.

Dream Job?

Broadway performer or doctor, maybe both?

And finally I found the page I was looking for: Biggest Crush? And there, written with Grace's obnoxious orange glitter pen, was the name.

Cameron Thompson

Cameron was Grace's next-door neighbor, and because we'd spent every waking moment from kindergarten on at Grace's house, we had all practically grown up together. It was no secret that as soon as we all decided to like boys, Grace decided to like Cameron. I knew it, Maddie knew it, even Cameron knew it.

Despite her suffocating parents, Grace almost always got what she wanted, and Cameron was no exception.

Of course, Grace wanted a lot of things.

My mind flashed back to the days before her death, her secret smiles and quiet text sessions. Maddie and I had known something was going on, but Grace only laughed and said she'd tell us everything...eventually.

I remembered passing Cameron in the halls at school after Grace was gone, his bloodshot eyes telling of too many late-night parties, too many early-morning detentions, and not nearly enough self-control. I figured he was probably the only person who missed Grace as much as Maddie and I did, but until this moment, it had never occurred to me that he might be hiding more than a nasty drug habit. That he might actually be hiding the truth.

I laid the slam book aside and pulled my knees to my chest. A twinge of pain registered as I hugged my legs and pressed the ugly bruise already forming from hitting the desk. Even though my room felt like a sauna, I shivered.

I pulled my laptop down from my desk and balanced it on my thighs, half expecting the email to be gone. I mean, there was still a good chance that this was some type of prolonged psychotic episode.

But the email was still there.

A strange feeling rose up in my chest, the feeling I thought I'd gotten rid of for good.

Hope.

Maybe I could do what our entire police force had proven incapable of doing. Maybe if I figured out what really happened that night, things would go back to the way they used to be.

Maybe.

Chapter 2

Last Fall

This was it. A rite of passage into the upper school of Pemberly Brown Academy. One of many traditions, or "Sacramenta," that PB students had honored for generations. Every year, at midnight the night before the first day of school, anyone who was anyone gathered at Station 10, Farrow's Arches, and stripped down for Nativitas, which was really just a pretentious Latin name for a midnight swim in Pemberly Brown Lake.

Grace had somehow managed to convince us that if we didn't sneak across town in the middle of the night, we wouldn't officially be upper-school students. So, against my better judgment, I found myself getting ready to run with the best of them.

Maddie, Grace, and I huddled behind a cluster of bushes, not quite ready to face the upper-school girls who pranced around in lacy black bras and thongs, followed by hoots and whistles from appreciative boys in boxer shorts. The upperclassmen didn't see much need for bathing suits, which made me extremely self-conscious about my own choice in swimwear. Earlier, my pink-and-white polka-dot bikini had seemed cute, but next to girls parading around in Victoria's Secret lingerie, the ruffles and ties screamed "first-year baby."

"Whose idea was it to eat mint chocolate-chip ice cream right before we left? You know I'm supposed to be on a diet, and now I'm all bloated." Maddie pinched at her chubby stomach as she struggled to free herself from a jean skirt that was at least two sizes too small.

"Oh, please, Maddie. You're like a curvy little Greek goddess. You've got to just own it!"

Grace pulled down her orange sundress, revealing striped, boy-cut underwear and a matching bra.

"Hey! Where's your bathing suit?" Maddie cast an annoyed look over at Grace's slim figure, which was revealed to full advantage in her underwear and bra. As usual, Grace was one step ahead of Maddie and me.

"Oops! Guess I forgot," Grace laughed. "Besides, you've got to admit these are way cuter than my lame one-piece."

Grace tossed her dress aside and started toward the crowd that had gathered on the other side of our bushes. I grabbed her shoulder.

"You're not really going to go out there in your underwear, are you?"

Grace gave me one of her patented "Live a little, Kate!" looks. "Come on, it's the same thing as a bikini." She glanced down at her slim legs and shot me a mischievous smile. "Hurry up and ditch your clothes—we're going to miss the run." She craned her neck, probably looking for Cameron Thompson.

Cameron was a rebel who completely lacked a cause. He was rich, spoiled, and good-looking in an angry way that Grace seemed to find irresistible. Despite his parents' attempts at portraying the picture-perfect family, Cameron was always in trouble. Black sheep? More like Black Plague. But Grace was "in love" in spite of all that. Part of me had always wondered if she loved his bad-boy image more than the bad boy himself.

A pair of tattooed arms snaked around Grace's creamy skin. The Black Plague himself was claiming what he considered rightfully his.

"Cameron!" Grace squealed and turned to him, her lips finding his. There was no denying the chemistry between the two, but they also shared an intensity that scared me a little. Luckily, after a few seconds of sucking face, Grace pulled away from Cameron, shoving him back playfully.

I couldn't be sure, but I thought I caught a flash of something in her eyes. Annoyance? Boredom? Fear? Whatever it was, it signaled that Grace would be moving on to bigger and better boys sooner rather than later. I couldn't help but be a little relieved.

"Okay, guys, see you in the water!" She grabbed Cameron's hand and made her way out into the gardens, her laugh echoing behind her.

Beyond the wall of shrubs I heard someone shouting over the crowd. It was the typical mix of Latin and teenage slang that Pemberly Brown was famous for century-old traditions mingled with twenty-first-century vices.

"All right, Maddie. Now or never." I stripped off my T-shirt and adjusted the straps of my bikini top.

Maddie grudgingly followed me out of the shadows, hunching a little in her tankini, pale skin glowing in the moonlight. I wanted to tell her that she'd look skinnier if she stood up straight, but I didn't have the heart.

We lined up with our fellow students, and I did my best not to stare at the curves of the older girls in their skimpy thongs or the tan chests of the guys. Tightening my ponytail, I waited for my cue. Finally a strong, deep voice called out, "*Incedo!*" The command set the clump of virtually naked students in motion as we all took off in the direction of the lake.

Instinct and years of tennis practice sent my legs into motion. The warm August air loosened my insecurities, and a smile tugged at my lips while my bare feet pounded against the grass. As I moved through the pack of bodies, I brushed against the warm skin of someone else's arm. When I turned my head, his smile caught me off guard. The white of his teeth contrasted sharply with his light brown skin, and his eyes practically matched the night sky around us.

Bradley Farrow.

He was one of the most popular guys at Pemberly Brown, captain of the lacrosse team and second-year class president.

Oh, and he was gorgeous.

He smirked at me and raised his eyebrows in a silent challenge, forcing me to slow down a little—he was *that* good-looking. Bradley laughed and quickly moved past me, splashing into the lake ahead with the rest of the runners. When I finally caught up, I dove into the cool water, my thoughts consumed by all things Bradley. I mean, we'd had a moment, right? The thrill of possibilities washed over me along with the murky water. I surfaced and scanned the lake for him, but he had disappeared into the crowd.

I could see Maddie cowering near the shore, her legs slightly bent, desperately trying to keep her body hidden, as usual. And there was Grace. I almost called out until I saw Porter Reynolds swim up next to her. Porter was roughly a seven out of ten on the hotness scale and had blood bluer than any color you'd ever find in a Crayola box.

He was one of those guys always trying to prove he was more hipster than WASP and forever trying to act just as cool (if not cooler) than his older brother, Alistair, reigning king of Pemberly Brown Academy.

Porter and Grace splashed at each other playfully until he stopped and reached over to wipe the drops of water from her forehead. He leaned in all serious and cheesy, and I could have sworn he was going to kiss her, but a wave of water yanked my attention away. Cameron was crouched beside me, staring at Grace in that creepy, intense way of his.

"Hey, Cameron!" I said it brightly in an effort to pull his attention from whatever was going on with Grace—even though Porter seemed to have already disappeared.

"She's so beautiful, you know?" He didn't take his eyes off her. "Grace, I mean."

"Um, yeah, she really is." I mentally crossed my fingers, hoping that he hadn't caught the moment between her and Porter.

Without warning, he pushed through the water to Grace. The second he reached her, his arms and lips once again claimed her as his own. I saw her hands pushing him back gently, her laughter ringing out across the water. Something about the way he touched her made me want to push through the water and rescue my best friend, but instead I went in search of Maddie. I'd rather hear her bitch about the size of her thighs than watch Grace make out with that sketchball.

This was going to be some year.

Chapter 3

Present Day

Wednesday morning, bus 315 jerked and stuttered around the stately neighborhoods surrounding Pemberly Brown Academy, and my head banged against the finger-smudged windows. The air reeked of the drugstore cologne boys bought after seeing ads in *Maxim*.

Between the fits and starts of the bus and the overwhelming smell of teenagers in heat, my head throbbed. Waves of nausea rolled through my stomach, and I was dangerously close to blowing chunks all over my squirrelly next-door neighbor, Seth Allen, who sat next to me.

Seth had put some serious effort into what he wore today. His uniform shirt was deliberately wrinkled with portions strategically untucked, making it clear that his overbearing mother must have been busy that morning. As usual, his cheeks were a feverish red, and his orange hair was wild, although he seemed to have used half a tube of man-product in an attempt to tame it.

Despite the carefully ironed crease down the center of each pant leg and the blinding whiteness of his brand-new Pumas, you had to give the guy an A for effort.

"So I'm pretty sure that Mr. Lansdowne is in some kind of cult," Seth said between bites of a breakfast sandwich. I knew without having to ask that this was not his first breakfast. For as long as I'd known Seth, he had always been trying to "bulk up." Based on his 130-pound frame, I think it was safe to say it wasn't working. As he chewed, he eyed Grace's pearls and my hand flew to my neck, suddenly self-conscious. I had worn them that morning on a whim, thinking they'd give me the courage to confront Cameron, but I was already regretting my decision.

"Mr. Lansdowne isn't in a cult. He just likes to walk at night." I rolled my eyes at Seth and went back to typing one last borderline-desperate message to Cameron. My parents were going to flip when they saw how many texts I'd used in the past twenty-four hours, but I had to talk to him. Alone. Grilling him about Grace was going to be awkward enough; confronting him in front of his stoner friends was unthinkable.

"Yeah, like anyone goes speed walking in long black robes." Seth stared at the pearls again. I opened my mouth to say something, but the bus hit a bump and Seth's knee knocked into mine. I scooted closer to the window.

"It's a bathrobe, you jackass." Couldn't old people be eccentric anymore? The only benefit of being seventy-five has got to be the fact that you can get away with acting insane and not give a damn about what everyone else thinks. I, for one, couldn't wait to be the crazy old pink-haired lady who walked the dog in her favorite Versace gown. And pearls.

I leaned my head against the bus window and shut my eyes,

praying Seth would get the hint and leave me alone so I could focus on not barfing. Although, puking on him might finally force him to ditch me like everyone else, not to mention make his shoes look a little bit more broken in.

Since Grace's death, everyone else at school had treated me like a social pariah, but for some reason Seth refused to give up. He was constantly trying to get me sucked into his crazy conspiracy theories about our neighbors and was always asking questions about Grace and my feelings (hence the intense pearl-staring).

The part of me that tried desperately to be a loner wanted him to leave me alone, but the part of me that longed for a friend made me want to show him the email. I mean, if anyone would believe me, it was Seth. But then I remembered Grace's warning: *They'll hurt you.* And I swallowed back the urge to spill my guts.

A ball of aluminum foil bounced off the back of Seth's head, and an even deeper flush crept over his cheeks. I rolled my eyes. Couldn't the burnouts in the back of the bus at least think of some more creative methods of bullying? Before I could stop myself, I spun around to see two first-years snickering with their uniform ties looped around their heads.

"Hey, Lame and Lamer!" They froze and stared at me, not quite sure how to react. "Just thought I'd let you know that you've managed to piss off *the* most powerful guy at Pemberly Brown. This guy," I said, gesturing at Seth's curls, "is Seth Allen *Brown*. His family, like, founded the school," I lied, "and he's probably texting the headmaster about your expulsion as we speak. Good luck!"

Lame looked like he might cry, and Lamer was already muttering about how sorry he was. I sat back down next to Seth feeling pretty pleased with myself as he gaped at me, his features tangled up with a mixture of embarrassment, amazement, and (God help me) love.

"Thanks, Kate."

"Whatever."

"Um…the pearls…" He stared down at them intently again. "Are they…"

But I had already tuned him out, shoving earbuds into my ears. My stomach sank as it always did as we drove through the iron gate, the bus ambling its way up a long, tree-lined lane. The massive oak trees created a shadowed canopy that hugged the edges of the road as we passed the lower school, then the middle school, and finally pulled in front of the upper school.

I used to think this last part of the drive was sort of magical, like I was entering a whole new world. But now the entire campus looked like a graveyard to me. A graveyard haunted by memories of Grace.

I sucked in my breath as the bus crept past the line of thick trees that marked the ruins of the chapel. I couldn't stop myself from pressing my face against the window, sure that if I tried hard enough I'd see her. But as usual, there was nothing left but rubble.

We had arrived.

Chapter 4

As we filed off the bus, I looked around at the Tudor-style buildings. The ivy climbing up the walls almost completely obscured the brick hidden beneath. Pemberly Brown Academy was one of those obnoxious private schools that took itself very seriously, and this was reflected in every square inch of the campus. Being a student there was a little like going to school on a movie set depicting the perfect private school: all archways, cobblestones, and antique-looking plaques bearing obscure Latin quotes.

Grace's long pearl necklace bumped against my chest in time with my steps, and I shot Seth a my-music's-too-loud-I-can't-hear-you look when he tried to ask a question about my schedule. Walking through the main doors of the upper school, I unconsciously slapped my palm against Station 1, a bronze plaque proclaiming, *Aut disce aut discede*. "Either learn or leave."

The Twelve Stations of the Academy had been placed at key spots throughout the campus to express the philosophies of the founders. In Latin. Pretentious much? Most of the students didn't take the time to translate, but as one of only ten students who had somehow gotten suckered into studying a dead language, I felt it was my academic obligation to memorize every single one. Guess I just have a way with useless information. Lucky me.

One of the many random traditions at PB was to touch a station plaque for good luck in hopes of acing a test or finally scoring the lead in the school play. Today I wasn't concerned with passing a test, just figuring out who had killed my best friend. Tall order for a good-luck ritual, I guess.

You'd never know it was just after 7:00 a.m. Students shouted across the hall, slapped shoulders, and gossiped loudly, making me regret my decision to skip my morning latte. The email from Grace had resurrected all the feelings that twelve months of therapy had tried to erase. Sleepless nights were only one of the side effects.

When I lost Grace, I didn't lose just one friend—I lost all of my friends. In fact, I lost everything. It was like a giant pair of scissors had come along and neatly snipped my life in two. There was now a distinct before and after, and I still hadn't figured out who I was in life after Grace.

I had spent the past year trying to convince my parents that Grace's death was more than just a freak accident. Instead of helping me, they had shipped me off to endless appointments with my shrink, Dr. Lowen, who I fondly referred to as Dr. Prozac. My parents thought I was delusional, distressed, withdrawn. They claimed that when I'd lost Grace, they had lost their daughter.

What they didn't realize was that I'd lost me too.

I checked my phone one last time before turning it to silent. Despite sending Grace email after email the night before, it didn't look like she'd be offering anymore help. She'd returned to silent ghost status. God, I just hoped she was okay. Wherever she was. But the email had given me a new purpose. I wasn't just sad or even angry anymore. Don't get me wrong: I *was* angry, but now my anger had a direction. It could be harnessed.

I spotted Bradley Farrow casually leaning against a locker, all smiles and dimples, his friends hanging on every word. The familiar feelings of guilt wound their way through my body just like they did every time I saw him. I should have been there to save Grace, but I had chosen Bradley instead.

I had failed her—just like everyone else.

Forcing my eyes down as I walked past Bradley, I noticed Maddie hovering next to her new bestie, Pemberly Brown's resident queen bee, Taylor Wright. Their ever-present bodyguard, Bethany Giordano, stood a foot or two away protecting the girls from the masses hanging out at Station 4, outside the main computer lab.

They obviously had never bothered to translate the meaning behind the station: *Liberae sunt nostrae cogitationes.* "Our thoughts are free." Something told me "free thought" wasn't a consideration for Queen Taylor and her bitches-in-waiting.

Bethany's eyes started at the top of my head and slowly made their way down to my plain, black ballet flats, assessing every inch of me. A sneer of disapproval twisted her dark features and made me want to punch her. Of course, I wouldn't dare. She was built like a line-backer. Not fat or even unattractive, just super-tall and sort of meaty.

She was the youngest of seven in a huge Italian family, and her six older brothers were all defensive linemen on college football teams. Grace, Maddie, and I had privately given her the nickname "Beefany" last year after it became clear she could kick the asses of half the guys on the lacrosse team.

As I knelt in front of my locker, I couldn't help but glance over my shoulder at Maddie and smile, remembering our inside joke. My eyes lingered on her emaciated legs jutting out from beneath the plaid skirt of her school uniform. She looked like she was living off Diet Coke and air. It was hard to believe this was the same girl who had once devoured an entire gallon of mint-chocolate-chip ice cream with me. She caught me staring and completely ignored me before turning and whispering something in Taylor's ear.

Taylor's bright blue eyes were frigid as she turned to look directly at me. She was the last in the line of Wright sisters, collectively known as the Three Ts, who ran the social scene at PB. Rumor had it that her two older sisters, Tinsley and Teagan, had worked an entire summer with Taylor to perfect her version of their patented icy stare. All that training had definitely paid off.

Although Taylor was stuck in the same boring uniform as the rest of us, her Tiffany jewelry—plus Chanel ballet flats, and a buttery leather bag that probably weighed more than Maddie—made her look ready for the runway.

The three girls stared me down for a few awkward seconds, and then Taylor burst out laughing. At one time that laughter would have been enough to force me into the girls bathroom for the rest of the day, but for once I didn't have time to obsess over the ice queen and her lackeys. I slammed my locker door shut and glanced at the clock.

They're called priorities. And Cameron was my number one.

I spotted him ducking out one of the side doors with his sketchy friends. Just before the door shut behind him, Cameron cast a quick look back and our eyes locked across the busy hallway. Even though he was the same guy I'd played capture the flag with in sixth grade and the same guy Grace had obsessed over since middle school, he looked like a stranger to me.

But I remembered the Cameron we'd grown up with. I remembered how he'd loved Grace in a desperate, almost dangerous way. And I remembered him going crazy with jealousy when she flirted with other guys.

Grace had hidden away a secret in the weeks leading up to her death. I'd always assumed she'd found another guy and that she was planning on dumping Cameron. But after the email, it was clear Cameron knew more about Grace's secret than he'd let on.

With his hands against the door, he cocked his head in a silent challenge before pushing through and letting the door slam behind him. He knew I didn't have the guts to confront him in front of his friends, but what he didn't know was that I had a killer Plan B.

Chapter 5

I made my way to Station 3, the school office, and touched the cold bronze on my way in. *Faber est suae quisque fortunae*: "Every man is the artisan of his own fortune." Around the corner, I saw Seth organizing files. He had study hall first period, and while every other student lucky enough to have a free first period could be found sleeping in, grabbing breakfast, or even—I don't know—studying, Seth spent his helping out in the school office.

"Hi again," I said, adjusting the bag on my shoulder.

Seth poked his head out the door and grinned from ear to ear. Then he glanced at the clock. "I thought you had English Lit first period."

I twisted Grace's pearls between my fingers and flinched when Seth's line of vision fell to the necklace again. He opened his mouth to say something, but I beat him to it.

"Yes, they're hers. Would you just stop looking at me?" As soon as the words left my mouth, I regretted them.

This was exactly what Dr. Prozac was talking about when he told me to "weigh my words." Seth looked hurt so I backpedaled.

"I'm sorry, it's just…I'm just…I don't know…tired. I didn't come here to pick a fight. I just…um…wanted to say hi…again." *And to find out the combination to Cameron Thompson's locker.*

Seth leaned against the gray metal filing cabinet, lost his footing, and almost fell on the floor. Once he recovered, he reached into his blazer pocket to pull out a plastic bag containing a crustless PB&J, completely unfazed by his own dorkiness. I guess in a way you had to respect him for that.

"It's okay. I was just going to say they look good on you. The pearls, I mean."

I suppressed the urge to roll my eyes and instead cracked a painful-looking smile. "Oh," I said, lifting the strand, "thanks."

"Hey, I hope you have a hall pass from your first-period teacher. Sinclair's been coming down hard on tardies, and I know how your parents feel about demerits."

This was exactly why Seth and I had never made the leap from next-door neighbors to real friends. He was always remembering inconvenient factoids about my life. Usually the very thing I was trying to forget.

"I'm just not feeling well. Girl problems." That ought to shut him up.

It did. He turned so red that for a moment his freckles disappeared, and he shoved the rest of the sandwich into his mouth.

"Oh, well," he said, with a mouthful of bread, "are you here to see the nurse? I can get her." He fumbled with the now-empty sandwich bag in his hands as his jaw worked on the sandwich.

"No, no," I said a little too quickly. "I just…well, this is really

embarrassing. I sort of forgot my locker combination. You know…
one of the weird side effects of this time of the month is forgetfulness."

His eyes found the ceiling, as though if he looked at me directly
he'd magically sprout ovaries. "I, well…I actually know where we
can look that up. What's your locker number?"

"Number 543," I lied effortlessly, crossing my fingers that Seth
was too flustered to recall my actual locker number.

Seth disappeared into one of the back rooms of the office and
reappeared shortly. He relayed the combination to me a little
breathlessly, either from running around the office or from the
sheer excitement of interacting with a girl. It was hard to say which.

I thanked him and repeated the combination over and over in
my mind as I ran the length of the hallway.

Minutes later I was at Cameron's locker, my silver monogrammed
bracelet clanging against the metal as I twisted the combination.
The lock clicked open.

I was in.

Without really knowing what I was searching for, I reached inside
and began digging around. Beads of sweat dotted my hairline, and
my heart hammered against my rib cage. My ears perked, and I
hoped that I'd be able to hear any footsteps coming down the hall
over the sound of my pounding heart.

I shoved aside books, notebooks, and a dirty-looking sweatshirt.
While I might not have known what I was looking for, I was pretty
sure it wasn't gray fleece reeking of boy.

The slamming of a classroom door shattered the silence of the
hallway and brought the meaning of "jump out of your skin" to a

27

whole new level. I craned my neck and let out a sigh of relief when I saw that it was just some first-year heading to the bathroom.

With my attention back to the locker, I pulled out a small composition notebook with the usual speckled gray-and-white cover. I flipped the pages, thinking it might be a journal. But before I could make out any of the words on the page, I heard voices around the corner. The sound of footsteps followed, and I knew my time was up.

When I shoved the notebook back into the locker, a piece of paper slipped out from between its pages and floated to the wood floor. I spotted Grace's name and a drawing of some sort.

The footsteps were coming closer, so I rearranged the junk in Cameron's locker and stood, one foot partly covering the piece of paper.

Someone cleared his throat behind me, and I swear I peed my pants a little. I turned around and looked straight into the eyes of Headmaster Sinclair.

Shit.

Chapter 6

Last Fall

It was the first week of school, and I had a bad case of what the upperclassmen liked to call First Year-itis. It hit all girls who started upper school at Pemberly Brown after coming into their own the summer before and leaving behind the braces, baby fat, and overall awkwardness of their middle-school years.

The most common symptoms included heart palpitations, flushed cheeks, and incessant giggling whenever a hot upperclassman happened to catch their eye. Sadly, there was no known cure.

My symptoms went into overdrive whenever I caught a glimpse of Bradley Farrow. After our "moment" during Nativitas, I was a goner, head over heels, crazy in love. He was hands down the hottest guy in school. Perfect mocha skin, eyelashes like paintbrushes, and six-pack abs that were discussed at length in the girls bathroom.

My locker was exactly seven lockers away from his, which meant that every time we changed classes, I was able to watch him out of the corner of my eye. Thankfully, I'd always had excellent peripheral vision.

I was in between English and Latin and was alternating between stealing glances at Bradley, blushing, and swapping out my books when I heard the loud giggling that almost always preceded the entrance of Grace and Maddie.

"Enjoying the view?" Grace giggled just loud enough to make Bradley look over to my locker and turn the corner of his mouth up in a smirk.

I had told her all about my crush after school the day before, and I'd been regretting that ever since. It's not that I didn't want her to know. Grace was my best friend, and I was dying to talk to her about all things Bradley. But she also couldn't keep a secret to save her life. It was only a matter of time before all of PB would be buzzing with rumors about my lame crush.

"Shhh! He's right there," I whispered and bugged out my eyes.

"Calm down, Kate. He doesn't even know we're alive," Maddie said. She tugged at the line of buttons down her uniform shirt in an effort to disguise the fact that a few were dangerously close to popping off. Maddie was one of those girls who should probably have worn a large but was always trying to squeeze into a small.

"Whatever, Maddie." I sighed dramatically and looked to Grace for support, but she just shrugged her shoulders in agreement.

"Stop being so touchy. I have great news." Grace grabbed my arm and began jumping up and down like a little kid who needed to pee. "Don't ya wanna know? Hmm…don't ya? Don't ya?"

I couldn't stifle my smile, so I gave in. As usual. No one could ever stay mad at Grace for long; she was just too entertaining. "Okay, okay. Tell me your big news."

"I'm ungrounded, which means I can go to the Spiritus bonfire on Friday night! I managed to convince my parents that it's required for first-years to promote school spirit."

"And they bought that?" I asked as my hands worked my long brown hair into a ponytail.

Grace's parents were crazy conservative. Emphasis on the crazy. She had spent most of her weekends grounded since she'd hit twelve and discovered makeup, boys, and other pursuits strictly forbidden by Mr. and Mrs. Lee. They had absolutely no idea she was dating Cameron, and they'd probably homeschool her if they found out.

"Well, there are conditions," Grace admitted.

"You didn't mention any conditions!" Maddie chided, yanking her skirt down another inch. If she'd just buy the right-size clothes, maybe she wouldn't look so uncomfortable all the time.

"Well, they have to drop me off and pick me up. But I figure if we all go together it won't be so bad…" She trailed off and gave us her best pretty-please-with-a-cherry-on-top look, a look that worked so well I'd begun to wonder if she practiced it in the mirror every morning.

Her dark eyes were all sparkly and hopeful, her mouth turned up in a nervous smile, and her straight, black hair hung like a curtain down her back. Who could resist?

Apparently Maddie.

"No way, Grace," she replied, smoothing her skirt." We're riding with Alistair Reynolds."

Grace and I stared at her, mouths agape. Alistair Reynolds was, well, Alistair Reynolds. He didn't actually do anything aside from hook up with younger girls, but he was from one of the oldest families in Pemberly Brown's distinguished lineage. The fact that he was Abercrombie hot and had a hefty trust fund pretty much cemented his number-one spot in the Pemberly Brown pecking order.

"How did you end up with a ride from Alistair Reynolds? Even Porter can't get a ride with Alistair, and they're brothers." Grace couldn't hide her shock.

Maddie rolled her eyes. "Oh, sorry. I didn't realize that it's such a stretch that a girl like me could get us rides from a guy like him."

I jumped in to save Grace. "Come on, Maddie. You know what she meant. It's Alistair Reynolds. He doesn't know we exist, right?"

"Well, if you must know, my parents are going out with the Reynoldses Friday night, and they said Alistair would take us to Spiritus if we wanted."

"So his parents are forcing him to take you and your friends so that they can go to the country club and get hammered?" Now it was Grace's turn to look annoyed.

"My parents don't get hammered…"

"Right. I guess Evian came out with vodka-flavored water." Grace had made the mistake of taking a sip of Mrs. Greene's water at the beginning of the summer, inadvertently solving the mystery of Maddie's mom's long afternoon naps.

"Enough!" I went into peacemaker mode and turned to Grace. "Mrs. Greene is super-nice and she's…well, just a little overtired sometimes, so lay off." Next I turned to Maddie. "You know we can't ride with Alistair, so just tell your parents that Grace's dad is driving us."

Maddie stuck out her lower lip like a child. "That totally defeats the purpose. I mean, this is *Alistair Reynolds* we're talking about here."

"Uh, actually this is your best friend we're talking about here. Come on, we'll ride with Alistair some other time." Grace shot me a grateful look. It was important to her to at least pretend she had a normal social life. There was no way I was going to let Maddie's social climbing ruin it.

"Fine," Maddie said, still pouting. She mumbled phrases like "not fair" and "have to suffer" and "Grace's stupid parents" as we walked to our next class.

"Kate Lowry for the win! Pineapple pizza is on me." Grace laughed as she walked backward in front of Maddie, trying to get her to smile. "You can't stay mad at me when our favorite pizza's involved. Right, Maddie? Right?"

This time she couldn't resist. No one could. Maddie's frown wavered, and her thin lips lifted into a smile.

"I knew you'd come around!" Grace's laugh filled the hallway but was cut short when Cameron grabbed her from behind, separating the three of us.

"I heard you guys talking," he said, pausing long enough for us to wonder how much he'd heard and why he was eavesdropping in the first place. "You didn't tell me you're allowed to go to Spiritus now." He talked to Grace as though Maddie and I were invisible.

"Oh, I just found out this morning," Grace said, smiling at Maddie and me. "I wanted to make it a girls night, though. You understand, right?"

Something in Cameron's eyes made it clear he didn't. "Of course, babe," he said, nodding. "I know how *important* your friends are to you." He said it with a hint of resentment. "I could use some time with the guys anyway."

Maddie and I exchanged a look. We both knew that Cameron was going to spend the entire night stalking Grace.

As we neared the World Language wing, I realized I'd forgotten my Latin notebook and had to turn around. "Crap, forgot something in my locker. I'll see you guys at lunch."

Grace planted a kiss on Cameron's cheek but threw her arm around Maddie. As I rushed back to my locker, I had to admit I was glad Grace was willing to spend time with us away from Cameron. He was demanding; I knew that balancing a boyfriend and your best friends couldn't be easy. After all, no one really wanted to share Grace.

I twisted the combination on my locker again and reached in to grab my notebook. But sitting on top of my messy pile of books and school supplies was a pristine cream envelope with my name written in calligraphy on the front.

I grabbed the card and looked around the crowded hallways. This definitely hadn't been there a minute ago. Who could have gotten this in my locker so quickly? There was no way it could fit through the slats, and Grace and Maddie were the only ones with the combination.

The paper of the envelope was velvety smooth. This must be what expensive felt like. I carefully opened the envelope, not wanting to rip the beautiful paper.

The text on the invitation was handwritten in the same gorgeous calligraphy as my name, and in the bottom right-hand corner there was a small design.

Katelyn Olivia Lowry,

Your presence is requested at Station 11 at dusk on Friday the 13th of September. Enter at the seal if you believe yourself worthy. Come alone. Tell no one.

Guess I was going to be doing some balancing of my own.

Chapter 7

Present Day

Miss Lowry, last time I checked, you were a second-year. Care to explain why you're rifling through a third-year locker that doesn't belong to you when you should be in your first-period class?"

Headmaster Sinclair was not a large man. In fact he couldn't be much taller than five-foot-seven, considering I was able to look him square in the eye and I had measured five-foot-five and three-quarters at my last doctor's appointment. He strutted around the halls like some kind of deranged peacock. Last year Grace and I had diagnosed him with an advanced case of little-man syndrome.

"Oh, hi, Headmaster. Cameron just asked me to grab his English Lit notebook. He went home sick, and he needs his notes to study for a big test tomorrow on…" I thought hard here. I remembered reading somewhere that when you lie, you should add a lot of detail—or wait, maybe you're not supposed to include a lot of detail. Whatever. I guess the point was to stay cool. "*Beowulf*…at least I think that's what he said." My voice was calm and steady.

The headmaster looked unconvinced, but luckily Cameron wasn't around to tell him the truth. I saw movement out of the corner of my eye as someone came out of the boys bathroom. Without thinking, I seized the opportunity and took a few steps away from Headmaster Sinclair.

"Whoa! Watch out." I ran right into Liam Gilmour.

Liam was one of those kids who had ended up at PB after getting kicked out of public school. There were all kinds of rumors about how he'd managed to get in a couple of years earlier, but I wasn't sure I believed any of them. I mean, if he really was a convicted felon who had somehow blackmailed Headmaster Sinclair to get into school here, wouldn't he be in juvie or something?

"I hope you have a hall pass, Mr. Gilmour."

"You know it." Liam flashed the stuffed armadillo that one of the science teachers used as a bathroom pass.

"Well, hurry back to class. You can't afford to be missing any additional lectures."

"Yeah, it's just that there's something majorly wrong in the boys bathroom. That last toilet is overflowing again. Just thought you should know."

Headmaster Sinclair muttered something that sounded distinctly like a curse and started walking toward the custodian's office.

"I trust you'll be forgetting that locker combination, Ms. Lowry," he threw back at me. "Now, get back to class. Both of you." Headmaster Sinclair gave us one last long look and disappeared around the corner of the hallway.

My hands shook as I bent down, grabbed the paper from beneath my shoe, and stuffed it in my pocket. When I straightened, I forced myself to look Liam in the eyes, not sure what to make of him.

"Overflowing toilet, huh?"

He laughed a little. "Well, technically it's not a lie. It was overflowing last week. You just looked like you could use a break."

"You have no idea. Well, thanks for the distraction. I really appreciate it." I studied him carefully. Liam kept a low profile, and the only thing really noteworthy about him—aside from the fact that he had amazing hair—was the rumor that his dad was some kind of gangster. Most of the girls at school avoided him in spite of his dangerous good looks. I guess he scared them a little.

But for some reason he didn't scare me. Maybe that was because I'd caught him sketching an incredibly detailed picture of Beefany—with horns and a moustache—in study hall. Even if the rumors were true and he was some kind of thug, anyone who could sketch Taylor's bodyguard as a devil-dude was fine by me.

"Well, thanks again." I suppressed the urge to stick out my hand. I had the worst handshake habit on the planet. My dad always forced me to practice firm handshakes, and while I was sure his training would serve me well later in life, it was the epitome of lame in high school.

"No problem." He nodded toward Cameron's closed locker. "Find what you were looking for?" His eyes were the kind of color that changed depending on the color of his shirt. Today they were a stormy blue, but tomorrow they could be green or gray. I'd always wished for that kind of eyes. Mine were just plain old brown.

"Maybe." I tore my eyes from his. They were making me kind of light-headed.

"Well, see you around." He squeezed my shoulder and walked away.

A quick glance at my phone confirmed that I was now way past tardy and into official class-cutting territory. I hoped Seth could work some magic for me in the office, like forging an official excused-absence note from the school nurse. Maybe he'd even "borrow" an entire booklet of absence slips. They'd come in pretty handy—for the sake of the investigation, of course.

Instead of turning toward my first period classroom, I slipped out a side door and into the courtyard to examine my findings. The air was already thick and muggy under the morning sun; summer wasn't quite ready to let fall take the reins. Eager for the shade of the path, I picked up my pace, sending Grace's pearls into an angry dance around my neck.

I had my sights set on Station 10, Farrow's Arches, tucked into the gardens of Pemberly Brown. Legend had it that if you and your boyfriend kissed underneath one of the arches, you'd end up married.

Amor vincit omnia. "Love conquers all."

My mind wandered to Liam and those stormy blue eyes. I shook my head. I had to focus. I couldn't make the same mistake twice.

The gardens were bursting the fiery oranges and reds of fall leaves and deep purple mums. I held my fingers out, letting the tips skim across the hedges that lined the path. Finally her bench came into view.

In Memory of Grace Elizabeth Lee.

After running my fingers over the grooves that spelled her name, I pulled the slip of paper from my pocket. A boy's block hand-writing had scrawled Grace's name above a crest carefully sketched in black ink. At first, it looked similar to the Pemberly Brown crest, but closer examination showed it was different.

The *P* and the *B* were missing, and on the door beneath an ornate crown was the letter *S*. I had no idea what it meant, but I had no doubt that the difference was significant. Why else would Cameron have saved it?

"What happened to you, Grace?" I whispered to the garden. In spite of the unseasonably warm air, I was suddenly freezing. When I looked up to see if a cloud had moved in front of the sun, a flash of plaid darted behind a bush nearby, long black hair streaming behind her. Grace.

I jumped up from the bench and craned my neck to see over the branches, but no one was there. The bush was completely still except for a couple of fat bumblebees buzzing and bouncing from flower to flower.

My pulse raced, the beat throbbing in my neck. Here I was trying to prove that I wasn't crazy, and I was hallucinating. This couldn't be good. As soon as I caught my breath, I headed back inside. The mind-numbing boredom of class sounded way better than waiting in the gardens for a ghost.

Chapter 8

Tennis practice after school was excruciating, particularly with the picture from Cameron's locker burning a hole in my book bag. By the time the late bus dumped me at home, I didn't even bother going inside. I plopped down on our porch swing and smoothed the wrinkled note out along my leg. The paper felt soft and worn, like it had been folded and refolded, read and reread. As I rocked back and forth, I was struck again by the similarities between Cameron's sketch and Pemberly Brown's crest.

They looked so much alike, but the Latin motto was different. Instead of the phrase *Veritas Vos Liberabit*, "The Truth Shall Make You Free," which was Pemberly Brown's promise, the words *Audi, Vide, Tace* appeared on the sketch. "Hear, See, Be Silent," I translated, thankful (for the first time ever) that my fifth-grade teacher had thought I'd be a good candidate for Latin.

I couldn't shake the feeling that I'd seen the words somewhere before. I stared at the picture, desperately trying to jog my memory. The crest featured the same door that every PB student had been wearing over their heart since lower school. But this wasn't quite the same.

I yanked my crumpled uniform blazer from the bottom of my book bag and compared it to Cameron's sketch. A crown was placed over the door in the sketch instead of the key on my blazer. And instead of the *P* and *B*, there was that letter *S*. I wondered if Cameron had gotten it wrong.

Pemberly was an all-girls school founded by suffragettes in 1890. In the early '50s, the school merged with the local boys school, Brown, to form one of the most elite private schools in the Midwest, hence the *P* and *B* coming together. The school's history was so riddled with legends and odd traditions that I wouldn't be surprised if this crest factored in somehow.

I had just typed the words "Pemberly Brown alternate crest" into the search engine on my phone when the loud thump of feet hitting ground interrupted me. I jumped up, startled.

When a mass of frizzy red hair came into view, I relaxed, releasing the breath I hadn't even realized I was holding. Seth had dried leaves stuck in his hair, and I recognized his well-worn copy of *The Biggest Controversies, Conspiracies, Theories, and Cover-Ups of Our Time: From the secret files of science, politics, occult, and religion* tucked under one skinny arm. He had a half-eaten candy bar clutched between his fingers. Paranoia must burn a lot of calories.

"Are you seriously reading that again?" I asked, shaking my head.

"I wanted to go back and reread the part about UFOs," he said with a shrug. "I saw something with my telescope last night that I swear wasn't a plane or satellite."

"Yeah, like the last time you saw a UFO and found out it was just a new cell-phone tower?" I looked up at the tree house he and his dad had spent weeks building when we were in fourth grade. "And I thought you were over the whole tree-house thing."

"For the record, I wasn't in the actual tree house, just sitting in the tree. There's a difference."

"Keep telling yourself that," I replied, unable to bite back a smile.

"So are you feeling better?"

I gave him a confused look and then remembered. Girl problems.

"Oh, yeah, much better. Thanks for your help." And I meant it. Seth may be a huge nerd and he could definitely be annoying, but he was about the closest thing I had to a friend. "And I might need another favor."

But before I could say anything else, Seth reached across and plucked Cameron's sketch from between my fingers.

"Sure. What is it?" Seth asked, examining the drawing.

"No! Not with that!" I said, grabbing it back. "I was going to ask you for an office excuse. For first period. Geez."

"Oh, okay. Sorry. I thought…I mean, I didn't mean to intrude." Red spread across his cheeks. He ran his fingers through his hair, shaking a few twigs out.

I reminded myself that he was just trying to help. He was *always* just trying to help, which I guess was part of the problem. I lowered the paper and held it out to him.

"It's this crest I found. Have you ever seen it before?"

"Here. Hold this," he demanded, handing me the candy bar. Taking the paper from between my fingers, he lifted it into the air as if that would help somehow. "Who gave it to you?"

"Nevermind." I pulled the paper back and held out his candy bar. I couldn't tell him that I'd stolen it.

"It's just that it looks really familiar. Does it have something to do with the Skull and Bones?"

I couldn't stop a snort of laughter. Leave it to Seth to find the least useful piece of information and regurgitate it back to me.

"Just forget it." I shoved the paper back in my pocket.

The conversation ground to a halt, and I noticed Seth staring at me in a weird, lovesick kind of way. I hoped he wasn't going to ask me out again. The last time had been awkward enough.

"Did you do something to your hair? It's…like pinkier. Did you put more pink in? Or maybe it's the necklace—I mean, Grace's jewelry—or…you know what I mean…you just look… um, different." The words tumbled out of his mouth, and at the end he sucked in a massive gulp of air.

"Don't, Seth. Just don't."

He lowered his head and shook it back and forth. "I'm sorry—I

46

shouldn't have said it. I couldn't help it." His voice shook, and I heard him mumble the word "stupid" under his breath.

"No, it's fine." I felt bad. I'm not always the easiest person to be around, and not that many people went out of their way to be nice to me. For some reason, a vision of Liam popped into my head.

"I guess what I mean is—thanks."

Seth's jaw practically hit the grass, and his entire face smiled. Eyes, mouth, forehead. Smile, smile, smile.

"So maybe we could, like, go to dinner sometime?"

"Has anyone ever told you to quit while you're ahead?" I began walking back toward my house, but I couldn't stifle a little giggle. The sound felt strange coming out of my mouth. It had been a while since I'd laughed. "See you on the bus tomorrow."

The door slammed shut behind me. As usual, my parents were working late, so I was alone again. You'd think I'd be used to it by now. Or maybe loneliness was one of those things you never really got used to. Somehow that thought made the house feel even emptier than it had just a moment before.

As I trudged up the winding staircase to my room, I felt the full weight of Grace's death on my shoulders. I found myself wishing that I could tell someone, anyone, the whole truth. Keeping secrets for a ghost wasn't all it was cracked up to be.

Chapter 9

Last Fall

The night of the Spiritus bonfire felt electric with energy. The air was thick with the smell of burning wood, and students crowded around the enormous bonfire in clumps—showing off new clothes, gossiping about each other, and waiting for something to happen.

The low sun cast an orange glow over Founder's Field, and Grace's eyes seemed to dance in the flames.

"I've got a secret," she taunted.

"You can't keep a secret to save your life," I laughed, running my fingers through my perfectly blown-out, brown hair. Grace had convinced me to wear it down, and I was a little self-conscious without my ponytail. The three of us had spent hours carefully selecting what we'd wear—denim skirts revealing tanned legs, dark jeans that hugged curves we wished we had, tank tops that only Maddie could fill out.

"Hey, that's not true. She never told anyone about that time in seventh grade when I split my jeans at the school dance. Not even you." Maddie jabbed me in the ribs.

Grace and I exchanged a knowing look and burst out laughing.

"You told? You bitch!" Maddie crossed her arms but smirked a little. "Well, yeah, then. You totally can't keep a secret. Spill."

"I promise I'll tell you guys everything after tonight, but for now my lips are sealed."

I laughed, but it sounded a little hollow, even to my own ears. I had a secret tonight too. My fingers wandered to the invitation still in my back pocket. Part of me hoped it was Grace's secret too, that we'd see each other at the chapel and squeal with delight.

There were probably only ten more minutes of daylight left. My stomach flipped. I wasn't sure what was going to be waiting for me at the chapel, but I couldn't wait to find out. I looked down at my phone, nervous. I wished the invitation had given an exact time.

Dusk was such a broad term. It might be dusk right now, for all I knew. Not to mention the fact that I was supposed to enter through some kind of seal. What could that possibly mean? The way I figured it, there was about a 99 percent chance that I would completely mess this up.

The thought that I might be missing whatever was happening at the chapel got me moving.

"Hey, guys, I've got to…"

I turned toward Maddie and Grace, but they were gone. I saw Maddie a few steps away hanging on to Alistair Reynolds's every word, but Grace was nowhere to be seen. Maybe we shared the same secret after all.

I started to casually make my way to the path in the surrounding woods that led to Station 11, the Pemberly chapel. *Ad vitam aeternam.* "To eternal life." The chapel was a relic from back when

Pemberly Brown was an all-girls school. The old building hadn't been used in years, and all the entrances were supposedly sealed, which added to my nervousness about finding a way in.

I was almost to the edge of the woods when I heard footsteps behind me. Was someone following me? Grace? I came to a quick stop, spun around, and was face-to-face with Bradley Farrow.

My heart stopped. I know it's cheesy and cliché, but when I turned around to find my face inches from Bradley's, my lips just a breath away from his, my heart stood still for just a second.

"Hey, Kate." He smiled his lazy smile and ran a hand over his head.

He knew my name. He actually knew my name.

"Uh…hi, Bradley." The boy I dreamed about at night and accessorized for in the morning was talking to me, and all I could say was "Uh…hi?" *Shoot me. Shoot me now.*

"What are you doing out here by yourself?" He glanced in the direction of the chapel and then looked right at me. I noticed that his eyes were so dark you couldn't even make out the pupils. The kind of eyes you could get lost in. "It's dangerous out here."

I couldn't be sure if he was joking or not, so I laughed, but it came out like a choked snort. *Nice work, Kate. I've heard guys just love a good snort.*

"I was just…um…walking?" I followed this riveting piece of conversation with a high-pitched giggle, which I unsuccessfully attempted to stifle with my hand. Who was this girl who could barely string two words together, snorting and cackling like a lunatic?

"Well, you shouldn't be by yourself." He shoved his hands in his pockets and actually looked a little shy. "Wanna take a walk with me?"

My entire body tingled with the possibility of a walk with Bradley Farrow. In fact, I'm fairly sure that if my body could talk, it would have screamed "*Yes!*" or more likely a completely inappropriate line from one of my mom's trashy romance novels like "Take me, Bradley. Take me *now!*"

So, yeah, I wanted to take a walk with Bradley more than just about anything in the entire world. The sky was pink and orange, the sun low on the horizon, and the smell of burning leaves tickled my nose. It felt like a night when anything could happen, a night made for long walks with cute boys.

But I was supposed to be at the chapel.

I stole a quick glance back at the path and figured that whatever was waiting for me could wait a little longer. It wasn't dark yet. Surely, whoever had sent the invitation wouldn't notice if I was just a few minutes late.

I looked up at Bradley, the last of the setting sun casting a warm glow over his entire face. His eyelashes picked up the light, and I realized I was close enough to see every. single. one.

"Sure, I can take a quick walk," I said, breathlessly.

He began to lead the way but slowed down so I could fall into step beside him. As we were walking, practically bumping shoulders, I felt his fingers slide down my arm and grasp my hand. I hoped he couldn't feel the goose bumps that had spread across my skin the moment he touched me or see the dorky smile on my face.

As we drifted farther away from the bonfire, I saw someone running toward the forest. When I saw the pearls bouncing around her neck, I knew without a doubt that it was Grace.

Chapter 10

Present Day

The text came late at night. Cameron was finally ready to talk. The thought of getting into a car alone with him scared the crap out of me, but after so many unanswered texts, I didn't really have a choice. I had to ask him about the drawing and Grace. If I was going to figure out what had really happened to her, I needed answers, and Cameron was the only person who seemed to have them.

And that's how I found myself scribbling a note to my parents about studying for a Chem test at Naomi Farrow's house. Yeah, she's Bradley's younger sister, but she was also on the tennis team with me and someone my mom remembered as "that nice girl with the gorgeous eyes."

If I got caught, this would probably end with my parents putting me under house arrest and forcing Dr. Prozac to move in to provide one-on-one coaching. Celebs might look cool rocking those ankle bracelets, but one of those things would totally clash with my wardrobe.

I sat in the formal living room we never used and waited for Cameron's car to turn into my driveway. I found myself wishing

I didn't have to do this alone. Not only had he transformed from a recreational drug user into a flat-out addict in less than a year, but it was looking more and more like he knew something about what had happened to Grace that night.

This was definitely not what my parents would call "a smart decision." Probably safe to add "smart decisions" to the long list of things that I'd lost over the past year. I hadn't made one of those in a long time.

I twisted the pearls that had permanently taken residence around my neck. Grace was my best friend. I hadn't been there the night she needed me most. But I was here now. And I owed it to her to find out the truth. She had said it herself: *Find Cameron. He knows.* Plus what did it matter? The worst had already happened.

Headlights swung across the living room, illuminating the stuffy furniture. I set the house alarm, pushed the button to the garage door, and expertly slid under, pearls bouncing as I jogged to his car.

"Hey," I said, climbing into his SUV. "Thanks for picking me up."

When Cameron didn't answer, I turned and was shocked at the sight of him. His light brown hair was matted and greasy-looking. Angry circles darkened his eyes, and his mouth hung slightly open.

I thought about getting out of the car—my hand even brushed the handle of the door—but before I could make a move, I heard the muffled click of the locks and Cameron threw the car in reverse, barreling down my driveway. Tires squealed as the Range Rover backed into the street.

What was I thinking? The car was suddenly too warm and too small. My pulse raced, and I started to panic.

"Maybe we could talk inside," I suggested. "Let's go back up to the house."

Silence from Cameron.

Instead of turning back into the driveway, Cameron put the car in drive and hit the gas pedal. Hard. We sped around the corner and came inches away from taking down a mailbox. My heart raced, and my whole body tingled with adrenaline.

"Cameron?" My voice sounded tiny. "Slow down…please."

The stoplight in front of us turned yellow, and I felt the car speed up instead of slow down. Yellow turned to red, and at the last moment, Cameron slammed on the brakes. We skidded to a stop, the rear of the car pulling to the side after the sudden loss of momentum.

A beer bottle rolled out from beneath my seat and hit my right foot. Cigarette butts littered the floor. And, oh God, was that a joint? Drugs, alcohol, and cigarettes—the car was like a rolling trifecta of substance abuse.

"What were you doing in my locker?" Cameron's question cut through the silence. He ran his fingers through his greasy hair and turned to face me.

"I…I don't know what you're talking about." The shakiness after my initial adrenaline rush reminded me that I was not out of danger. Not by a long shot. My legs twitched, preparing to jump out of the car at a moment's notice, and my heart pounded in my chest, warning me not to get too comfortable.

"Cut the shit, Kate." He threw something that landed in my lap. When I picked it up, I realized it was my silver monogrammed bracelet. It must have fallen off while I was rummaging through Cameron's locker. The worst part was that I hadn't even noticed it was missing. How could I have been so stupid?

"I know you went through my locker. Did you find what you were looking for?"

He'd caught me, and I had no idea what to say. "Cameron, I just want to go home. Please. I think I might be sick," I begged.

As hard as I fought them, I couldn't avoid the tears. They fell quickly, leaving salty trails down my cheeks.

The light turned green, and Cameron hit the gas pedal with so much force that his entire body shifted and my head hit the back of the seat. The beer bottle rolled back to its original hiding place.

"That drawing you stole is important. You have no idea what you're getting into. You ruined everything. Things with me and Grace were supposed to be different." Cameron was gripping the steering wheel so tightly that his knuckles were almost as white as mine clutching the sides of the seat.

His words cut through me. *I* was the one who ruined everything between him and Grace? If *he* wasn't such a psycho, *we* wouldn't even be having this conversation. My fear was replaced with anger…well, most of it.

"I know you were there that night," I whispered. My entire body began to shake when I heard the words escape my mouth. "It wasn't just some random accident, was it?"

For a second, I wondered if he hadn't heard me. And then Cameron swerved the car onto the shoulder and came to a screeching halt.

For what felt like hours, neither of us said a word. The exhausted motor hummed in the background, and Cameron held his face in his hands.

A few minutes later, he lifted his head, reached over, and grabbed me roughly by the shoulders. If this were a movie, all fifteen years of my life would have flashed right before my eyes.

"You have no idea who you're dealing with, Kate." His voice was slow, controlled. "You snooped around, found some stuff you don't understand, and now you think you've got it all figured out." He slammed his fist down on the dashboard so hard that the entire car quivered beneath me.

"News flash, Kate!" A vein on his forehead pulsed in sync with my pounding heart. He reached over and gripped my upper arm. "You don't know anything!"

Wrong. I did know one thing: I needed to get the hell out of that car.

I clawed at his arm with my nonexistent nails, and he released his grip as though he'd woken up and didn't know where he was.

"Kate, wait…"

I fumbled around for the door lock, grabbed at the car handle, and practically fell out of the car and onto someone's front lawn. The second my feet hit the ground I took off down the sidewalk.

I heard Cameron open his door, but I'd already put a respectable distance between the two of us.

"Wait! You don't understand. Let me explain." He let out a howl filled with rage, pain, and grief. The noise was almost inhuman.

I had to get away from him.

I must have looked ridiculous sprinting down the street,

because I earned myself quite a few honks and more than one "Yeah, baby!"

Just as I was congratulating myself on my impressive endurance, one of the straps of my flip-flops broke and left me limping down the sidewalk. A halo of tangled fuchsia hair framed my face, I could feel the makeup melting off my eyes, and I was carrying one of my shoes.

But at that moment, I wasn't really thinking about how I looked. Instead I obsessively looked over my shoulder for Cameron and his Range Rover. The memory of his fingers wrapped around my arm forced me to pick up my pace despite my broken shoe.

And then, like a mirage, it appeared before me. The caffeine-fueled haven where nothing bad could ever happen. The white letters on the green sign spelled out "Starbucks," but it should have said, "Safety."

I hobbled inside, thankful that I'd stuffed the twenty dollars my parents had left for takeout into my pocket before I left the house. Maybe if I had a venti Frap and calmed down a little, I could call someone for a ride home.

Of course, nothing ever goes the way you plan it. It's like Newton's Law or something. Or wait—maybe it's Isaac's Law? Whatever. It's that law where some guy basically says that the worst-case scenario almost always happens. And that night when I stumbled into Starbucks, I was like a walking hypothesis doomed to prove his theory absolutely, unequivocally right.

Chapter 11

It occurred to me as I walked into Starbucks with one bare foot that I might not qualify for coffee, given their "No shirt, no shoes, no service" clause. Fortunately the barista ignored my broken sandal and took my order for a full-fat, full-sugar, venti Mocha Frappuccino with extra whipped cream.

As soon as she announced that my drink was ready and handed me the cup, I took one long sip of the cold, sugary concoction and felt my muscles begin to relax. I turned around and plopped myself into a comfy overstuffed chair in the corner.

"Ahem." The sound came from the couch behind me. I turned around to see Liam Gilmour lounging on the couch like he lived there; tall coffee in his hand, shit-eating grin on his face.

In that moment I almost wished I was back in the car with Cameron. It would have been less humiliating. Well, less humiliating and potentially fatal, but at that moment Cameron seemed like the lesser of the two evils.

"Uh...hi," I managed to stutter while running my fingers through the rat's nest situated on top of my head. My hair was a lost cause. Pink + frizz = disaster, so I casually wiped the mascara from beneath my eyes.

"Rough night?"

"Yeah, you could say that." I gave up trying to pull myself together and took a long sip of my drink. As I peeked over the rim of my cup, I realized that Liam was even cuter than I'd remembered. I recalled my promise earlier not to care, not to get involved, but I couldn't help it. I noticed. His retro T-shirt clung to his arms and waist, promoting some band I'd never heard of, and his jeans were perfectly broken in. But the most surprising thing about Liam had to be that he really looked at me.

I wasn't used to that.

One of the unexpected side effects of your best friend dying and your other best friend publicly disowning you was that people stopped looking directly at you. They stared at my hair or feet or sometimes (and you know who you are) even my chest, but no one ever looked me in the eye. It was like the grief in my eyes burned with such intensity that no one could look directly into them.

Uncomfortable, I glanced down and pretended to examine my fingernails.

"Do you need a ride home or something?" he asked eyeing my grubby foot.

"No!" After the word left my lips, I realized it might have sounded a little abrupt. "I mean, no thanks. I'm fine. Really."

He looked me up and down. "You don't look fine."

I bristled. Yeah, I was a complete freaking train wreck, but the last thing I needed was some random hipster-gangster hybrid reminding me of that fact.

"I'm fine," I repeated tonelessly.

"Listen, I'm not leaving you here with one shoe on. I'll take you home. It's no big deal."

I looked down at my dirty foot. Who was I kidding?

"Fine. Can I just finish this first?"

I needed some time to pull myself together before going home. My parents were going to have lots of questions when I walked into the house looking like a mess, and I needed some time to mentally prepare.

"See, that wasn't so hard now, was it?" The corners of his mouth turned up ever so slightly in victory. Bastard.

The door swung open, and I turned to see who had arrived, thrilled to have a minute to think about how to fill the impending awkward silence. I should have been ready for what happened next. After all, I was walking, talking proof that the theorem of worst-case scenario was a law as concrete as gravity. Unfortunately when Maddie, Taylor, and Beefany breezed through that door, I almost fell off my chair.

There was no hiding the horrified expression on my face, just like there was no hiding my hideous hair, my broken shoe, my dirty foot, and my three-thousand-calorie drink.

I won't lie. I have indulged in occasional (okay, fine—frequent) revenge fantasies involving me looking gorgeous, flirting with the hottest boys, and pretty much kicking ass in general, while Maddie, Taylor, and Beefany are relegated to the sidelines because they're dressed all wrong and feel awkward and out of place.

But the reality was that I was here in Starbucks trying to pull myself together after I had literally run for my life. And there they were, looking like they'd just spent the afternoon at a spa and were in the mood for a quick, calorie-free drink before they headed to some fabulous party that I, of course, knew nothing about.

When I looked back at Liam, I saw that his face had darkened. He was staring directly at Beefany, of all people. Creepy. At least I could kind of understand why guys obsessed over Taylor. I mean, she was gorgeous. Blond, flawless, poised. But Beefany? Yeah, she was pretty, but she probably had five inches and twenty pounds on him. The look on his face made all the rumors about Liam's shady family and rocky past a little more believable.

Taylor and her posse must have felt our eyes on them, because Taylor whispered an order to Maddie, sending her rushing over to the barista. After a few more hushed words to Beefany, they glided over to our little corner. Beefany did all the talking while Taylor just stood there reeking of perfection.

"Hey, guys, it's so nice to see some fellow PBers out and about," Beefany said, her voice rasping like she'd just come off a weeklong chain-smoking binge.

"Uh, hi. I was actually just getting up. Kate, I'll be right back." Liam looked at me and nodded to the bathroom.

Way to throw me under the bus, Liam. But Beefany swooped in before he could escape.

"Don't you go running off." She placed a meaty hand on his shoulder and pushed him back down. "What would your date think?" She looked directly at me and raised one perfectly manicured black eyebrow.

I stared into her eyes for a second but was drawn to her strong fingers as she massaged Liam's shoulder. He shot me an apologetic look, but he didn't push her away. I threw up a little bit in my mouth.

"So I hate to do this when you're on a date, but I really need to talk to you, Liam. In private." Beefany turned, her long black hair swinging over one shoulder, and began walking toward the corner of the coffee shop without even bothering to wait for a response. To my complete and utter shock, Liam promptly followed.

The only upside to my bucket-sized Frap was that I had something to keep me busy while I tried to pretend that our school's reigning queen bee and my ex–best friend weren't standing a few feet away whispering about me.

Instead I focused on observing Liam and Beefany. I'd had no idea they were even friends, but they were deep in conversation. Liam's back was to me, but Beefany was laughing and touching his arm, stealing glances in my direction every so often. Liam was tall, but Beefany was taller. When she whispered in his ear, her cheek grazing his, my skin crawled. I glanced up at Taylor, who watched with a small smile playing on her lips.

Finally the happy couple headed back in my direction. Liam's face was completely blank as he sank back into the couch. Taylor whispered something in Beefany's ear, and I had no doubt that she was pulling the strings on this entire awkward encounter. Apparently, Beefany saved Queen Taylor from getting her hands dirty.

"Well…I'll let you two get back to your little date. Hope you feel better, Cat. You look like you've had a rough one. Ciao!" Beefany said with a final flip of her hair.

"It's…Kate. My name is Kate," I said. But the two of them were already laughing among themselves on their way out the door. I wondered if Taylor had told Beefany to get my name wrong, the icing on my cupcake of humiliation.

Maddie obediently waited near the exit, holding three iced black coffees with her spindly arms. She must have expanded her diet to include ice and coffee. Impressive. Taylor walked right past her, and Beefany followed. Neither of them bothered to help Maddie with the drinks. Typical.

I turned back to Liam, who was staring into space, lost in thought, with the same dark expression on his face. He finally snapped out of his daydream and looked back at me. He wrinkled his forehead a little before his mouth twisted into a smile.

"Did she just call you 'Cat'?"

I tried to look annoyed, but I started laughing right along with him.

"Yeah, she hasn't once gotten my name right. We practically grew up together, and last week she called me Christy and now…Cat. Must be a royal decree from Queen Taylor that no one should get my name right."

"Yeah, well, we're not all loyal to the queen," he said, his face darkening. "Ready?" He took the last sip of his coffee.

"Yep. Let's get out of here. You're sure you don't mind?"

"Don't mind a bit, Cat."

"Very funny," I said, rolling my eyes. I waited for him to walk toward the door, but he just stood staring at me for a second. My cheeks flushed, and I examined my feet.

"I should probably get your number, though, you know, in case you ever want to refuse a ride from me again."

My mind flashed back to the darkness in his eyes when he'd stared at Beefany and then the cozy little conversation that followed, but I listed the numbers anyway. For the first time in the after-Grace, I felt a shivery wave of desire. As usual, my timing totally sucked.

A piece of hair hung in his eyes as he typed, a slight smile playing on his lips. He was hot, but he was also a distraction. And I didn't need any of those right now.

Of course, if I was the kind of girl who doodled potential married names in my notebooks, you can bet your ass my margins would have been covered with "Kate Gilmour" when I did my homework that night.

But I wasn't that kind of girl. At. All.

"Got it," he said, sliding his phone back in his pocket and pushing through the door.

My phone vibrated on my way out. I had one new text from an unfamiliar number.

bc youll prob need a ride again sometime

I smiled. Turns out there was a lot to like about Liam Gilmour.

My phone buzzed again and I glanced back down, expecting another text from Liam. Even though he was only a few feet away from me, I liked this game.

Seeing Cameron's name made my stomach sink.

we need 2 talk

Game over. I deleted the text. I wasn't sure what I needed from Cameron, but I knew I wasn't ready to talk to him. At least not yet.

Chapter 12

My cell phone buzzed on and off throughout most of the night. Every time I checked, it was Cameron. There was something scary and kind of obsessive about his persistence. Truthfully, I was terrified to talk to him. I just wasn't sure I was ready to hear whatever he might confess.

I promised myself that I'd deal with him tomorrow, when the long shadows in my room weren't making me so jumpy and the branches that scraped against my window didn't sound so much like fingernails. The morning seemed like a much safer time to hear the truth about Grace.

As usual, things seemed more manageable in the light of day. Yeah, I'd gotten approximately thirteen texts and missed ten calls from my dead best friend's stalker boyfriend, but I was sure I could handle the situation. I'd wait until my parents were both home and call him back. You know what they say, safety first.

In the meantime, I decided to proceed as normal, and a normal Saturday for me always included a trip to the mailbox. One of my sole responsibilities as the only child of Greg and Beth Lowry was to get the mail every day. Apparently, Mom and Dad had a thing for their responsible daughter retrieving the mail and leaving it in a tidy pile on top of our granite countertops.

Getting the mail was one of the only artifacts of the "old Kate" that remained in place. I think it gave my parents some kind of false hope that their perfect daughter was buried somewhere underneath the sullen teenager who'd replaced her over the past year. The reality was that I didn't complain about the chore because it came in handy when demerits were mailed home.

Analyze that, Dr. P.

As I stood at the mailbox, I learned that my search for Cameron had landed me a demerit for cutting English Lit. I guess Seth never came through with that excused absence. I'd have to open that bad boy and forge my dad's illegible initials.

But the small package at the bottom of the heap was what made my stomach flip-flop.

It was a manila envelope lined in bubble wrap, addressed to me. Besides the fact that I pretty much never received mail (unless you counted those freaking demerits), there was no postage, no return address. But I didn't need either of those to know who had left the package in my mailbox. The handwriting was the same blocky script used to scrawl Grace's name next to the mysterious crest.

I looked left and then right, half expecting to hear Grace yell, "Gotcha!" in between fits of giggles. But the only person around was Seth, making his way down the driveway to his own mailbox.

"You okay, Kate?" he yelled over. He was chowing down on what looked like a s'more, and I had a vision of his family gathered around a campfire in their backyard roasting marshmallows and singing songs. Who made s'mores at 11:00 a.m. on a Saturday? He bypassed his mailbox and headed straight for me like some kind of Kate-guided missile.

"Hey, did you get some bad news or something?"

He craned his skinny neck and attempted to zero in on the bunch of mail I held. I pulled the pile to my chest and shook my head.

"I'm fine, Seth, seriously." I wiped at the corner of my mouth with my finger, trying to clue Seth in on the string of marshmallow dangling from his lip. He didn't take the hint.

"So I'm planning on heading up to the um...observatory later tonight. I have those new neighbors under surveillance. Wanna come? We can research that weird crest thing or whatever. Our Wi-Fi works great up there."

"Just to be clear, by 'observatory' you mean tree house, right?"

Seth's cheeks caught fire. "Well, yeah, but I've added some really cool stuff since the last time you saw it. There are chairs and a telescope, and it's, like, really private." He stuffed the rest of the s'more in his mouth and nodded his head as if he'd just told me he'd reserved us a suite at the Four Seasons.

"Yeah. Not a selling point, Seth." I turned around and started back up my driveway.

"So I'll take that as a maybe?" he called out hopefully behind me.

"No. Take it as a no." I didn't even bother turning around to tell him. Cameron's weird package was calling to me. I held Grace's pearls to my chest and picked up my pace.

Once I was back inside, I threw the mail pile on the counter and rushed up the stairs to my room. I ripped open the envelope before I even closed the door, and something fell to the wood floor. A delicate silver charm engraved with the words *Audi, Vide, Tace* sat nestled in the chain it was connected to. I crouched next to it and dumped the contents out of the envelope. An invitation almost identical to the one I'd received over a year ago slid to the hardwood floor. Only this version was addressed to Grace.

The same creamy card stock caressed my fingertips, and I cursed myself for losing mine. I still couldn't believe I'd been so careless, and it made me want to cry thinking about how different the past year would have been if I'd only managed to hang on to it. There would have been an actual investigation into Grace's death, and maybe even answers.

I examined Grace's invitation closely, and as far as I could tell, the only difference was that instead of a drawing in the bottom right-hand corner, where mine had been, hers appeared in the bottom left. Clearly the drawings were a part of a bigger picture. Cameron's careful block letters appeared on a sticky note taped to the back.

Kate,

You know Grace. She couldn't keep a secret.

And I'm sick of keeping mine. I don't know why she was there that night. But I was supposed to be with her. She told me to wait for her in the chapel basement, but I saw her with some other guy and I didn't bother to show. It's my fault she died. I should have been down there to save her.

You have the symbol I drew, and now you have this charm I found the day after she died. That's as far as I could get. There's more to this story, and if anyone can figure it out, it's you. It's over for me.

Cameron

I rubbed my eyes, trying to understand what all of this meant, and then I reread Cameron's final words: "It's over for me."

Oh, God.

I fumbled in my purse for my phone and with shaky hands scrolled through my contacts until Cameron's name was highlighted. After three rings, I figured the phone would go to voice mail, but a man's hoarse voice filled my ear.

"Hello?"

"Is Cameron there?"

"Who is this?" The voice on the other end of the phone was harsh, and for a split second I thought about hanging up.

"My name is Kate. I'm...um...a friend from school." I wondered if he'd remember me as the girl who always played with Grace.

"This is Mr. Thompson, Kate, Cameron's father." His voice cracked on that last word. "Do you know where he is? We've been looking everywhere...he never came home last night."

"I...um, I'm sorry, but I don't know anything. I was actually hoping to find him too."

"He left his cell phone here, but it's completely empty. He deleted all the contacts, all the emails, all the texts. We know nothing." Cameron's father sounded desperate, pleading. "Please call us if you hear anything from him. We've just filed a missing person's report, but the police think he ran away. There's just not much we can do…" His voice cracked again, and I was almost positive he'd begun to cry.

"I'll let you know if I hear anything, okay?" My words barely came out a whisper.

"You do that."

"I'm so sorry…" But I knew by the way my words echoed into dead air that he'd already hung up.

I rolled Grace's pearls between my fingers and wished that she was here to help me through this. Through all the years of our friendship, Grace had been the fearless one. She would have known what to do and would have given me the courage to do it. I squeezed my eyes shut. Maybe if I tried hard enough, I'd be able to feel her or she'd sense that I needed her and send me another email.

But when I opened my eyes and checked my phone? Nothing.

If I hadn't broken into his locker, Cameron would probably be under the bleachers right now, geeked out of his mind. But I had found the sketch. I had accused him of killing Grace.

Cameron was gone, and it was my all fault.

Chapter 13

Last Fall

B radley and I had finally reached the lake in the center of campus, and I wondered if he remembered me from the night of Nativitas. Maybe he'd spent the past few weeks at school searching for the girl in the pink polka-dot bikini and had only now recognized me.

Navy blue bled into the orange of the horizon, and dim pinpricks of light dotted the sky as stars began to make an appearance. I looked up at Bradley through eyelashes layered in Maybelline mascara, admiring his profile and unable to believe that this was really happening to me, Kate Lowry.

Bradley sat down on one of the benches surrounding the water, and I hesitated, not sure how close I should sit to him. Opting for the other side of the bench would be all kinds of awkward, but I wasn't going to plop down into his lap either. I finally settled on taking a seat about a foot away from him. As soon as I sat down, he scooted toward me, close enough so our knees touched, and a surge of electricity shot up through my leg.

My knee was touching Bradley Farrow's knee. Holy crap.

I adjusted my denim skirt so it covered more of my thighs and twisted the bracelet around my wrist.

"So it's a nice night, huh?" he asked, turning toward me.

"Uh, yeah. Beautiful," I managed to stammer in response, my mind spinning, my leg burning from his touch.

"I'm surprised you didn't have somewhere else to be," he commented, with a slight smile.

For a second I wondered if he knew about the invitation, but then he grabbed my hand and I couldn't think about anything except the warmth of his fingers. A rush of courage coursed through me. I was here. Bradley liked me. I could do this.

I opened my mouth to speak, but Bradley cut off my words with a kiss. His lips were soft and warm on mine, their gentle touch a tease. I opened my mouth slightly, eager for more, relaxing into his chest. But just as suddenly as it had begun, it was over. Bradley jerked away.

My face burned with humiliation. What the hell had I been thinking? He probably thought I was a huge slut or something. Or maybe my mouth still tasted like the pizza we had eaten at Grace's house. I tried to analyze the expression on his face: boredom, confusion, revulsion? I couldn't be sure.

I felt his eyes searching the space behind me and noticed a subtle nod of his head. Was somebody there? I whipped my head around and watched a person run back toward the direction of the bonfire. God, I hoped they hadn't seen Bradley push me away.

Bradley's hand felt limp in my own, and when I turned back to him, I struggled to read his face. He wasn't half smiling like before, and his eyes darted around, looking everywhere except at me.

He pulled his hand out of mine and ran it over his shaved head. "Hey, sorry…" He pulled his phone from his pocket. "I didn't realize the time. I've got to run, but I'll see you around." He gave me one last smile before jogging into the darkness and back toward the bonfire.

I was speechless. The worst part was that I knew exactly when it had all gone wrong. I was a terrible kisser, and everyone at school would know all about it on Monday.

I did my best to fight the tears, but I couldn't hold them back. I felt so…rejected. But as I swiped at my cheeks and wallowed on the bench, I remembered. A wave of nervousness washed over me. The invitation. The chapel. The night sky was now close to black, well past dusk.

I was late.

I jumped up from the bench and ran toward an opening in the woods. The path was faster but scarier than sticking to the open, rolling lawn of campus. I took off toward the trees and figured being scared was my punishment for wasting all that time with Bradley. Or maybe my reward for being the worst, most disgusting kisser on the planet.

Leaves crunched rhythmically under my feet, and the cool night air bit at my arms and legs while my imagination ran wild. I imagined someone chasing me and not being able to hear their footsteps. I imagined a dangerous animal attacking me from the shadowy depths of the woods. I even imagined getting lost *Blair Witch* style and never being able to find my way out. I tried to push the scary thoughts away as I ran, but that was impossible. They flooded back with each step.

I heard the snap of a tree branch a few feet away and froze. I could just barely make out the pad of footsteps over the sound of my racing heart.

I wasn't alone.

But it was only after I saw the flames that I began to scream.

Chapter 14

Present Day

Number of times I'd refreshed my email since I'd sent my last message to Grace: 548.

Status of my inbox as of 1:14 a.m.: empty.

Number of times I'd stared at my phone praying for a text or some kind of communication from Cameron: 1,326.

In five hours my alarm clock would scream in my ear and force me to get my butt out of bed and to school. Needless to say, tomorrow wasn't going to be a good day. Not only did I have to make it through nine interminable classes, but I also had a tennis match after school. And no doubt everyone would be buzzing about Cameron's disappearance by then. Somehow, in light of recent events, studying for quizzes and hitting a little yellow ball over a net seemed really pointless.

Just as I shut my laptop to attempt to sleep, my phone buzzed in my ear. I jumped up, shaking, thinking it might be a message from Cameron or maybe even Grace. I was wrong.

It was a text from an unfamiliar number.

Station 2. 2 a.m.

It had to be from Cameron. I had to go to him. I had to try to fix this mess.

I looked at the clock: 1:32 a.m. I didn't live far from the school. It was only about a ten-minute bike ride. Of course, that would mean breaking my "no bike riding in public" rule, but considering it was pitch-black outside, I could probably bend on that a bit. After all, it's only considered public if people can actually see you, right?

Before I could change my mind, I threw on Grace's pearls (they make pajamas more presentable) and crept out of the house and into the garage to unearth my bike from beneath the piles of junk.

The wind tossed my hair around as I pedaled through the darkness. I had no idea why Cameron would want to meet at the clock tower in the middle of the night, and I was more than just a little terrified. But when I drew the predawn air deep into my lungs, I could feel the adrenaline race through my blood. Something about riding a bike just feels so free. Too bad it looks so dorky.

I got to the clock tower just in time to see a white-cloaked figure ascend the first flight of stairs, candle in hand.

There would be no Cameron, no answers, no fixing what I'd broken. It was Candela, another Sacramentum, a tradition that would do nothing but make me more exhausted than I already was.

According to a Pemberly Brown legend, a second-year girl was attacked by a boy on campus in 1971. She went to the police, but they didn't believe her. Once word spread that she had accused one of the most popular boys at school of rape, she was tormented by the other boys and supposedly hanged herself at the top of the clock tower.

Every year, eleven second-year girls gather to ascend the stairs of the clock tower, eleven flights total. Each girl carries a single candle that she holds in the window on one of the levels of the tower until all are lit. The eleventh girl climbs to the very top and waits for the girl's ghost to appear.

I hung back, debating whether to go home or move in closer. The decision was made for me when I felt someone grab my hand and lead me forward.

It was Naomi Farrow, Bradley's gorgeous sister, not a hair out of place, dark eyes flashing. She didn't say a word—silence was the unspoken rule—but handed me a white cloak exactly like the one she wore. She gestured that I should put it on, so I pulled it over my T-shirt and pajama pants.

She smiled and gave me a white candle that she lit with the one she held in her hands. Her face flickered in the candlelight, and her eyes shone with secrets. Again she grabbed my hand, and I followed her to the clock tower.

The girls were lined up at the plaque that marked Station 2, the clock tower. *Tempus edax rerum.* "Time is the devourer of all things." The girls looked ghostly, the candlelight casting shadows where eyes and mouths should be. I couldn't stop myself from looking for Grace's face among the white phantoms. My eyes widened a bit when I saw Maddie but no Grace. Obviously.

I stood behind Naomi and realized that I was the eleventh. I'd be climbing to the top, the last unlucky girl to wait for the ghost.

One by one, the girls climbed the steps, and one by one the windows leading to the top of the clock tower were lit. If I weren't so terrified of what I'd find at the top, the sight of them would have been oddly beautiful. But climbing the stairs to meet a ghost hit way too close to home.

I watched Naomi walk slowly to the tower. Girl number ten. I saw her candle flicker past each window as she wound her way up to the tenth story. When she finally stopped in front of her window, it was my turn.

I tried to hold my candle steady, but my hands were shaking so much that the hot wax dripped down and burned my skin. My legs were barely able to support my body as I climbed each flight.

When I passed Maddie on the sixth floor, she turned to look at me. Her face was blank, but her eyes were wide and glossy and sad. God, I missed her. I lifted my fingers in a wave, but she shook her head quickly and turned away. As usual, there was an invisible wall between us that she never let me breach.

I walked on without a word, a new purpose in my steps. I could do this. I had to do this. I was Kate Lowry, not some lame-ass prom queen who was afraid of her own shadow. If a ghost really was at the top of the tower, I was sure I'd be able to handle it. That is, if you define "handling it" as dropping my candle, booking it down the stairs, and sprinting back to the safety of my bedroom.

I crept up the final flight of stairs, terrified that the tiniest noise would stir whatever might be waiting up there. The old gears of the clock churned and creaked, and every tick and tock made me jump and search for the girl with the noose looped around her neck.

When I finally approached the window with my candle, I saw her. She stood in the middle of the courtyard, plaid skirt, inky hair spilling down her back. Her body was turned toward the dense woods that surrounded the campus. But before I could scream, deep voices rang within the tower, slicing through the silence.

"*BOO-AH-HAH-HAHH!*"

The voices came from each level of the tower and were followed by piercing, high-pitched screams, one of which was my own. When I swung around, heart pounding, to confront whatever or whoever was there, I came face-to-face with Alistair Reynolds and Bradley Farrow, both dressed head to toe in black.

I shoved Bradley's chest, pushing him backward. His large frame only moved an inch, and he held his hands up as if to surrender. But before I could lay into Alistair, I remembered who I'd seen out the window. I whipped my head back around and screamed through the opening.

"*Grace!*"

I scanned the dark ground below, looking for her. I locked in on her running into the woods, her hands pushing weeds and twigs to clear the way.

I took off down the stairs, my candle long since extinguished in my rush to get out of the tower. On each level, girls in white stood with boys in black, all staring wide-eyed at the crazy girl running down the stairs. But by the time I made it out into the open, Grace was gone.

Slowly the black and white figures trailed after me, offering concerned looks. Tears that I hadn't realized were falling blurred my vision.

I had lost her again.

I leaned against the cool brick of the clock tower and slowly sank down into the grass, cradling my head in my hands and feeling even more lost. Alistair and Bradley reached up to pull off the black hoods covering their heads, revealing faces darkened with face paint.

Bradley tried to reach down and touch my shoulder, but I jerked away, not wanting his hands anywhere near me. It was hard to believe that a year ago I would have given just about anything for this kind of attention. But as soon as I felt the pressure of Alistair's fingertips on my other shoulder, the anger returned, and all at once I figured it out.

"It was you. You sent her on purpose!" Tears gathered in my eyes, spilling down my cheeks and landing in the corners of my mouth. "You found someone who looked like her. Who looked like Grace..." My chin shook as the words spilled out. "You think this is funny? You think it's funny to...to trick me!" I looked at the boys standing in front of me, accusing each of them.

"I don't know what you're talking about," Alistair said. "We just wanted to scare you guys—that's it."

Bradley bent down in front of me.

"We didn't send anyone who looked like Grace, Kate. We wouldn't trick you." His face looked soft and sincere, and all at once my anger was replaced with embarrassment. God, I was just so freaking tired of all of this.

"Just…just leave me alone." A few more tears slipped out of the corners of my eyes. Alistair was the first to walk away, and slowly the rest of the group followed until they had all disappeared into the night.

I sat for a while, hoping that if I closed my eyes and opened them again I would be at home in my bed, the entire night a bad dream. But when I opened my eyes, my back was still against the hard stone of the clock tower, my hands gripping the damp lawn.

My left hand sank into the soft earth as I struggled to stand, but my right hand pressed into something hard and cold beneath the grass. A small rectangular stone was almost completely hidden by clover, but as soon as I ran my fingers over the carving I knew exactly what it was.

The crest.

Chapter 15

I practically sleepwalked through the following day, nodding off in World History and sleeping so soundly in Latin that a pool of drool formed on my notebook.

I woke up to Porter Reynolds elbowing me in the rib cage. Grace had thought Porter was the dreamiest boy in our grade, and he was actually kind of cute in that I've-never-worked-a-day-in-my-life-and-probably-never-will kind of way. But to me, his intentionally unwashed hair and cheesy smile screamed "douche bag." Not exactly the person I wanted disturbing my beauty sleep.

My thoughts were interrupted by my five-foot-nothing Latin teacher. "Ms. Lowry, *evigila! Ne dormias inter disciplinam. Evigila!*" Oh, so that's why Porter was waking me up. Looks like I owed good old Porter a mental apology. Sorry, dude.

"*Mihi ignosce, magister,*" I managed to mumble.

"*Poenam meris,*" she said in her obnoxious, fake Latin accent. I mean, aren't all Latin accents fake? Considering that Latin is a dead language, how does anyone even know what it's supposed to sound like? It's not like there's an eight-track of Julius Caesar giving one of his famous speeches lying around somewhere.

In spite of the fact that I'd slept through most of Latin, I was able to make out the word "punishment" in there. Crap. Two demerits equaled a phone call from the headmaster to my absentee parents. I mentally added the impending parental contact to my list of worries, right underneath global warming.

Grace was, of course, number one on my list.

After class, my name rang through the hallway. I turned, expecting Seth or maybe even Liam, but instead met Alistair Reynolds's eyes. Two Reynolds brothers in one day? Someone must have spritzed me with eau de old money or something.

"Oh, hey, Alistair," I said, trying not to sound too disappointed. As I looked up at him, I flushed again after thinking about my outburst the night before.

"I want to apologize," he said, running a hand through his shaggy hair. "It was a stupid idea, and I'm really sorry you got so upset."

"It's not a big deal. I was just super-tired," I mumbled, avoiding his eyes.

"Can I make it up to you?" He wore a sly smile as he leaned casually against the bay of lockers. It was impossible to tell if he was being serious or not. I kept looking around the hallway expecting Bradley Farrow to pop out and scream, "*Gotcha!*"

Alistair sensed my hesitation. "Well, I mean, unless your boyfriend will get mad."

Students rushed by us trying to make it to their ninth-period classes in time. I couldn't deny the feel of their eyes on us as they passed. Surely each one was wondering why a boy like Alistair would ever talk to a crazy girl like me. As I considered this question, I thought of Maddie and her infamous crush on him. I thought about how hurt she would be if I accepted. For a second, I even thought about how good that would feel.

"You don't have to do that," I said, forcing myself to smile. "But thanks for offering. It's really…um…sweet of you."

He pulled his hands to his chest, covering his heart and feigning heartbreak.

"Ah, denied!" he joked. As he walked backward, he slammed right into someone. Well, not just someone—Liam Gilmour.

"Hey, watch where you're going, dude," Liam said with a quick glance at Alistair and a long look at me.

"Sorry, man. Just trying to stay on my game." Alistair raised his hands at Liam and winked at me. Suddenly his whole playboy shtick seemed very tired.

"Interesting." Liam rolled his eyes.

"Always," he responded to Liam, but he didn't take his eyes off me. "Anyway, call me, Kate. I'll be waiting." Alistair winked again and walked off in the direction of his next class.

"Didn't realize trust-fund d-bags were your type." Liam shook his head. "Too bad. These guys gave me some tickets to a show tonight in exchange for designing posters for their band. I thought it might be your thing, but maybe I was wrong."

Holy shit. Did Liam Gilmour just ask me out on a date? "I… um…I have a tennis match…and bands aren't exactly my thing, unless you count the Beatles…" I trailed off.

"Whatever. I get it. It's cool." He looked down at his feet and then back up at me. "Just be careful with those guys, okay? They're not who they pretend to be. Or maybe they are." He shook his head. "Just, I don't know…watch out. Oh, and the Beatles? They totally count." He ducked into a classroom and vanished just as quickly as he'd appeared.

Awesome. I'd somehow managed to make the cheesiest guy in school think I was going to call him while simultaneously blowing off the one guy I might actually be interested in.

Universe: 1. Kate: 0.

• • •

Directly after school, Naomi and I were paired to warm up before our tennis match. As soon as I heard Naomi's name, my face flushed. She probably thought I was insane after the previous night. But I couldn't exactly ask my coach for a different partner. I jogged onto the grass court, thankful that Naomi waited along the baseline instead of meeting me at the net.

Over the summer Naomi had grown her hair out and had some serious work done on her eyebrows, transforming from an ugly duckling to a full-on supermodel. The best part was that Naomi seemed totally oblivious to her mini-transformation. She adjusted her sports bra, smoothed her perfect hair, and gave a little wave to one of the football players practicing nearby.

Well, maybe not totally oblivious.

"Hey, Kate!" she called, hitting a couple balls in my direction. She looked obnoxiously well rested despite having participated in a secret ceremony the night before. "You can serve first."

Okay, so we weren't going to discuss what had happened the night before. I was actually a little relieved to focus on warming up my serve instead of obsessing over Candela. Soon Naomi and I were hitting back and forth and laughing between shots. I'd forgotten how much I missed laughing with a friend.

But before I could get too comfortable, I spotted a bus pulling into the parking lot and, out of my peripheral vision, caught a glimpse of somebody hiding behind one of the huge oak trees surrounding the courts. Naomi hit a killer backhand that whizzed so close to my head that it moved tiny wisps of hair near my ear.

"Oh! Sorry!" she yelled. "I thought you were ready."

With my eyes glued to the tree, I approached the net and walked onto Naomi's side of the court.

"Kate?" Naomi laughed uncomfortably.

I narrowed my eyes and zeroed in on the navy-blue-and-hunter-green plaid of a uniform skirt.

"Who's there?" I called, dropping my racquet and gripping the fence with my fingers.

The girl took off into the woods, so I ran the length of the fence and out the door after her.

"Kate?" Coach Schafer screamed after me. "Kate!"

I tried to keep up with the girl, her dark hair splashing against her back as she ran, but she had too much of a head start.

"Grace!" I yelled into the woods, even though I hadn't yet seen her face. "Wait!"

My feet slowed, but my chest only heaved harder when I stopped next to a white birch tree.

"Now what?" I asked absolutely no one.

I had my answer when I heard the soft sound of sobbing and followed the noise. The crying grew louder as I exited the woods and ended up underneath Farrow's Arches. And there right in front of me sat a huddled form sobbing on Grace's bench.

The girl had her legs pulled to her chest and her forehead on her knees. Her hair was light brown. Not the girl I'd chased into the woods. Not Grace. I considered turning around, but she lifted her head and caught my eye before I could disappear.

Maddie.

"Kate?" she whispered. "What're you doing here?" She wiped at her cheeks and lowered her legs to the ground, adjusting her athletic shorts.

"Nothing," I said, but I remembered my tennis dress. "I mean, just taking a walk before my match."

Maddie's phone buzzed, and she pulled it out of her book bag to read the message. Panic washed over her face, making her look way older than fifteen and not in a good way. Part of me still couldn't believe that this shadow of a person was my old best friend—the pudgy, happy girl who concocted schemes to get us a seat at the best lunch table or to score us an invite to an upperclassman's party. Guess she didn't have to worry about stuff like that now that she was Taylor's bestie-in-waiting.

"I have to go," she said hurriedly, shoving a pile of books back into her bag. Sadness stabbed me when I noticed her place the bright pink journal I'd given as a gift for her thirteenth birthday into the bag. Well, at least she hadn't burned it.

"Bill and Jude?" I managed. I knew joking with Maddie about her not-so-protective parents was a stretch, but I thought maybe it would clear the air a little.

"No, it's...Taylor. We were supposed to meet at three-thirty, and I'm late," she said, bending to grab her bag.

"Wait...Maddie?" I asked. "Have you seen...I mean...did you see a girl running through here before I came?"

Maddie's entire demeanor changed. She was fuming, which seemed a little extreme based on the question. I mean, it's not like I asked her when she last ate something white.

"Kate, people always run through the gardens. Hello? Cross-country," she snipped and scratched at her leg, clearly agitated by my question.

"Oh...right," I said, rolling my eyes.

Her nails left angry red scratches down her legs. She was such a bad liar.

I brushed my fingers over an oil-rubbed bronze plaque that dedicated part of the Memorial Garden to Abigail Moore, 1956–1971. Legend said that her sister had planted the peonies, Abigail's favorite flower, after she died.

Throughout the years, the story surrounding her death changed depending on who was doing the telling. Some kids said she was killed in a drunk-driving accident. Others said she was the one hanging from the clock tower. And still others said she had turned up in the lake. Like so many PB legends, the truth had gotten lost somewhere in time.

I glanced over at Maddie, surprised she was still standing there.

"Remember the pee-on-mes?" I gestured to the plaque.

Our first year at the lower school, right after we became insta-friends, Grace, Maddie, and I used to crack up over our inside joke about the beautiful flowers.

"God, Kate, are you ever going to grow up?"

I looked up at her, eyes flashing. How dare she? Who was she to judge the person I'd become after she refused to talk to me for a year? The sad truth was that I would have given anything *not* to grow up if that meant having Grace here with me now.

But when I examined Maddie's face, she didn't look angry anymore, just sad. In that moment, I wanted us to be friends again. I didn't care about Taylor or Beefany or how cruel Maddie had been to me in the weeks after Grace's death—or even how cruel she was being right now. I just wanted to talk to one of the girls who used to know me better than anyone else on this planet. I wanted at least one of my best friends back.

"I miss you."

For a second, Maddie looked into my eyes and transformed back into the chubby girl who had shared countless secret-filled sleepovers with me. But then something changed in her face.

"You don't seem all that lonely. I saw you talking to Alistair today in the hall." She raised her thin eyebrows and shook her head at me in disgust. "I have to go," she said. And just like that, she turned and walked away from me.

As usual, she didn't look back.

Chapter 16

After Maddie left, I decided to head home. I couldn't go back to the courts. By now the matches would have already begun, and all the girls, plus my coach, were probably planning an intervention to save my crazy ass. Besides, I was itching to do a little research on Station 2 after my discovery in the grass the night before. I hoped that the clock tower would lead me to the meaning behind the crest and its connection to Grace.

I took the long way back to the locker room to avoid the tennis courts, hopped on a late bus, and ten minutes later was home. As soon as I walked through the door, I headed straight for the answering machine and hit Play. Coach Schafer's frantic voice filled the kitchen, and when I heard someone walk into the kitchen behind me, I hastily hit Erase and turned around.

"Deleting incriminating messages?" my dad asked, the lines around his mouth and near his eyes deeper than ever.

"Uh…no. That was an accident. You scared me," I said, searching for an excuse.

"Don't bother, Kate. I've already spoken to your coach. She called me on my cell. You ran off before a match? Two demerits? What the hell is going on?" He grabbed a drink out of the fridge and sat down.

The thing is, I would have loved to sit down next to him and tell him the whole unbelievable story, but I couldn't. Telling my dad would only confirm my parents' suspicions that I was completely insane. Instead of seeing Dr. Prozac, I'd probably be stuck in the freaking psych ward.

Dr. Prozac's big theory was that I avoided getting close to people for fear of losing them. But the truth was that I felt safer when I kept everyone at a distance. It was more efficient. Hurt less, too.

So instead of pulling up a chair and telling my dad everything, I settled for a quick, "I'm fine," and hoped he'd leave it at that.

He didn't.

"I wasn't born yesterday, Kate." He stopped, unable to finish. "I can't…I just can't go back to the way things were last year. Your hair is bad enough. We thought we were going to lose you…"

He trailed off, looking confused and more than a little scared. I felt awful. Of course he didn't understand. How could he? I hadn't given him the chance. But what was I supposed to tell him? If I started blubbering about emails from dead best friends, my parents would accuse me of obsessing again.

Just this past summer, I had been deemed well enough to stop taking the cocktail of drugs that were supposed to help me move on. All they really did was make me forget what being alive felt like. I couldn't risk telling him and going back to that place. Not when I was supposed to be helping Grace.

"I'm at a loss here, Kate. But your coach seems to think a different after-school activity might help. She suggested you join the Concilium. She said this girl, Taylor something, is in charge of the meetings and that she's a great role model. I'm hoping she's right."

"I'm not joining some stupid club." I gripped the table and dug what nails I had into the wood. "I have tennis to worry about."

"You know, you're not the only one who lost someone, Kate. You think I don't wish I had my daughter back?" His face was old and sad. "If your coach thinks a new club will help, we'll try a new club. Your first meeting's tomorrow. And detention starts Tuesday."

"Fine." I swallowed the egg-sized lump in my throat.

"Fix this, Kate," he said, resting his hand on my shoulder. "Come back to us. We miss you."

I laid my head down on the kitchen table and watched my dad walk back into his office. I wished everything could be as easy as finding the girl I used to be and forcing her to come home.

Unfortunately she seemed just as lost as Grace.

Chapter 17

I used bubble letters to draw the words *Audi, Vide, Tace* in the margin of my notebook when I should have been taking notes during a PowerPoint presentation on Dostoevsky. The previous night, I had Googled just about every combination of the three Latin words, adding "symbol" and "Pemberly Brown" and "crest" into the mix. The only semi-helpful result had been an Ohio Historical Society web page featuring an article referencing the history of Pemberly Brown.

Apparently Brown, the boys school, had closed in 1950 to merge with the local girls school, Pemberly. The decision was a controversial one at the time, but Brown was low on funding and faced competition from other private schools in the area, so it was either merge with Pemberly or cease to exist. A picture of Brown's old crest showed that it had featured a lion holding an ornate-looking key. I was sketching what I remembered of the crest when I felt a hand on my shoulder.

"Kate?" My English Lit teacher, Ms. Cole, tapped my desk and raised a curious brow when she saw my bubble letters in the margin. "Careful with that," she whispered as she placed a note on top of my notebook and walked back to the front of the room to continue her presentation.

Before I could even begin to wonder about her last comment, I realized that the note was an early-dismissal slip from the office. I had a sinking feeling in my stomach as I gathered my books and stuffed them into my bag.

On my way to the office, I made a mental list of the potential reasons for an unplanned dismissal. It definitely couldn't be a good thing. As far as I knew, no parents in the history of the world had ever left work early to yank their kids out of school for a surprise vacation to the Bahamas.

With each step, I imagined more dire circumstances. What if my mom had been in an accident, or one of my aunts or cousins was dead or…Cameron? Had they found him? Was he alive?

When I pushed through the office doors, my dad was waiting for me.

"You're already signed out." The expression on his face didn't look like one he'd have after someone died, but he wasn't wearing his vacation clothes either. "All set?"

"Yeah. But where are we going?" I asked as I followed him out.

"Dr. Lowen had an eleven o'clock opening, so I made an appointment."

"I thought I didn't have to go every week anymore. Why are you doing this to me?" I couldn't say the words without whining. I sounded like a three-year-old.

"Since you won't talk to your mom and me, you need to talk

to someone. Maybe this week you can tell Dr. Lowen about what you were doing when you should have been in first period or playing tennis."

I glared at my dad and shook my head. It was probably safer not to talk. There was no telling what might come out. During the entire drive to the doctor's office, the elevator ride to the seventh floor, and the forty-five-minute wait in the office, my dad and I said exactly four words to one another.

"Which floor again?"

"Seven."

When the woman behind the desk with a five-o'clock shadow (a walking, talking cautionary tale against women using razors to shave facial hair) finally called my name, I jumped out of my seat at the opportunity to escape the waiting-room game.

The guy next to me covertly examined me in his peripheral vision; the woman under the cheesy painting of a little girl at the beach snuck glances behind magazine pages; and the boy with the black-painted fingernails looked out from beneath heavily lined eyes, all of them trying to determine what particular brand of crazy had landed their fellow patients in the waiting room. I wondered what they came up with when they looked at me. Did I have the classic "I see dead people" look in my eyes?

I wound around to the back of the office and opened the familiar door. Dr. Prozac was sitting behind his huge mahogany desk. And, no, I didn't lie down on some couch. I sat in an uncomfortable chair with wooden arms that matched the desk. I forgot how much that chair sucked.

Me: Long time, no see. (Dr. P. looked up at me over his old-man glasses and smiled his careful smile.)

Prozac: Kate, you know how much I look forward to our chats. How's everything going?

Me: Fine. (If only shrinks would let you off the hook after the word "fine." If only everyone would.)

Prozac: How's school? I haven't seen you since (he looked down at his notes) last month.

Me: Good. (If having only one friend who also happened to be your nerdy neighbor was good.)

Prozac: So what brings you here? (He took off his glasses and placed them on the desk.)

Me: My dad. He says I need a safe place to talk. (I yawned even though I didn't have to.)

Prozac: Do you miss Grace?

Me: (Long pause. My throat went completely dry. I couldn't for the life of me form the words to answer. I hoped Dr. P. couldn't read minds. There was no way I could tell him the truth about Grace and still make it out of here without ten different antidepressant prescriptions.)

Prozac: What are you thinking, Kate?

Me: Well, now that you brought her up, I'm thinking about Grace. (Dr. P. put his glasses back on and checked his notes again.)

Prozac: Have you been thinking about her a lot lately? Are you having any of those same feelings you had after the funeral?

Me: No, no. I'm fine. (What feelings? The anger that came after trying to tell everyone there was more to Grace's death and having no one believe me? The betrayal I felt after my parents checked me into the hospital for depression instead of listening to me? Or maybe he was referring to the good old-fashioned guilt I felt about ditching my best friend at the moment she needed me most.)

Prozac: How are you sleeping?

Me: Fine. (If you don't count staying up all night refreshing email.)

Prozac: Have you been using any of the "exercises" we practiced? (Dr. P. formed quotations with his fingers.)

Me: Sometimes. (Mental note: never make quotation signs with fingers. Ever.)

Prozac: How's tennis?

Me: (Very long pause. This was a loaded question and I liked to see how long I could make him wait for my answer. My record was three and a half minutes.) I'm sure my dad told you, but I have to take a break.

Prozac: A break? (Dr. P. pushed his desk chair out a little and uncrossed and recrossed his legs. Hard to trust a male leg-crosser.)

Me: (I narrowed my eyes. I found it highly annoying when people beat around the bush.) I'm pretty sure you know about me wigging out during my match and being forced into the Concilium. This is a safe place, Dr. P. You can just come right out and say what you want to say.

Prozac: (Laughed. Well, as close to a laugh as he got. It actually sounded more like a cough.) Yes, Kate, your dad mentioned the match. Want to explain?

Me: (Began an impromptu staring contest. I liked to see who

would blink first. I usually won. I think Dr. P. liked it too.) I just...
got distracted.

Prozac: (Blinked and glanced at the clock.) I want you to work
on something for me between now and next week. Any time you're
feeling overwhelmed, like you want to run away, tell people you
need a break. No one can read your mind, Kate. But people will
understand if you need a time-out.

Me: You mean like when a kid gets pissed and rips a toy away
from someone and his mom sends him to his room? (Back to square
one—weekly visits. Next came the tiny green-and-white pills.)

Prozac: Only the adult version. Like a breather. We all need
breathers. And Kate? (He stood up and took his glasses off.) Give
Concilium a chance. You might be surprised what you'll find there.
You can make next week's appointment on your way out.

I got up from the chair without answering, hoping I could play
the "I didn't hear you" card. But Dr. P. followed me out and told
the receptionist to book my appointment.

"See you next week" never sounded so depressing.

Chapter 18

That evening as I pretended to do homework, I accomplished nothing more than spreading every clue I'd gathered to date around me on my bed. The mysterious crest, Grace's invitation, her email, Cameron's letter, the Latin charm. Everything.

I even had our slam book, just in case Grace's answers held some clue that I was missing. I ran my fingers over the puff paint, rhinestones, and glitter, and closed my eyes and made a wish like I was a little girl again. I wished for the ability to understand the meaning behind at least one of the clues. I wished that I'd make good on my promise to Grace.

But nothing.

I flopped back onto the pillows on my bed, thinking back to Candela and the stone I'd uncovered beneath the grass. There had to be more to the clock tower than the legend of a girl's suicide. I looked around my bedroom knowing I'd never find the answer here. Grabbing my book bag and dumping out the contents, I carefully placed every clue inside and rushed out my door.

"Dad!" I yelled as I descended the stairs two at a time. "I have to go to the library for a project!"

"Hold on, Kate. I can't hear a word you're saying," he called from the kitchen. I rounded the corner and waited for him to turn off the faucet. "Okay, what now?"

I adjusted the book bag on my shoulder. "I have to run back up to school to get a book from the library. It won't take me that long."

"Kate, your mom's on her way home, and I've just ordered dinner. I can't take you now."

"It's okay. I'll ride my bike."

The look of shock that came over my dad's face was priceless. "I thought you had a rule against that."

"It's important. I'll be back in time for dinner." Before he could say anything else, I ran out the door and into the garage, breaking my no-bike-riding-in-public rule for the second time in a matter of days.

Good thing my social life was already in shambles. These kinds of leaps are much easier to take when you don't have far to fall. Besides, taking off on my bike really was kind of fun. Maybe it was time I embraced my inner nerd.

• • •

I waved my student ID in front of the sensor and pulled the library door open when I heard it unlock. Only a few of the buildings on campus were open 24/7, and the library was one of them. Like it said on the plaque outside the door that marked it as Station 9, *Scientia est potentia*. "Knowledge is power," and power never sleeps.

"And you were just going to rush on by," I heard a raspy voice call out. I didn't have to turn around to know that Dorothy would be smiling. I could hear it in her voice. Ms. D. manned the librarian's desk after hours and made sure no funny business took place on school grounds.

"Hey, Ms. D., of course I was gonna say hello. I'm just kind of in a hurry," I called back. She went by Ms. D. or Officer D. depending on who you were talking to. A large woman in her late sixties in charge of security on campus, she wore her wiry gray hair closely cropped to her head and could easily defeat most of the boys on campus in an arm-wrestling match.

One of PB's many random traditions was for every fourth-year boy to challenge Dorothy before he graduated and left the Academy behind for one of the Ivies. I think only a handful of boys had actually beaten her after all these years, but she would never confirm or deny her stats.

"Well, I can't stand in the way of your studies, now, can I?" Ms. D. raised her hands in surrender, and her entire wrinkly face smiled.

"You know I'd hold you responsible," I laughed and pushed open the glass doors to Pemberly Brown's library.

I headed straight for one of the computers to check out the catalog. I typed in the words "Pemberly Brown history" and crossed my fingers that someone had written a book about PB and that the book could be found on the first level of the library.

"What's a girl like you doing in the library after hours?" a smooth voice whispered behind me.

I whipped around to find Porter Reynolds smiling lazily at me with his guitar slung over his shoulders. Porter could typically be found mooning around campus with his beat-up guitar, playing three tired chords over and over again while singing along in a monotone yet somehow poetic voice.

A handful of girls trailed after him who either suffered from First Year-itis or were raging gold-diggers who loved the sound of their last names hyphenated with "Reynolds."

"Just doing some research for a school project. What brings you out and about? Serenading study groups?"

"Aw, come on, Kate. Just because you're immune to my charms doesn't mean I don't have anything to offer." He fake pouted and looked even douchier than usual. "I'm just waiting on my ride and thought I'd grab some reading material." He held up copies of Jack Kerouac's *On the Road* and *Howl and Other Poems* by Allen Ginsberg. God, he was such a cliché.

"Do you even know what beat poetry is?" I couldn't stop myself from asking.

"Beat poetry? Never heard of it. But girls totally dig guys who carry books around." He inched his way closer to me and flung his arm around my shoulders. "So what do you think, Kate? Is it working? You wanna head down to the stacks?"

"Oh, yeah, it's totally working. Let's get going." Porter's eyes lit up. "Do you think Ms. D. would be interested in a threesome?" His face fell, making him look like a kid who had just found out he wasn't getting a pony for Christmas.

Porter swore at me under his breath before he slunk off, presumably to harass some other unsuspecting girl. I turned back to my search. The computer made the crackling sound that let me know it was thinking and…bingo.

The results pulled up a book called *Pemberly Brown: 150 Years of Excellence* by Calvin Markwell. But my heart sank a little when "stacks" was listed as the location. The idea of going down to the stacks alone almost made me regret turning down Porter's invitation. There were always rumors of strange noises and ghostly figures roaming down there. I used to laugh the stories off, but now I wasn't so sure.

After jotting down the book details, I did a quick scan of the library to see if I was alone. When my eyes fell on Dorothy, I considered telling her I was headed for the stacks and to come looking for me if I didn't reappear within fifteen minutes. But what was I, five? Besides, there was an emergency button I could push to call Ms. D. if anything did happen. I put on my big-girl pants, slung my book bag over my shoulder, and headed for the stairs.

As I descended and the shelves came into view, I leaned over the railing and stood on tiptoe to see if anyone else was browsing for books along with me. The coast appeared to be clear. I wasn't sure if that was a good thing or a bad thing.

I found the right row and ran my fingers along the leather-bound books until I landed on "Markwell." Voila. *Pemberly Brown: 150 Years of Excellence*. I pulled the large maroon book from the shelf, held it to my chest, and headed toward a study carrel.

I opened directly to the index, and there it was on the opposite page: the crest. Well, almost. This version had the words "Pemberly School for Girls" written around the shield and date of establishment. I wrinkled my forehead in confusion.

So the mysterious crest was really the old Pemberly crest? But why would someone have had a necklace engraved with *Audi, Vide, Tace*, Pemberly's old motto, at the chapel the night Grace died? And why was there an *S* on Cameron's drawing? This just didn't make any sense.

Next to the Pemberly crest was the Brown crest with the lion and key, and beneath both was a picture of the current Pemberly Brown crest. The paragraph below explained that Pemberly had altered its crest when the school merged with Brown. Pemberly brought the door; Brown brought the key. Together, the schools established a new motto that would better represent unity.

The marker I'd seen outside the clock tower must have marked Station 2 before the merger. But what did that have to do with Grace?

I glanced at my phone. Time was slipping away. Running my fingers over the headings, I found the page number where information about the Twelve Stations began and flipped to the chapter I needed. I got distracted when I came across the picture of a beautiful woman a few pages before the station information. The caption beneath the photo listed her as head architect of the 1950 merger, Josephine Fitzgerald Reynolds.

As I continued reading, the section explained that she redesigned the entire campus, transforming what used to be the upper school into the lower and middle schools, and designed a new upper school from the ground up. Go, Josephine.

My stomach grumbled, reminding me that dinner was probably getting cold, but I still had work to do. I flipped the pages the rest of the way and saw the familiar picture of the clock tower. It was built in 1893 when Pemberly Brown was just plain old Pemberly. Watches were a luxury, and the tower was built to establish standard time on campus.

I skimmed through information about the huge pendulum that made it run and stopped to read the section about the girl who had supposedly hanged herself on the eleventh floor. The historian said the information could not be substantiated and that it was considered legend. He went on to describe Candela, Nativitas, and some of the other rituals associated with Pemberly Brown.

I turned the page a little annoyed at the so-called historian. I guess I wanted to believe that some of the Academy's legends were actually true. As I continued reading, I noticed that at the top of the following page, the text did not line up. When I lifted the page, I realized that a perfect square had been cut away, removing an entire section of text. I sat back in my chair and chewed on a jagged fingernail.

What had been removed? Lifting a chunk of pages from the chapter, I let them fan away and noticed additional holes in the pages. For a second, I couldn't believe what I was seeing.

Pemberly Brown had secrets that someone didn't want students to discover.

"How's it going down here?" Dorothy's voice shattered the quiet, and I almost fell out of my chair.

"Oh, fine, I guess. Just can't seem to find what I'm looking for today." I slammed the damaged book shut, annoyed that I'd have to make a trip to the public library or order a copy online and wait for it to be delivered. I didn't have time for this.

"Maybe you're just not looking in the right place," Dorothy said as she walked down the stairs.

"Well, I'm starving, so the rest of my research will just have to wait." I packed up my bag and was startled to feel Dorothy's hand on my back.

"Just be careful. Strange things have happened around here, and some things are better left alone," she said, nodding at the book on my desk.

"Yeah, I guess," I replied. Dorothy had probably seen a lot of interesting things go down over her thirty years at Pemberly Brown.

She patted my shoulder twice and headed back in the direction of the stairs.

After the last of her footsteps disappeared, I returned to the book, opening it back up to the page that showed the merger of the school crests.

"What does it all mean, Grace?" I whispered, rubbing at my burning eyes. All at once I felt exhausted. I lifted her pearls from around my neck and wrapped the necklace around my wrist, playing with the beads. I was officially out of answers. Not that I'd had any in the first place.

I pulled the book to my chest and entered the stacks to return it. I made my way back to the row where Calvin Markwell's book belonged and started to slide it back onto the shelf, but a piece of notebook paper was tucked into the open space.

Tick tock, stay away from the clock. We're watching.

I heard a book slam a row over. I wasn't alone.

"Ms. D.?" My voice shook as I called out her name and shoved the heavy book back in its place. Through the gaps in the books, I caught a glimpse of someone running down the row next to me.

"Porter? This isn't funny. You're going to be in huge trouble..." My voice trailed off as I heard another book come crashing down behind me.

I took off toward the exit, cursing the emergency button for not being exactly where I needed it. The opening at the end of the row came closer and closer, so I slowed down and listened.

I couldn't see anyone through the books and could only hear the sound of my own ragged breathing. I peered around the corner, but no one was there. I had to make a break for the stairs. I shot forward and hurled my body upward, taking the steps three at a time.

When I landed in the library foyer, Porter was busy romancing a couple of first-years who giggled inanely at something he'd said. Their conversation ground to a halt as they took in my frazzled state, mouths gaping. I ignored their strange looks and headed straight for Dorothy's desk, the note wrinkled in my sweaty palm.

"Ms. D.," I huffed, "did you see anyone go down to the stacks after you left?"

"Kate, what happened?" Ms. D. asked as she stood up, a concerned look on her face. If Ms. D. were allowed to carry a gun, I'm pretty sure her hand would have moved to the holster at that moment.

But instead of slapping the note on her desk and requesting a handwriting analysis, I crumpled the paper into a ball and shoved my hand into my pocket.

"Oh...um...I just got a little scared. I heard noises and...I just wanted to see if...someone else was down there."

Ms. D. narrowed her eyes, probably considering whether or not she should call the police.

"I want you to file an incident report." She handed me a form. "Submit it to Headmaster Sinclair personally when you go to school tomorrow." She shook her head back and forth slowly. "I've told him countless times those stacks are trouble. I can't be in two places at once," she mumbled. "Maybe he'll listen to a complaint directly from a student."

I didn't have time to argue, because the clock behind her desk read twelve after seven. My parents were going to kill me.

"I'm actually late, but I'll fill this out and turn it in tomorrow." I swung my book bag around and pushed the paper inside.

As I pedaled in the direction of home, my legs burned with exertion and my mind spun with questions. Maybe Ms. D. was right and some secrets were meant to stay buried. But then Grace's face flashed through my mind.

Some secrets were worth the trouble.

Chapter 19

As I waited for the traffic light to change at an intersection, I saw lightning streak through the blackness. A few seconds later, thunder rolled. I pulled the crumpled note from my pocket and took in the crooked letters for a second time.

We're watching.

The wind picked up, and I couldn't stop myself from twisting around to see if I was being followed. Fat raindrops landed on the note and swirls of red ink bled into the droplet, blurring the letters below. Soon the words of the threat were as muddled as the clues I'd gathered.

My phone vibrated from the pocket of my jeans as soon as the lightning struck again, and the skies opened up. Completely drenched within seconds, I pulled my bike beneath a tree, sure it was one of my parents calling. They were probably worried about me riding in a storm. After the whole tennis-skipping debacle the week before, I couldn't afford to be screening anymore calls.

But it wasn't my mom or my dad. In fact, it wasn't a phone call at all.

I had mail.

To: KateLowry@pemberlybrown.edu

Sent: Wed 7:16 PM

From: GraceLee@pemberlybrown.edu

Subject: (no subject)

We're running out of time.

Go to the arches.

The truth is with the benefactor.

I need you.

Chapter 20

Last Fall

I wished whoever was screaming would stop. My head was pounding, and oddly enough, my throat felt raw. It wasn't until I brought my hand to my neck that I realized the sound was coming from me.

Flames licked at the old chapel, searing through wooden beams that broke like matchsticks and collapsed. As the chapel fell in on itself, puffs of sparks floated up into the night sky. I stood in front of the wooden building and watched it burn, hypnotized by the oranges and blues of the fire. Finally the heat reached my face and arms, snapping me out of my daze and sending me tearing through the woods to find Maddie and Grace. Someone could be in there. I had to get help.

By the time I made it out of the woods, fire trucks and emergency vehicles were already on the scene. Firemen were directing students away from the bonfire and maneuvering their trucks as close to the burning chapel as possible. I searched the crowd for Grace, praying that I was wrong about seeing her in the woods, hoping she hadn't been summoned to the chapel as I had.

But she was nowhere to be found. And neither was Maddie. Tears welled in my eyes, but I forced myself back to action before they spilled over the edges. I didn't have time to cry. Not now.

Blue and red emergency lights spun on top of police cars and were reflected in the shocked faces of students and teachers. People scrambled around cupping hands around their lips, battling against the wail of the sirens. Names were being shouted, girls were sobbing, and people were hugging each other and thanking God when they found their friends. We all understood that this was more than just a fire, that this was more serious than the loss of a building.

I wound through the clusters of students, searching for Grace and Maddie. They were nowhere to be found. When I finally saw Seth's familiar crop of red curls, I ran to him.

"Seth!" I threw my arms around his neck. I just needed to touch someone. "Have you seen Maddie and Grace? I can't find them anywhere!"

Seth's cheeks were completely pale, making his hair look brighter than usual. "Relax, Kate. Everything's going to be fine. I haven't seen them, but I'm sure…"

I was already off and running for the teachers before Seth had time to finish. My best friends were in that chapel. I just knew it. I had to get them out. I had to save them.

The teachers were clustered around Headmaster Sinclair, looking nearly as shocked and scared as the students. Fresh fear sliced through my heart.

"I need to get by!" I shouted as I shoved my way through the mass of administrators and made my way to the headmaster. "Headmaster Sinclair!" His face was flushed, and I watched a droplet of sweat zigzag from his sideburn to his chin.

I grabbed his arm. "I think my friends are in there!"

The teachers froze, and for a second I couldn't hear anything except the shouts of the firemen and the crackling of the fire.

"That's impossible." But in spite of his words he looked worried. "No one has used that building for years. All the entrances are sealed." But he was wrong. There was a way in, because I was supposed to have found it.

"I saw one of them walk into the woods earlier, and now I can't find either of them."

"Who is it?" one of the other teachers asked from behind me.

"Grace Lee and Maddie Greene."

There were some murmurs. No one else had seen them around the bonfire since the fire had broken out. I could hear the concern in their voices.

"Come on. We'll alert the fire chief." The other teachers watched us anxiously as we walked away.

The headmaster grabbed my shoulder as we made our way toward the firemen. "Are you sure they didn't leave with friends?"

"They'd never do that. Grace's parents are strict, and they're supposed to be picking us up tonight." I continued to scan the crowd, praying that I was wrong. That I'd hear Grace's and Maddie's voices or catch them coming back from the woods with Cameron or even Porter.

"And, there's this." I dug around in my back pocket for the

invitation. They had to see it. Other people could be stuck in that building. Who knows how many people had received the same mysterious note in their lockers? But as I dug around in my pocket, there was nothing but the wrappers from a few sticks of gum Grace had offered all of us in the car on the way over. Headmaster Sinclair's face twisted with anger as he snatched the crumpled paper from between my fingers.

"Young lady, this better not be some kind of joke. There's no time for this." He cast the foil down and it reflected orange and yellow flames as it floated to the ground. I shoved my hand into my other pocket, desperate to feel the creamy card stock of the invitation that had been there minutes ago.

"Wait!" I cried. "I know it's here somewhere." But Headmaster Sinclair was already talking to another frantic student.

I rushed through the crowd and pushed my way to the front of the group where students, their faces glowing orange, stood staring at the hose, which now was bursting with water. I saw Bradley Farrow rubbing at his eyes, almost in disbelief, and Alistair Reynolds, wide-eyed and shocked.

"My friends!" I screamed at the top of my lungs. "They're in there!" By now tears were streaming down my face. I tried to push further, to run with the firemen, but students held me back. "Grace! Maddie!" I screamed, my voice cracking.

A young fireman who held part of the hose inched over to where I stood screaming.

"It's going to be okay. Do you hear me? It's going to be okay. No one's used the chapel for years. There's no way in."

"No, you don't understand. My friends are in there. I had an invitation..."

I threw myself forward, one last attempt to shove my way through the human barrier, but the bodies were too thick. I was forced to turn back into the crowd, ducking and pushing, searching for the faces of my friends in the dancing light of the bonfire.

And then I found her.

"Maddie! Thank God!"

"Oh, Kate! I thought...I mean..." Her head whipped around, her eyes searching wildly. "Where's Grace? Is she..."

A sharp pain spread from the center of my chest. It felt like my insides were breaking. "I thought she was with you," I screamed. I grabbed both of her hands, my eyes wide, my voice frantic. "Maddie, did you get an invitation last week? Something about meeting in the chapel tonight?"

She looked past me, her body shaking violently.

Tears ran jagged down my cheeks. "I know this is awful, Maddie, but I'm scared. I think someone wanted us to be in that chapel when it burned. There's something going on..."

Instead of answering, Maddie wandered away from the direction of the fire like she was sleepwalking. The sound of sirens wailing in the distance forced me in the opposite direction. I shoved through the masses of people huddled together, blinking back thick smoke and waving away particles of ash that danced against the sky like snow. But in my heart, I knew the truth. I was already too late.

Grace was gone.

Chapter 21

Present Day

"Attention everyone." Taylor rapped a small gavel on the lectern and called the Concilium to order. I'd never realized it before, but I think this was one of the first times I'd actually heard her speak. She usually forced her underlings to do all the talking for her.

"We have a lot to cover today, so I'm going to hand it over to Bethany." She sighed prettily and gave Beefany the gavel, lowering herself into one of the front seats, her eyes drilling into mine with a look cool enough to give me frostbite.

Alistair Reynolds and Bradley Farrow booed when Beefany took the lectern, so she began rapping the gavel furiously against the wood.

"Come on, you guys! Can you at least pretend to be mature for ten minutes?" Beefany's face was red; she was clearly flustered. Even Taylor narrowed her eyes in the boys' direction, her normally impassive face wrinkled with frustration.

"Yeah, we're all yours once you start saying something worth listening to," Alistair shot back.

Taylor stood up. "Enough. This isn't the time or place." Her blue eyes sparked with anger. After a couple of muttered references to "bitches" and suggestions about exactly what Taylor could do with the stick shoved up her ass, Bradley and Alistair quieted down and kept their loudmouthed heckling to whispers.

Taylor took her seat, and Beefany began her lecture on the importance of maintaining Pemberly Brown traditions and updating alumni contact information. Her voice went up more than an octave when she spoke in front of a crowd, resulting in an earsplitting pitch that probably had dogs across town howling. I had my notebook in front of me, pen poised so I would look like I was taking notes, but really I read Grace's email over and over again, trying to figure out what it meant.

So far, I'd been able to figure out that I needed to talk to the person who had donated the arches. I was 99 percent sure that the arches referred to were Farrow's Arches, so the benefactor must be a part of the Farrow family. But that's where it got tricky. By my calculation, more than twenty Farrows had attended Pemberly Brown. Bradley and Naomi were the first to come to mind, but they had a slew of cousins, aunts, uncles, and even grandparents who had been students over the years.

I'd already done a little research and knew the arches themselves had been donated by Bradley and Naomi's grandfather Cornelius. Aside from the fact that he was loaded (big shocker there) and had founded Cleveland's largest real-estate development company, there wasn't really all that much information about him.

Apparently, in addition to being the school's first African

American student, he was the first PB student to earn a full scholarship to Harvard. According to the articles, he had donated the arches as a way to show his appreciation for the gift of education. When he proposed to his wife at the dedication ceremony, Station 10 was complete.

I knew I had to start with Naomi or Bradley, but the thought of confronting them made me want to puke. What could I possibly say? "Oh, hey, I got this email, and I think you might know something about how Grace died. Spill. Oh, and sorry about randomly ditching our tennis match last week." Or better yet, "Bradley, I know it's been a little awkward since our 'kiss' last year, but tell me the truth—did you set fire to the chapel?"

Beefany rapped the mini-gavel again, and I had to wonder if she and Taylor shared custody of the stupid thing. A snort of laughter escaped my lips when I pictured Taylor prying the gavel out of Beefany's meaty fingers every other weekend.

"Excuse me, Kerry? Do you have something to add?" Beefany barked from the lectern, staring directly at me. Her husky voice had returned.

"Er, it's Kate, and, uh…no," I stammered.

"Well, Cade, our last order of business is Homecoming. I need some help hanging signs around the school today. Are you familiar with how to use a staple gun?"

I had the urge to tell her most monkeys were proficient in staple-gun usage, but Taylor shot me a chilly look from her throne on the sidelines and I found myself nodding my head instead. Beefany and her queen had spent the past year pretending I didn't exist, and now all of a sudden they wanted me to help hang posters? Surely this was a sign of the impending Apocalypse.

"Great, let's get moving then. Everyone, you know the drill." Beefany stalked toward me carrying a rather sizable staple gun. "Come on, Cade. Grab those posters and try to keep up." I glanced back at Taylor and saw that she hadn't even bothered to get up from her chair. Instead people were waiting to talk to her like they were in some sort of receiving line. Unbelievable.

Beefany's thick fingers wrapped around my bicep, and she dragged me to a bulletin board outside the classroom. She thrust a poster into my hands and gestured that I should hold it up. Before I could even straighten it, she attacked the poster with the gun. Apparently staple conservation wasn't a primary concern for Beefany.

"Didn't I see you with Liam Gilmour at Starbucks last week?" she asked, pausing to reload the gun.

I'd never noticed how smooth her olive-colored skin was until I stood right next to her. She was prettier than I'd given her credit for. Exotic even.

"Um, yeah," was the only response I could manage.

"Just watch yourself around him. You know what everyone says about the drug money." She affected an awed whisper for the words "drug" and "money."

"Didn't stop you from throwing yourself at him," I said before I could stop myself. *Geez, Kate, jealous much?*

Beefany froze in her tracks and spun around to stare directly into my eyes.

"Liam Gilmour is off limits. You don't know anything about him, Cade. And trust me when I say it's safer for you that way."

She didn't bother to wait for a response. She turned around, straightened her shoulders, and began walking, her black waves rippling with each step. As we turned the corner, we ran directly into Liam, who had obviously heard Beefany's words echo through the empty hallway.

I glanced at Beefany, curious to see how she'd respond after seeing him, but his presence didn't seem to faze her. I guess girls like Beefany didn't know that embarrassment was an actual emotion.

"Well, am I right or am I right? You are off limits." He went to open his mouth, but Beefany pushed her finger to his lips. "We should talk." Her sharp brown eyes seared into mine, but she addressed Liam "in private."

I tried to gauge his reaction to Beefany's demand. For someone who claimed to hate the Beefster and her queen, he agreed rather readily, and I was again left completely confused. What kind of hold did she have over him? Did they have some kind of history together?

They walked toward a nook in the hallway, and again Beefany hissed something into his ear, her arm snaked around his waist. At that moment, he seemed so submissive, so unlike the Liam Gilmour I thought I was getting to know.

Our "date" at Starbucks seemed like a figment of my imagination, our moment in the hall a fake. Taylor had probably put Beefany up to it as an experimental form of torture. I could imagine her whispering, "Let's see if we can get Kate to think a guy actually likes her. It'll be hilarious."

As soon as they finished talking, Liam gave me one of his patented boy nods and walked away. I had been dismissed. I hated when people, especially guys, made me feel that way. Every time it happened, I remembered that night with Bradley and my own stupidity.

Beefany walked back over to me. "No hard feelings," she chirped in the same nails-on-a-chalkboard voice she'd used at the Concilium meeting. Considering that she had the staple gun pointed directly at my chest, her comment felt more like an order than an apology.

I briefly considered making a grab for the gun to put myself out of my misery, but in the end I just nodded and followed along. Sometimes life was easier that way.

Chapter 22

I paused in front of the doorway to Station 5, the student detention room, or more accurately, hell. In huge letters, *Abyssus abyssum invocat* hung over the door. "Hell invokes Hell."

Happy Tuesday.

I yawned for the thousandth time since stumbling out of bed, cursing the administration for implementing morning detention. Starting your day in the dark was wrong on so many different levels, although I guess that was their whole point. That or they couldn't risk detention interfering with after-school sports. Ah, priorities.

Today I spent my entire forty-five minutes alternating between staring at the second hand of the clock and watching a pool of drool expand on Porter's now tattered copy of *On the Road*. Did I mention he and I were the only two in the room? Well, three if you counted Mr. McAdams, my ancient World History teacher. I wondered how Headmaster Sinclair had managed to rope Mr. McAdams into morning-detention duty. He was probably on probation or something. Brutal.

Finally the morning bell rang, rousing Porter from his

slumber and forcing Mr. McAdams to lower the newspaper he was reading.

"Get out of here," he mumbled. "It's just you and me tomorrow, Kate."

There had to be a law against that. I'd have to ask my dad.

Before I'd finished gathering my books, the door opened. Mr. Farrow, voted number-one DILF three years running by the fourth-year girls, current CEO of Farrow Developers and president of the Pemberly Brown Academy Board, made his way in. Now this was getting interesting.

"John McAdams?" Mr. Farrow asked. "Clayton Farrow." He walked forward with his hand outstretched. "The principal sent me to find you. My daughter, Naomi, has you for history."

As they shook hands, Mr. Farrow's eyes wandered and landed directly on me.

"Ah, yes, Naomi," Mr. McAdams said. "I received the email about her being out this week. I'll meet you in the office with her assignments."

Mr. Farrow smiled, exposing two rows of straight, white teeth. "Great. I'll be down in a few minutes. I just need to grab some books from her locker."

As I attempted to sneak out of the classroom, I felt a strong hand on my shoulder. "We've missed you at the matches, Kate."

Mr. Farrow's eyes bore down on me, and for one ridiculous second I felt like he was reading my mind. Maybe that was one of the skills they taught at Harvard Business School. "I miss it too." I flashed him a rueful smile. It was the truth.

"Do you mind showing me the way to Naomi's locker?"

My eyes widened a bit, and I had the sudden urge to shout, *Ding, ding, ding!* My mind flashed back to Grace's email: *The truth is with the benefactor.* Not only did I have the opportunity to ask Mr. Farrow some questions, but I'd also get a glimpse inside Naomi's locker. This had to be a sign from Grace.

"No problem, Mr. Farrow. Just follow me."

We made our way down the hallway and saw a few students arriving at their lockers to gather books for first period.

"Is everything okay with Naomi?" I asked, unsure how to begin my interrogation.

"Oh, yeah, absolutely fine." He looked around the halls. "Can you keep a secret?"

I nodded my head. Not bad. Ten seconds of conversation, and Mr. Farrow was already telling me secrets.

"Naomi's actually attending Chris Evert's tennis camp, which starts tomorrow. We were able to get her in at the last minute, but with my being on the board, it wasn't the best reason to miss three days of school. So we went with tonsillitis instead."

I smiled and tried not to look disappointed. Did I really think he was going to tell me that Naomi stayed home from school because she felt guilty about her involvement in Grace's death?

"Oh, good. Glad to hear she's okay." I searched my mind for a way to get him talking about Grace, anything aside from tennis camp.

"Has the board made any decisions about further memorials for Grace?" I tried to ask casually, but when Mr. Farrow's features softened, I knew I'd failed miserably. I needed information, not pity.

"It's got to be tough for you, Kate. I forget how close you and Grace were." He hesitated a minute and again looked around the halls as if he wanted to make sure we weren't overheard. "The truth is, we're going to rebuild the chapel as a memorial for Grace, and the Farrow family has decided to donate the funds. This is just between you and me. The official announcement won't come from the board for another few weeks, but you deserve to hear it first."

I wasn't sure how to react to the news. On one hand it was generous, but on the other it seemed calculated somehow. As if the Farrow family was paying some kind of debt.

"Wow…that's just…wow," I managed to stammer, articulate as ever.

"I know this is hard for you, Kate. But we all need to move on."

I slowed in front of Naomi's locker and felt grateful for having something to say.

"Here we are!" I said, doing my best cheerleader impression to mask my suspicion.

Mr. Farrow consulted a scrap of paper and began turning the combination lock. After a few spins and murmurs he tried to open the locker, but it was still stuck.

His phone began to ring. "Excuse me, Kate. I've got to take this. Do you mind taking over?" He handed me the scrap of paper with Naomi's combination scrawled across it.

"Uh, okay. I'll just gather the stuff you'll need." But he'd already made his way toward a quiet corner of the hallway. I looked up to the ceiling, said a quick thank-you to Grace, wherever she was, and got to work.

Ever so casually, I snaked my hand inside the locker trying to find something, anything that could help me decode Grace's email. I found a few energy-bar wrappers, an old piece of gum, and even our tennis-team picture, but nothing about Grace. I had just about given up when I heard the tinkle of something metal hitting the ground at my feet. I scanned the ground and saw the glint of something small and silver.

Good things really do come in small packages. I wound the necklace with the tiny charm of the crest through my fingers and smiled. It was identical to the one Cameron had left me with Grace's invitation. And all the evidence I needed to confront Naomi.

When I heard Mr. Farrow's heavy footsteps, I grabbed Naomi's Chemistry book out of the locker.

"Sorry about that, Kate." He took the book from my hands and bent to pull the rest. "Thanks for all your help." He winked at me and shut the door of the locker.

"No problem, Mr. Farrow," I replied with the same goofy smile stuck on my face. "Tell Naomi to have fun this week."

"Will do. You take care of yourself, okay?"

I nodded and gave the tiny charm in my hand a squeeze.

I wasn't sure who the emails were really coming from, if Grace was still somehow alive or even a ghost. I wasn't even sure if I'd ever hear from her again.

But I did know one thing for certain—someone was looking out for me.

I raised my eyes to the ceiling again and smiled.

Chapter 23

I grabbed my bag and made my way to the nearest girls bathroom. Once I was safely tucked into one of the stalls, I powered on my phone and called Naomi. She answered on the first ring, sounding worried.

"Kate? Everything all right?"

"Oh, yeah, um…sort of. But I really need to talk to you. I just saw your dad, so I know you're leaving, but do you have time to meet before you go?" I heard the bathroom door open and shut, and some girl who sounded disturbingly like Beefany asking someone else if her shoes made her legs look fat.

"I don't know," Naomi was saying. "I still have to pack, and it's not like you can just ditch school…"

"Come on," I whispered. "It's really important. Plus I have fifteen minutes till first bell."

"Okay, okay. I'll meet you at the tennis courts. I'll tell my mom I want to get one last round of practice in before my flight this afternoon."

"Perfect! I'll see you there."

As promised, Naomi pulled up a few minutes later. I curled my hand into a fist, hiding her charm deep within the folds of my palm.

"Hey," she said, walking toward the weathered bench I sat on.

Naomi wore a pair of low-slung jeans with a pristine white button-down set off by a chunky, beaded gold necklace and a pair of gold ballet flats. Her outfit probably cost more than my entire wardrobe combined. It was hard to imagine someone who looked this good setting fire to the school chapel.

"Thanks for coming. I'm guessing you didn't tell your mom you were coming to play tennis?" I squeezed my fingers tighter, suddenly nervous.

"Yeah, my mom vetoed that idea. I told her I forgot my lucky tennis dress in the locker room."She plopped down next to me on the bench. "So what's up?"

I opened my hand and showed her the charm. "I found this in your locker." I watched Naomi carefully for her reaction.

Her eyes got a little bigger, and she looked at me and then looked away. "That's weird. I've never seen it before. What were you doing in my locker anyway?"

"Helping your dad get your books for the week," I answered, looking her straight in the eye. "What does it mean, Naomi? I know it has something to do with what happened to Grace."

Naomi made a grab for the charm, but I closed my hand around it again. She wasn't getting off that easily.

"Tell me the truth, and I'll give it back."

"It's not my truth to tell." Naomi reached out her finger and traced the letters "G+C 4 EVA" that were carved into the back of the bench. She finally looked up at me. "If I tell you something about that night, will you give it back to me?"

"Depends."

She looked back down at the ragged-looking heart and the letters trapped inside and sighed. "I saw something the night of the fire. I was supposed to be at the chapel, but I was late, and by the time I got there...it was...." She shook the thought away and looked up at me again. Her striking eyes were desperate, begging me to understand.

"I had no idea Grace was in there. I...I saw someone running away. A boy in jeans with longish dark hair. All I really saw was the back of a Rolling Stones T-shirt. You know, the one with the tongue hanging out? "

"That describes about 90 percent of the boys at our school."

"I know...just...that's all I can say, okay? It's more than I should have said..." She looked around, almost like she expected to get caught.

"So you got an invitation too?" I asked, although I already knew the answer.

"Wait here." She ran back to her car, opened the passenger-side door, and sat on the seat with her long legs hanging out. Once she found what she was looking for, she rushed back over to me.

"Here," she said, holding out an invitation. It was identical except for the picture. Hers was in the upper right-hand corner. "I hope it helps."

I opened my book bag and pulled Grace's invitation from the

pocket. I placed the two side by side, but until I moved them diagonally, the pictures didn't meet. When the two cards touched at the corners, they formed half of the crest. Looking at it now, I couldn't believe I hadn't see that before.

"Is it Grace's?" Naomi whispered.

"Yes." I shuffled the cards together and put them back in the pocket of my bag.

Naomi stared into the woods. "If you tell anyone, I'll lie and say you stole it." The air between us shifted a little. "And trust me, you don't want my friends as your enemies." She pushed back the cuticle of her thumb. "You're close. Probably too close."

"Who else was there that night?"

Naomi sighed and ran her hands through her hair. "You know I can't tell you that. But I promise they didn't have anything to do with Grace's death."

"Please…" I was ready to start begging, but Naomi just shook her head and stood to leave. She hesitated before getting back into the car, but she didn't say another word.

Looking down at the cards on my lap, I knew without a doubt my missing invitation would have filled in another corner of the crest. But who had the fourth piece?

Chapter 24

That evening, my parents were working late as usual. I used the twenty dollars they left on the counter to order my favorite Pad Thai. I'm not sure if it was the peanut sauce, the solitude, or maybe the small charm of the crest I'd been staring at all day, but I was feeling sorry for myself.

I dragged my desk chair over to my closet and pulled down another box of Grace memories. As part of my healing process, Dr. P. had prescribed packing away all of the things that most reminded me of Grace. Theoretically, that was supposed to curb my obsession with her death. But in reality I just fixated on the boxes stacked in neat rows at the top of my closet. *Thanks for that, Dr. P.*

The second I lifted the lid, I smelled her. The scent was a mixture of Johnson's Baby Shampoo (she swore by it) and vanilla, essential Grace. Tank tops, sweaters, T-shirts, dresses, even a pair of jeans were folded in the tub, all of them belonging to Grace. Well, at least they used to.

We'd shared clothes constantly, Grace borrowing the outfits she wished her mom would let her buy, me borrowing the ones Grace cast aside, many still with tags. I pushed my hand to the bottom, gently lifting my favorite piece. It was her orange cashmere sweater. Grace had given it to me to wear to one of our eighth-grade dances.

"It'll look better on you," she had said. Grace was as impulsive with her gifts as she was with everything else in her life. "Make your eyes pop." I had doubted it at the time, but on the night of the dance, with the orange reflecting onto my face and my skin practically glowing, I had never felt prettier.

Pulling the sweater on over my T-shirt, I shut my eyes and imagined away all of the heartbreak and sadness of the past year. And as if on cue I heard the ding of the new-email sound from my laptop.

I knew it would be from her before I even opened my mailbox.

> To: KateLowry@pemberlybrown.edu
> Sent: Tues 9:03 PM
> From: GraceLee@pemberlybrown.edu
> Subject: Re: (no subject)

> The writing is on the wall.
> Look into the heart of Brown.
> Our time is almost up.
> They're coming for you.

My stomach twisted as I read and reread that last line. *They're coming for you.*

I still didn't know who "they" were; I wasn't even sure if it mattered anymore. What mattered was uncovering the truth.

My eyes drifted back to my box of memories. Guess Dr. P. was right. It was time to put the past behind me. I slid the sweater up and over my head, carefully folding the material and placing it back into the box. As much as I cherished all of my memories of Grace, they weren't going to bring her back. But figuring out what really happened that night just might.

Chapter 25

The heat had finally broken, making it the perfect fall morning, but I was too tired to appreciate the weather. Instead of sleeping, I had spent the entire night rereading Grace's email and checking the lock on my window.

Between bites of toaster pastry, Seth chattered about the new neighbors being secret agents. He couldn't say for sure whether they were working for the CIA or for Russia, but apparently he'd seen both of them sneak out of the house late at night wearing earpieces.

I was 99 percent sure they were trapped in a loveless marriage and using Bluetooth headsets to make late-night booty calls, but instead of bursting Seth's secret-agent bubble, I stuck with "ahhing" and "hmming" my way through the conversation.

My mind was elsewhere, and I could not turn it off. One line from Grace's email played over and over again.

Look into the heart of Brown.

Did some rule force ghosts to speak in riddles? Why couldn't Grace just tell me what the hell was actually going on?

I'd already Googled my butt off trying to find out something, anything about the "heart of Brown." Clearly the reference was to the old boys school and most likely involved one of the three Brown buildings that still dotted the perimeter of the upper school's campus.

But I was fairly certain the buildings were used for storage, and I knew for a fact they were locked. Even if I did manage to figure out the right building and get inside, how was I supposed to know what I was looking for?

I was left with only one choice.

"Seth." Apparently he was enjoying the conversation he thought he was having with me, because he didn't hear me interrupting him. "*Seth.*" This time I elbowed him. He rubbed his ribs and finally stopped talking and actually looked at me. "What do they use the old Brown buildings for?"

He needed a second to process my seemingly off-topic question. I could almost hear the gears in his brain working.

"Storage, mostly. At the end of every school year, teachers weed through the department closets and haul old sets of textbooks, outdated student files, and other random junk down there. Why?"

"I just have an art project about Brown's architecture and wanted to check them out."

"I can get you in. I'll walk you over. Just meet me at the office after ninth period."

I leaned my head against the cool window. I didn't have the energy to think about what a field trip to the old buildings would be like with Seth buzzing in my ear. As I stepped off the bus,

I wondered why this couldn't be easier. Why couldn't I run across campus right now and throw open the door to the heart of Brown and find Grace's big, fat clue staring me in the face?

For one, I couldn't skip anymore classes. I had suffered through two days of morning detention (one of the days alone with Mr. McAdams—apparently there wasn't a law against that if the door was left open, which thankfully it was), and I was already on Headmaster Sinclair's shit list. Not to mention my parents who were on the brink of giving Dr. P. consent to use shock therapy to zap the Grace obsession right out of me. Worse (and about five thousand times scarier), I seemed to have someone on my trail. Someone comfortable using threats to get what he wanted.

So instead of booking it over to Brown, I mentally explored the edges of campus, searching for imaginary clues as I navigated the maze of hallways to my locker. After screwing up my combination three times, I stopped and focused on the numbers. When a voice said, "Hey, Kate," I jumped, yanked my locker open, and slammed the metal door into my head—in that order.

Liam.

"Holy…" I threw my hand to my chest, covering my pounding heart.

"Oh, I…didn't mean to scare you. Just wanted to say hi."

I turned back to my locker without even acknowledging his presence. Did he really think he could humiliate me in front of Beefany and then show up at my locker to flirt a few days later?

"Oh, so you're allowed to talk to me now? Bethany won't get pissed?"

He blushed, and I felt myself waver just a little bit. God, why was it so cute when boys blushed?

"I…well…it's a long story. I just…I don't know. It's not like that…anymore." He looked down, suddenly fascinated with one of his shoes.

"Could've fooled me." I grabbed my English Lit book and slammed the door to my locker shut.

"Yeah, right," Liam said, turning away from me. "But enough about Bethany. Um…" He met my eyes for a second but then glanced back down at his shoes. "Do you think maybe we could, like, hang out sometime? If concerts aren't your thing, we could grab a coffee again or something."

I stared at him. What exactly did Liam want with me? He seemed to like me, but clearly he had a history with Beefany that didn't seem to be over.

"Sorry. Not interested."

"Listen, we got off on the wrong foot. Give me a chance. I'll prove you wrong."

I stared at him and he smiled this amazing, heart-stopping smile, and I wanted to say yes. I wanted to spend more time with him, to learn more about why he was always covering every available inch of notebook paper with cartoons and doodles, to hear about how he got started designing band posters, why he liked music so much, whether or not he'd really blackmailed the headmaster to get into PB. I suddenly wanted to know all of that and more. I wanted to know who Liam Gilmour really was.

And then out of the corner of my eye I saw Bradley Farrow stop at his locker a few down from us. He nodded in my direction and gave me one of those secret smiles that made me want to punch his perfect white teeth in.

"Kate? Kate? Did I lose you?" Liam looked at me expectantly, his smile hopeful and a little apologetic.

"Yes, I'll go out with you," I said, unable to stop my eyes from wandering over to Bradley as I said it. "But don't screw this up." I managed to remain serious at first but then allowed the corners of my mouth to curl up just a little.

"Does today after school work?" he asked.

"It would, but I'm being forced to go to the Concilium meetings. I could probably just blow it off," I said. Hopefully no one would notice my absence. Not that I contributed much.

"Cool, I'll meet you by the parking lot doors after ninth period."

Crap. I had totally forgotten about my date with the decrepit buildings of Brown. Minor change of plans.

"Actually, do you mind if we meet at four? I have a bunch of questions for Ms. Haverton about trig." I wasn't sure how long it would take me to dig around Brown. I hoped an hour would give me enough time to find whatever it was I was searching for.

"No prob," Liam said. "See you at four."

It took all I had to hide the smile threatening to overtake my face.

I spent the rest of the day walking on air. I was almost excited enough to forget all about lost best friends and the writing on the wall.

Almost.

Chapter 26

The second hand of the black-and-white clock hanging above the marker board was painful to watch. It made its way around each number, patiently ticking a slow circle. The clock wasn't in a rush, but I was.

As soon as the last bell rang, I grabbed my stuff and booked it toward Station 3, where I knew Seth would be waiting. I had an hour to find whatever it was I was looking for.

Faber est suae quisque fortunae. I repeated the Latin phrase hanging above the office's glass doors over and over in my head. "Every man [or woman, in my case—those Romans were a bunch of sexist pigs] is the artisan of his own fortune." Seth, for better or worse, was a time suck. And time was not on my side. As I rounded a corner, I noticed a desperate-looking group of first-year boys and took matters into my own hands. Those sexist Romans would have been scandalized.

"Hey!" I yelled out, but no one looked. "Boys!" All at once, seven heads turned and looked up at me. I felt like Snow White and I'm not even that tall; they were just *that* short.

"They're giving away free doughnuts in the office." I pushed past them and continued down the hall to where Seth was leaning against the glass walls of the office, arms crossed, keys in hand. It crossed my mind to run up, swipe the keys, and tear out of the building in the direction of Brown. I knew I could outrun Seth, but I also knew that would break his heart, and I wasn't in the mood.

"Hey, thanks for waiting." As I stood with Seth, the same group of boys stormed into the office. A worried look crossed my face. "I wonder what's going on."

Confused, Seth stretched his neck out and stood on his tiptoes to peer through the glass. "I've gotta get back in there. Mrs. Newbury needs backup. We'll have to go to Brown another time." Seth made a move to leave, but I placed my hand on his arm.

"I have a deadline." I tried to mimic Seth's signature kicked-puppy-dog look. "I'll take Naomi," I lied. I knew he wouldn't want me to go alone. "And I'll bring the keys right back, promise." More puppy-dog eyes. If I'd had a tail, I would have wagged it.

Seth thought about my proposition for as long as he could. Mrs. Newbury really was struggling in there, all raised hands and darting eyes. She looked totally confused and even a little scared. Doughnuts were not a joking matter.

"Okay, but you can't tell anyone, and you have to come right back. I mean *right* back. If someone finds out I loaned out my keys, I'm dead. *A dead man*, Kate!" Seth's eyes bugged out of his head.

After he showed me which ones to try, I bolted out of the building. I guess I didn't need to be concerned about not getting enough exercise since breaking from tennis. With all the running I was doing, I should have joined cross-country.

I flew past a bunch of first-years hanging out in the gardens. As usual, it was quite the hot spot for the squealing girls of Pemberly Brown. If the legend about kissing your boyfriend under Farrow's Arches wasn't enough to lure them inside the garden, there were always the carved wedding stones that made up the garden pathway. Nearly everyone knew a couple who had met at Pemberly Brown and ended up married with a gorgeous stone on the wedding walk to commemorate the event.

It was a source of endless fascination to see how incestuous the school really was. I mean, it couldn't be normal to have hundreds of couples graduate from the same prep school and eventually marry, right? And even worse, they ended up breeding and sending their own kids to PB. I swear they put something in the water.

I jogged past them—laughing, talking, doing normal teenage girl things—and hated them just a little. They were a reminder of how abnormal my life had become.

Fortunately the girls barely spared me a second glance, and I moved deftly along the twisting path through the gardens to the campus beyond.

I spotted the three remaining buildings that made up Brown's old campus. While they were beautiful from the outside, they hadn't been used for anything aside from storage in years. According to the administration, the buildings would be too costly to renovate after years of neglect, plus they were too far from the main campus to be of any use.

The wind picked up. I noticed gray clouds looming overhead and caught a whiff of that just-before-it-rains smell. Another storm was on its way. I didn't have much time if I was going to make it back to the office to drop off the keys and then out to Liam's car without getting completely soaked.

I ran to the nearest building and tried one of the keys. I slipped it in, but the key wouldn't even turn. I tried the remaining two with no better luck. Had Seth screwed up the keys? I stood on my tiptoes and tried to look through the small glass window situated near the top of the door. I couldn't see much.

I hadn't set out to add breaking and entering to my growing list of misdemeanors, so I jogged over to the next building, hoping one of the keys would work. *Please, Grace, help me find whatever it is I'm supposed to be looking for.* I sent my silent plea up to the stormy sky as the clouds rolled ominously—and hoped for the best.

When I approached the door to the next building, I saw that something had been traced into the layer of dirt on the window of the door. A heart. The heart of Brown.

My breath caught in my throat. This was it. I slipped in one of the keys and wiggled it back and forth. It moved a quarter of an inch but no more. I slipped the next key in and did the same. As soon as I began twisting, I felt the lock give way beneath my fingertips and knew I was in. Relief flooded through me as I pulled the heavy door open and took a step inside.

Dust danced in the dim light of the doorway, catching in my throat and nose. When the door slammed behind me, I wasn't sure what was worse, the claustrophobia or the dust-induced coughing fit.

But then I thought of Grace, of her funeral, the coffin, her buried under the ground. In that moment, more than anything else, I wanted to turn around and run away. I wanted to climb into the warmth of Liam's car and forget all about this dusty, tomblike building.

Instead I forced myself to imagine the real Grace, my best friend, who deserved so much more than secrets and lies. I pictured her crooked smile and lifted the hem of my blazer to cover my mouth. I was going in.

Led only by the meager light streaming through the window by the door, I navigated through the hallway. To my left I spotted a plaque mounted to the wall, similar to the stations at the Academy. I brushed off a thick layer of the ubiquitous beige dust and read: Brown School for Boys, *Cor Unum*. "One heart." I was in the right place.

I continued down the hallway. Classroom doors were open on both sides of me, but boxes, desks, chairs, and other random pieces of furniture blocked the line of windows and any light they would have let in. As a result, it grew darker and darker as I moved away from the door. I finally came to the end of the corridor, and the hallway split in two directions. I could go either left or right. Crap.

I looked both ways as they had taught me at Safety Town and noticed something shiny on the wall to my left. It was a tiny metallic sticker of a heart. Guess I wasn't the first person to seek the heart of Brown. My finger briefly lingered over the sticker, and I figured the choice had been made for me. I turned left and had only made my way a few feet into the hallway when I saw it.

I'm not sure if it was intentional or not, but the door itself looked like a giant heart. It had two rounded peaks at the top and then subtle panels that formed a deep V.

I drew in as much air as my blazer would allow and pulled the door open. The air reeked of incense, but it was free of dust. I dropped my hem from over my mouth and breathed deeply.

The room itself was large and clean. The ceilings were higher than those in the hallway, and it was clear that the room was used regularly. All of this should have lent the room an airy feel, but someone had made the ridiculous decision to paint the walls black. Dim light filtered through a row of high rectangular windows, but the dark paint seemed to suck the daylight out of the room.

I saw a switch to my right near the door and flipped it on out of pure habit. Black light showered down from the ceiling, and the walls came to life. They were covered with names. Chase Roman. William Vaughan. Kellan Wood.

"The writing is on the wall," I murmured to myself and looked around in awe. Every single one of the names belonged to a boy. I spun around in a circle, taking in each of the names until I saw one that I recognized.

Richard Sinclair. Or, as I knew him, Headmaster Sinclair.

I pulled my slam book and a pen out of my book bag and got to work. I wrote, "The writing is on the walls," and underlined it three times. Next, I listed Headmaster Sinclair's name, circled it, and then jotted down a few of the other names that stood out to me.

When the sound of shattering glass ripped through the silence, my blue pen streaked across the page, crossing through part of Chase Roman's name.

A small object covered in paper skidded across the floor and landed at my feet. My heart thudded to life in my chest, hammering so hard and fast I thought it might burst. I briefly considered booking it out of there without the message that had come crashing through the window, but my curiosity overcame my fear. Paper beats rock, I thought as I unwound a rubber band securing the paper and flattened it out on my thigh. In bloodred ink and block handwriting, the note read:

Ashes, ashes, we're going to take you down.

Lightning flashed in the distance, and I instinctively counted, "One-one-thousand, two-one-thousand, three-one-thousand…" as I waited for thunder. At four-one-thousand, thunder cracked. I tossed the note and rock into my book bag and ran through the dark hallways.

The air around me felt charged with electricity, possibilities, and danger. I knew I'd never be able to run fast enough. Sooner or later I'd have to stop and brave the storm.

Chapter 27

Half screaming, half laughing, we rushed from Liam's Jeep through the door at Starbucks, both shielding our heads from the pouring rain with our blazers. As soon as we pushed through the door, every head in the coffee shop turned like Pavlov's dogs to check us out.

"You get the seat, I'll get the drinks," Liam suggested, handing me his dripping blazer. "Skinny Frappuccino, right?"

"Um, have you met me? I'm a full-fat Frap kind of girl. I don't subscribe to 'skinny' drinks." I considered asking for extra whipped cream to really make my point, but I figured that might be overkill.

I headed over to my favorite couch and threw my wet body down onto it. In spite of all the Beefany awkwardness, I was happy to be here with Liam again. He made the threat I'd received at the heart of Brown feel a little bit farther away than it had felt fifteen minutes earlier.

But when his blazer vibrated on the couch cushion next to me, I jumped, my heart pumping blood through my ears. I guess I wasn't quite as removed as I thought. His phone slid partway out of his pocket, and I hoped whoever was calling or texting wouldn't cut our date short.

I shifted my shoulders a few times and realized that with my soaking-wet shirt sticking to my skin, comfort was virtually impossible. Liam was still waiting at the counter for our drinks, so I draped both of our wet blazers over the couch cushions to save our seats and ducked into the restroom.

By the time I made it back to our spot, my hair had been partially dried under the hand dryer. I'd also ditched my wet button-down for the semi-dry tank top underneath and wrapped Grace's long pearls around my neck three times instead of twice. Liam sipped a black coffee, and my Mocha Frappuccino sat chilly and inviting.

But when I moved my blazer aside, I noticed a small white note sticking out of the pocket. I hadn't put anything in my pockets. In fact, I'd been careful to put the rock and the threat in my bag for safekeeping. My eyes flickered to Liam, who smiled at me.

"I'll be right back," I mumbled, slipping the note into my palm. "I think I left something in the bathroom." Yeah, my sanity.

I hurried back through the restroom door and, after bending and peeking beneath the stalls to make sure I was alone, opened the paper.

Hush, little Kate, don't say a word. We hear everything.

Same block handwriting, same bloodred ink. Despite my damp

tank top, I felt feverish. Paranoid, I scanned the ceiling—for what? Cameras? The bathroom suddenly felt too small, so I pushed back through the doors, seeing each customer in an entirely different light than before I'd walked through the door.

A young kid wearing a black trench coat sat a few feet away from us. I stared hard at him and wondered. An older couple chatted animatedly near the door; the man met my eyes for a second but returned to his partner's. Was he watching me? A girl around my age sipped coffee and typed into her laptop a few tables over. Could she have left the note?

And then there was Liam sipping coffee, his uniform shirt unbuttoned to reveal a vintage T-shirt underneath. His cell phone vibrated in his blazer pocket again, and I watched his face darken as he examined the screen. He looked toward the door and then back at his phone. Could I really trust him? Suddenly I wasn't so sure.

I felt a little sick, and I had no idea what to do next. I couldn't just whip the note out of my pocket and demand to know who had written it. If Grace were here, she'd clap her hands together and jump up and down at the thought of something *actually* happening. She would have told me to sit my ass back down, suck on my Frappuccino, and keep my eyes and ears open. So I returned to the couch just as Liam finished typing a message.

"Is everything okay?" Liam asked with a concerned look on his face, sliding his phone on the table.

"Sure." I said, but it sounded more like a question. I picked a piece of lint from my uniform skirt, letting my mind wander again.

And, big surprise, it wandered straight back to the heart of Brown and all the pieces of Grace's puzzle. On top of the names, the heart of Brown was used as some sort of meeting place. And then there was that crumpled note I'd stuffed into my book bag.

Someone not only cared enough about me being there to send the threat, but even more disturbing, they *knew* I'd be there. And apparently one note wasn't enough. They'd followed me here and delivered a second ultra-freaky warning. Clearly I was getting a little too close for comfort. Otherwise why would they bother? Too bad I still didn't have any idea what all of this really meant and how it might connect to Grace.

"Hello? Kate? You still with me?" Liam's voice made me realize that I'd been staring blankly at his shoes.

"Sorry, I was just thinking about..." Headmaster Sinclair? No, that was just gross. The Brown School for Boys? That was just weird. Rocks? Weird and geology focused. I shrugged.

Liam shifted in his seat uncomfortably, and I wondered if something more than just our awkward conversation was making him edgy.

"I'm gonna grab a water. You need anything?" Liam asked, standing up.

"Um..." I thought for a second about all the things I needed, but I waved my hand and shook my head.

As soon as Liam entered the line to order, his cell phone vibrated again. I craned my neck to evaluate his position in line and casually reached to retrieve his phone—in the name of my investigation, obviously.

On the screen, Beefany's name was listed next to two new text messages. Without thinking I opened the first text.

Remember what we talked about.

I cleared his screen and tossed the phone back on the table, annoyed. What exactly was going on between them? And what exactly was going on between us?

After paying for his bottle of water, Liam lowered himself into the couch and shot me a smile I couldn't possibly return. His phone vibrated again, and as he typed, I considered all the things he might be saying to Beefany, things about me, things about threatening notes. At this point, he could have been typing just about anything. I took one last sip of my Mocha Frappuccino and set the half-full cup on the table. Things had to be bad for me to abandon a Frappuccino.

"I'm out of here." I pulled my damp blazer off the couch and threw it over my arm. Liam's forehead wrinkled as he looked up at me and then over to his phone, which had just begun to vibrate for the millionth time. I could almost hear the struggle playing out in his mind. *Kate or Bethany...Kate or Bethany.*

"Oh, and, you might want to get that. Rumor has it that Bethany doesn't like to be kept waiting," I snapped, adjusting my blazer. Before I could grab it, a piece of crumpled notebook paper floated into Liam's lap. On it was my drawing of the crest with the words *Audi, Vide, Tace* underlined repeatedly. I almost snatched it up myself, but Liam grabbed it and took in the picture.

"What's that supposed to mean?" Liam asked, silencing his phone.

"I just wouldn't want Bethany to get upset." I cursed myself for admitting I'd snooped in his phone but figured it didn't matter.

I was leaving. "Have fun texting about me." I turned to go, but I felt words bubbling up in my throat that needed to be said. "I should have known you'd be a liar too."

Liam reached up and grabbed my arm. "If you're so into the truth, why don't you tell me what this means?" He held up the picture of the crest.

I opened my mouth to say something and quickly snapped it back shut. I stood there stewing for a few seconds until Liam broke the silence.

"So, what does it mean?"

I wasn't in the mood to be cooperative. "Why does she keep texting?"

"If I told you there's nothing going on with Bethany, would you believe me?"

"If I told you I don't know what the picture means, would you believe me?"

He took a swig of his water. I sat back down and reached for my Mocha Frappuccino. No use letting it go to waste.

"There's nothing going on with her," Liam whispered.

"I don't know what it means," I said.

And that was it. We both had our secrets. We were stuck: willing to trust each other enough not to lie but not enough to tell the whole truth. As I looked at him, his damp hair wavy, his wet shirt clinging to his skin, I wanted to believe him, to trust him.

"So let's start over." Liam shook the hair from his eyes, which had magically switched back to light blue. "I think I remember one of the questions I wanted to ask you."

"Wait. You planned a question to ask me?"

"Well"—he turned a little red—"yeah, but only if things were going really bad, which, in light of recent events…"

I laughed one of those belly laughs that always seem to catch you by surprise. It felt good.

"So…what are your favorite things? You know, what do you *really* love?"

"Um…" I laughed, a little uncomfortably now, because it was kind of a personal question. "Well, I can't live without Mocha Frappuccinos," I said, rattling my near-empty cup. "I love infomercials, and even though I know it's total bullshit, I check my horoscope daily." The conversation had taken a 180, and my face flushed with something I hadn't felt in a while. Something like happiness.

"So what did it say today? Mystery date with a hot guy?" he asked with a laugh.

"Yeah, a hot guy who spends half the date texting with some other girl." A shadow passed over his face, and I felt bad for ruining the moment. But, hey, the truth hurts.

"Yeah, what an asshole," he joked halfheartedly. "Although, now that I think about it, *my* horoscope might have said something about meeting a girl with a big secret."

Laughter shone in his eyes, and I considered telling him everything. Yeah, he might think I was totally crazy, and I'd probably be putting myself in danger, but I was ready to be done with the secrets and lies.

I stuffed my hands into my pockets, my fingers brushing against the note still crumpled inside. Suddenly the words that were on the tip of my tongue were gone, and I knew this wasn't even close to being over.

Chapter 28

If someone held a feeling chart up in front of me (you know, the one with all the cartoon faces that guidance counselors use to help us describe our emotions?) and asked me to show how I was feeling, I could probably have pointed to each cartoon face listed.

My emotions were all over the place. One second I was terrified, fearful that someone was out to hurt me. Then the next I was captivated by the thought of finding a boy I actually liked. And then, as always, there was the bottomless sadness of not being able to share any of this with Grace.

Despite my confusion, I knew I had work to do, and I wasn't about to let a guy come between me and the truth, no matter how charming he seemed.

And that's how I found myself working Google again with Saturday afternoon drift, drift, drifting away. I started with the usual "Richard Sinclair" and got about a million random hits. Duh. Next up: "Richard Sinclair, Pemberly Brown Headmaster." I got a bunch of hits with a Pemberly Brown–approved bio. Boring. But one hit was about Richard and Robert Sinclair, brothers who had broken all kinds of track records during their years at PB.

I stretched my back, cleared the search box, and tried "Robert Sinclair, Pemberly Brown, Ohio." Bingo. A PDF of track-and-field records from 1970 came up. Backing out of the PDF, I clicked on results linking to school newspaper archives. I skimmed one, an interview with Robert about his track career. In one answer he mentioned his younger brother, Richard.

I backed out of the article and clicked on another. This one was far more interesting than the fluffy interview. Apparently Robert Sinclair had been accused and acquitted of attacking a girl in his grade at Pemberly Brown. The article discussed the impact on his track career.

The paper left out the girl's name to protect the innocent while noting that other publications hadn't been so kind and that the victim had been bullied by classmates as a result. Now this was getting interesting. The headmaster had a brother who had been accused of attacking a girl? Somehow I didn't find that hard to believe.

Unfortunately I couldn't find the girl's name anywhere on the site, leaving me with no other choice—I needed to go public. And by public, I mean the public library, where the books I needed wouldn't have pieces sliced out of them.

Faster than you can say "acquittal," I grabbed my stuff, hopped on my bike, and ten minutes later was locking it to the rack outside the library. I know, I know, I was one leisurely ride away from sporting spandex shorts and one of those aerodynamic helmets. I shuddered at the thought.

Pulling open the ornate doors, I stepped into the atrium and breathed in the smell of musty books. They smelled like answers.

The old wooden floors creaked beneath my feet, and books sighed as people turned pages. Every time I visited the library, I admired the stately rooms that housed row after row of books. Some eccentric millionaire had donated his mansion to the city for a library back in the '40s, and even though the floors were chipped and the paint was peeling in many of the rooms, the library still oozed a stately elegance.

It was a library you could get lost in. Tiny rooms with oversized armchairs and small side tables were peppered between larger rooms lined with tall shelves of books. The sterile buildings that usually housed books paled in comparison.

I wove my way through room after meandering room before I finally found the help desk.

"How may I help you?" The man behind the desk looked up at me over his glasses.

I figured I might as well get the easy stuff out of the way first.

"Do you have a book called *Pemberly Brown: 150 Years of Excellence* by…" I glanced down at my slam book, "Calvin Markwell?" The library was my last chance for good old Calvin. Every online bookstore said the book was out of print.

It might have been my imagination, but I swear the librarian sitting a few feet away from him stopped typing as I asked my question.

"Let me see if we have any copies. We just began allowing some of the reference materials to go out on loan." He typed into his computer and looked up at me with a smile. "You're in luck.

Pemberly Brown: 150 Years of Excellence by Calvin Markwell. Computer says we have one copy available. Follow me."

I gave him a smile, but it wavered when I felt the other librarian's eyes on me again. I followed the nice old man, eager to get away from Eva Eavesdropper over there.

The library was set up in a similar way to the Academy library, only on a much larger scale. Bookshelves loomed around me, and computer terminals dotted each section.

"Say, you don't happen to know Officer Dorothy?" the man asked as he led me to the nonfiction section. "She mans the PB library after hours."

"Yeah, she's awesome! Everyone loves Ms. D."

"Well, you'll never believe this, but she was my History teacher way back when. If you don't find what you're looking for here, just ask her. She knows everything there is to know about PB."

"Oh," I said, confused. "Thanks for the suggestion. I'll have to talk to her."

I wondered why Ms. D. would have stopped teaching History to take a job in security. Definitely an interesting career move. Plus she'd never mentioned it before. Granted we weren't all that close, and I'm sure it wasn't the type of information you really wanted to broadcast, but still.

"Here we are." The man stopped in front of the reference section. "There should be one copy available. It's leather-bound, maroon, I think."

He bent to check the titles, but I knew after my quick scan that the book was not on the shelf. I shouldn't have been surprised.

"Hmm, I'm not seeing it. Someone might be using it within the library, or maybe it was an error. But I can hold a copy for you when it becomes available."

Time was one of the many things I really didn't have a lot of at the moment, but it was worth a try. "Um, yeah, that'd be great. My name is Kate. Kate Lowry."

He wrote my name down in a small notebook and asked if he could help me with anything else. Before I could speak, the librarian who had been giving me the once-over at the desk stalked toward us.

"Thanks, Charles. There's a young lady who needs your help at the reference desk. I can take over from here. Kate, is it?"

"Actually, I need to look through some old newspapers." I didn't trust her, but she was being forced on me, so I'd have to be flexible.

"May I ask what you're looking for?"

"I'm just…um…researching Pemberly Brown during the seventies for a paper."

She cocked her head slightly to the side. I wondered if she was equally concerned with every library patron's information searches. If that was the case, her job must have been exhausting.

"Let me take you to the newspaper archives on the microfilm machine. You'll find what you're looking for down there."

"Show me the way," I said as the librarian led me toward a stairwell. Just as we were about to step down, a voice broke through the otherwise silent space.

"Hey, Kate!" The sound came from behind a huge stack of books. The librarian stopped in her tracks and shushed the voice, throwing a stern look in my direction. I couldn't suppress a groan when red curls emerged over the stack.

"Oh, hey, Seth."

"What're you doing here?"

"Research." I hoped he'd disappear back behind his pile of conspiracy theories.

"On what?" I really should have known better. After all, this was Seth Allen.

"Um…on a long-lost cousin of my dad's. It's extra credit for World History if I research someone in my family tree," I lied, rolling a single pearl of Grace's necklace between my fingers. "She went to PB in the seventies."

"Want some help?"

I was about to decline his offer, but then I remembered that my search involved something called a microfilm machine and I reconsidered.

"Yeah, I guess."

The librarian stood at the top of the stairs tapping her foot—she sure meant business. "Ready?" she asked.

We nodded and followed her down the winding staircase to the bowels of the library. A quick wave of nervousness washed over me when I recalled my last experience with a library's basement, and I silently thanked Seth for being nosy enough to want to help.

Two lonely microfilm machines sat tucked into a corner next to drawers overflowing with microfilm rolls. It looked like the place where old school filmstrips went to die.

"Have a seat," the librarian said.

I sat in front of one machine, and Seth pulled up a chair.

"Have you ever used one of these before?" she asked.

"No," I responded.

"Yes," Seth chimed in.

"Oh, good," she said handing me a huge roll of film labeled, "The *Cleveland Plain Dealer*: 1970 to 1975."

Without thinking twice, I handed the roll over to Seth. He expertly loaded the film and pulled up the first article.

"Oh, and Kate?" the librarian asked from the foot of the stairs. "I hope you find what you're looking for."

"Um, thanks," I said, but she had already started walking back up the stairs. "What was her deal?" I mumbled.

"What? I thought she seemed nice." Seth glanced back toward the stairs before slyly pulling a bag of Cheetos from his jacket pocket. "Please tell me you've tried Google already," he said while messing with the focus knob.

"What do you think I am? An idiot? I couldn't find anything. Trust me, the library was a last resort."

"Okay, okay. Let's just start. What're we looking for?"

"Anything related to an incident on Pemberly Brown's campus. Technically an assault."

"I thought you said this was a project about your dad's cousin, family-tree research." Seth looked me dead in the eyes, the corners of his mouth stained with orange powder.

Crap.

"Oh, yeah, um…I'm working on that project too. But first I'm researching a paper for my Women's Studies class about the history of assault against women at PB."

"Oh, okay." Seth pushed the button and the print became a blur, and I let out a huge sigh of relief. I couldn't believe Seth was buying this crap. Maybe love really was blind.

Seth whizzed and whirred his way through 1970.

"Anything?"

"Keep going. I'll tell you when to stop."

By the time we got to May 1971, an hour had passed. This wasn't going to be as easy as I had thought. By July my eyes had glazed over, and I was pretty sure that even if I did see something having to do with Pemberly Brown, I wouldn't realize it.

But then the machine made a strange clicking sound, and even though Seth turned the knob, the film was stuck.

"That's strange. I'll go get the librarian." Seth pushed out his chair.

"I thought you said you've used one of these." I turned the knob manually and backed up the film. When I pushed the Forward button, the strip got stuck again at the same place. As I reversed it, I noticed a thin line in the film. I gently pulled at it to get a closer look.

"Is that tape?" Seth asked. "Someone must have tried to fix it." He leaned his head in super-close to mine. His breath smelled like artificial cheese, and I resisted the urge to stuff a piece of gum in his mouth.

"Wait." I loaded the film again and pulled up the article right before the split in the film. There was nothing on the screen about an assault. I manually turned the film forward and stopped directly after the piece of tape. "Somebody cut out an article."

"No one even uses microfilm anymore. I'm sure it just broke or something. Keep going. I've gotta get back upstairs soon."

Leaning in close to the screen, I saw the remainder of an article in the upper left-hand corner.

-berly Brown accused a fellow student of assault. The minor accused was an accomplished student and athlete, and police theorize Moore killed herself after friends and classmates turned against her. Along with her family, Elisa Moore, the victim's sister, is speaking out-

"I think this is it," I said, biting my thumbnail. "But it's all broken apart, and I need an address, I mean...for the project."

"Why? It's not like you can interview her. She's dead." Seth pointed out helpfully.

"Yeah, but there's always her sister." Opening my slam book, I noted Elisa Moore's name and shoved the book back in my bag. "Thanks for your help with the machine, Seth. I could never have figured it out by myself." I pulled the film out of the machine, placed it back in its canister, and tucked that in the drawer along the wall.

"Wait. How will you find the address?"

"I'll figure it out," I said, swinging my bag over my shoulder and rushing to the stairs. But before I started up, I softened, thinking of everything Seth had done for me. "Hey, I saw a commercial for some special on the History Channel about..."

"Conspiracy Theory Week," Seth cut me off. "DVRed."

"Well, I thought it looked…um…interesting." The lie rolled off my tongue, and Seth looked like he'd died and gone to heaven.

"Well, it's a date then! I'll call you later."

"Uh, yeah. Sounds great." I rushed up the steps thankful to have a friend in Seth, even if that meant I'd have to sit through hours of the History Channel. In surround sound, no less.

Back on the main floor of the library, I found an empty computer terminal and started limbering up for some serious Google-fu.

The last name "Moore" was like "Smith." Googling it produced almost three million hits. The white-pages listings were pretty bad too. More than three hundred results were listed for "Moore" in the area alone.

"Elisa Moore" was a little different. There were only two Elisa Moores listed, and one was an Elisabeth. Under Elisa's name was the name "Palm Manor Extended Care Facility," as well as the address. According to my complex mathematic calculations (basic arithmetic done on my cell-phone calculator), if Elisa was living at a nursing home, she must have been the victim's older sister. Pulling up Google, I typed the address in the box and clicked the search button.

Within thirty-three seconds, Google spat out directions. God bless the interwebs.

Chapter 29

I scooped the last two soggy Cheerios onto my spoon and slurped. I'd made the mistake of sitting to the left of my dad, so every time he turned a page of the Sunday paper, he sent a puff of nasty newspaper smell in my direction. Nothing ruined breakfast like nasty newspaper smell.

Dad was in his "lounge" clothes. Translation: he wore khaki pants and a button-down shirt instead of his usual suit and tie. He must have been planning to take the day off.

"You're up early," he said. I watched the pupils of his eyes change size.

"I have a project to do today."

He lowered the paper and smiled. "Need some help? I'm free today." He nodded to his "lounge" clothes as if I couldn't see them for myself. My dad loved helping with school projects—well, at least he used to. I think he secretly missed tinkering around with science fair experiments and helping me spray-paint Styrofoam balls to create atom mobiles.

"Nah, it's a group project for World History. But I'm kind of excited. We get to go to a nursing home and interview some of the residents."

He stared at me a second, and I fidgeted, sliding my tongue over my teeth and wondering if a Cheerio was stuck in the front or something.

"What?" I asked, covering my mouth with my hand.

"Nothing. It's just, well…" He put the newspaper down. "I haven't seen you excited about anything in a long time."

I had to give him credit. He was right.

My phone buzzed, and my dad sighed as he watched me touch the screen.

Liam's text read, *On my way.*

"Let me drive you," my dad said. "It'll be like old times."

I lifted the bowl to my mouth and sipped the sugary milk.

"My ride's on the way."

Today was all about killing two birds with one stone. I wanted to spend time with Liam, and I wanted to get information about what had really happened to the girl in the clock tower and how that connected to Sinclair's brother and Grace. Oh, and, of course, I needed a ride. So I guess I killed three birds. (Thank God I'm not a vegan.)

Unfortunately I had to tell a few lies to get there. Like Seth, Liam thought we were visiting my dad's distant cousin for an extra-credit family-tree project in World History. And now my dad thought I was doing a group project for the same class. I was weaving quite the tangled web.

I shot Liam a quick text back telling him to honk when he got to my house. No reason for my dad and Liam to meet. Especially when they'd both been fed slightly different lies.

As I placed the empty bowl in the sink, I glanced at my dad, who sat holding the newspaper but looking straight past it. He was probably trying to remember the last time I'd agreed to let him help me.

"Thanks for the offer, though, Dad." I briefly considered walking over and kissing his cheek but opted for an awkward pat on the back instead. He gave me a vague smile as Liam's honk rang out through the kitchen.

I grabbed my coat and shot through the door before my dad could demand an introduction.

"So when are you going to start driving me around?" Liam joked as I ducked into the car.

"My birthday's not till June, so it'll be awhile. Unless you want to hit up the backseat of my dad's Saab and listen to him yell at me about hand-over-hand turns." I rolled my eyes and Liam laughed, shifting the car into reverse.

"So how are you related to…"—he squinted his eyes trying to remember her name—"Elisa?"

"She's one of my dad's second cousins or something," I lied again. "I'm supposed to interview her about…um…growing up during World War II." I'd kind of pulled that one out of my ass, thanks to Seth's lame-o documentary. I tried to do the math to figure out if Elisa could have grown up during the war, but it was a little too early in the day, and I couldn't exactly whip out my phone for a quick calculation.

"You don't have to come in if you don't want. I don't have that many questions, so it won't take long."

"Nah, I'll come along. All of my grandparents are dead, so I've never really had the chance to talk to anyone that old."

As sweet as it was that he wanted to talk to Elisa, I panicked a little about not being able to ask her the right questions with Liam in the room. Even though I really didn't have a clue as to what the right questions were. I couldn't exactly show up in an old woman's room and ask her for the details surrounding her sister's death.

Liam made the turn into Palm Manor Extended Care, and my stomach clenched just looking at the front door. I wasn't sure how I'd ever make it to Elisa's room. I twisted the pearls around my neck, attempting to channel a little bit of Grace's courage. I was going to need it.

"How can I help you?" the woman behind the desk asked, barely looking up from her computer screen.

"We're here to visit with Elisa Moore." My voice shook. I hoped it wasn't obvious.

The woman typed something into the computer and asked us to sign the guest book.

"Ms. Moore's room is 306. Just follow the signs," she said, pointing. "You'll wrap around a bit, and her room will be on the right."

We thanked the woman and followed her directions. Elisa's door was cracked open, so I knocked lightly.

"Come on in," said a young-sounding voice.

Great. Did Elisa have a family member visiting? What would

Grace do now? Well, if she'd just knocked on someone's door and gotten the okay, chances are she'd enter the room. I pushed open the door and came face-to-face with a friendly looking nurse who was washing her hands at the bathroom sink.

"Hi, there," she said. "Have you come to visit with Ms. Moore?"

I nodded my head while Liam hung back.

"Well, she'll be so happy, even if she doesn't show it. She hasn't had a visitor in some time, and I think she could really use a little cheering up. Come in, come in."

A twin bed was neatly made, and an older woman sat in a wheel-chair positioned in front of the window. Her light brown hair was pulled into a low chignon. As she kneaded her hands, I clenched and unclenched my own.

"How are you related to Ms. Moore?" the nurse asked.

I glanced at Elisa and sent a silent apology in her direction regarding the lie I was about to tell.

"Elisa is my dad's…cousin," I whispered, hoping that Ms. Moore was hard of hearing, which really was kind of a terrible thing to hope.

The nurse walked ahead of us and placed her hand lightly on Elisa's shoulder, but the woman didn't move a muscle.

"Ms. Moore, you have visitors! Isn't that nice?"

Elisa continued to stare out the window, and just when I thought she'd never answer—or that maybe she didn't even talk—she turned to the nurse and nodded her head. Her face was smooth, aside from a few wrinkles near her eyes and around her mouth. The nurse smiled as she came back toward Liam and me.

"Ms. Moore has good days and bad days, but I think you caught her on a good one." Her smile broadened. "Her memory goes in and out, so be patient." She squeezed my shoulder and left the room.

I sat on the bed near Elisa's wheelchair and figured I should introduce myself.

"Hi, Eli…er…Ms. Moore. My name is Kate Lowry," I said and extended my hand. She didn't move or even turn to look at me, so I awkwardly dropped my hand, barely resisting the urge to start chewing on my fingernails. "And this is Liam," I finished lamely.

"It's nice to meet you, Ms. Moore," Liam said in his polite talking-to-elderly-people voice, even though she really didn't look all that old.

Elisa did nothing but stare out the window.

"It's such a beautiful day today. Look at all that…foliage." Okay, I'm a complete sucker for trying to fill silence, but "foliage" was a stretch, even for me. Liam shot me a look that said, *Did you really just say that?*

"Um, we're students from Pemberly Brown. My dad tells me you went to school there." I watched her carefully, praying that the name of our school would trigger some kind of memory for her, but her eyes remained stubbornly blank. It was like she didn't even know we were there.

I wanted to ask her about her sister, but I couldn't go there with Liam in the room. I had to get rid of him somehow.

"Hey, Liam, why don't you see if you can snag us all some pudding or something?" I suggested.

Liam gave me a weird look, but he agreed and left the room to find a nurse.

As soon as he was out of earshot, I began firing questions at her. "Ms. Moore, do you remember a Robert Sinclair? He went to Pemberly Brown? I think you might have gone there too."

She didn't move a muscle. I was starting to wonder if she was even breathing.

I heard Liam's voice drift in through the open door. Something about chocolate or butterscotch. I didn't have much time.

"Elisa!" I touched her shoulder and spun her around to look at me. "What happened to your sister? What did they do to her? Why did she hurt herself?"

Her eyes widened when she looked at me. They were a muted, glassy blue, and they reflected fear and something else. Maybe recognition.

"She was your age." Her voice was stronger than I would have guessed, and her creepy eyes were focused on something behind me.

I took a step back, not knowing what to say, and followed Elisa's line of vision, terrified that Liam was back and that he'd heard me badgering an unstable old woman. Instead I saw a framed picture of a girl. The picture was yellowed, but the image was a familiar one. She looked like the girl in the plaid skirt with her long dark hair. She reminded me of Grace. I felt queasy.

"We would talk for hours lying next to each other in the grass. She told me everything." Elisa's skin looked paper-thin, and she sounded miles away. As if she were reading a script.

"She had her whole life ahead of her. We talked about what we

181

would do when we left. We talked about falling in love and moving away. Because that's what sisters do."

I glanced at the door, praying Liam hadn't been able to decide between the pudding flavors or that maybe Elisa's strange condition made him uncomfortable and he'd take his time.

"I told them what I thought happened. I told them she was acting differently. She never recovered after that night. And then when she went to the police, they started in on her. I knew they would kill her. No one believed me."

She reached her frail arm toward the picture frame and tried to move her body forward. Afraid that she'd lose her balance, I grabbed the frame with shaking hands and placed it on her lap.

"She never came downstairs for breakfast, and I knew the worst had happened." Elisa lifted the frame and cocked her head.

Liam walked into the room with the pudding and opened his mouth to say something, but I quickly shook my head and gestured for him to stay quiet.

"Will you go try to find the nurse?" I whispered to him. "She's not right."

Liam rushed back out of the room, and I knew I had to work fast. There wasn't much time. I took Elisa's hand in mine again.

"Did Robert Sinclair hurt your sister?" I asked, even though I knew the answer.

"Her bed was empty because she was in the tower."

"What tower?" But as soon as the question left my lips, I understood. The clock tower. Abigail was the girl hanging from the beams. It wasn't a legend after all. She was a real person with real problems and a real family who had been destroyed by the loss.

Spidery wrinkles formed along Elisa's forehead as she remembered. "Station 2. She was at Station 2 all along. Her sisters couldn't save her. The brothers got her. They did this. They took her from us. And they lied. All they tell are lies." Her eyes bulged, and her hands clenched the arms of her wheelchair so tightly that her knuckles turned white.

I stood and ran to the door, looking wildly down the hallway, praying someone would come to help. The sound of broken glass made me rush back over to Elisa's wheelchair. But when I got there, her face had rearranged itself back into a blank stare, as though her earlier outburst had never happened. I gathered the shattered glass from the frame and placed the fractured picture of the young girl back onto Elisa's bedside table next to a vase of beautiful pink peonies.

I was almost fifty years too late, but I placed my arm around her shoulders and tried to comfort the fragile woman with the broken heart.

Chapter 30

After I got back from the nursing home that afternoon, yet another email was waiting for me in my inbox.

To: KateLowry@pemberlybrown.edu

Sent: Sun 4:21 PM

From: GraceLee@pemberlybrown.edu

Subject: (no subject)

You're looking in all the right places
And never finding the right things.

The answers lie within the heart of Brown
Where the Brothers live.
Find them.

I had to get back to the old Brown buildings. I was sure I was missing something that would tie the headmaster's brother back to Grace, but I had no idea what it was. And who was I supposed to look for? Brown had closed more than sixty years earlier. There were no boys to be found.

I sat on my front porch, staring at the sheets of falling rain. Why'd it have to rain right now? I mean, how was I supposed to follow up on leads without a reliable mode of transportation? I'd already texted Liam twice, and a third time would venture into Stage 5 clinger levels of desperation.

My only remaining option was riding my bike to the clock tower in the pouring rain, and that was obviously out of the question. It was getting dark, and to avoid getting flattened by a car, I'd have to wear a helmet, reflective clothing, and probably a poncho. Enough said.

And then, as if the gods had sent him down from above to answer my prayers, Seth appeared in midair. Well, technically he jumped down from his lame-ass tree house, but at that moment he looked like a pocket-sized, redheaded superhero to me. He had his windbreaker thrown over his head and was running toward his front door.

"Hey, Seth!"

He spun around, his face all scrunched up.

"Come over here. Get out of the rain!" My chipper voice sounded a little false. Better tone it down a notch before he got suspicious. Seth ran over and under the porch roof. "Hanging out in your tree house again? You're so lame."

"I was just checking out the neighbors. They installed a new satellite dish, and I think they're using it to communicate with their FBI handlers."

"Sounds cool. So what are you up to tonight?"

Seth was visibly taken aback by my question. I made a mental note to be nicer to him in the future. He was acting like an abused animal, shocked at the tiniest bit of affection. It made me feel like the worst person in the world.

"I was just, you know, hanging out. Gonna do some homework, eat dinner…watch some more Conspiracy Theory Week, if you're…"

"No, no, no," I said, cutting him off before the invitation left his lips. "I just wanted to see if you're interested in taking a road trip to…" I began but was interrupted.

"Of course!" Seth said, not letting me finish. "Just let me ask my mom if I can borrow the van. It's raining, but I'll convince her to say yes!"

"Seth, you have no idea what you just agreed to. What if I said, 'to see if we can score some crack'?"

"Then I would have reminded you of the drug-free pledge we all had to sign last year. Where do you wanna go anyway?"

"I actually have to run back up to PB. I…um…forgot something…at one of the…uh…old Brown buildings."

My response didn't even make Seth think twice.

"I'll go get my keys!" Seth threw his jacket over his head again and ran toward his front door to get permission. "Mom!" I heard him yell before the door shut behind him.

Seth probably would have agreed to drive me to the end of the earth in his mom's white minivan, and for that I was eternally grateful. I mean, come on, every girl should have a Seth Allen in her life.

While Seth begged for permission, I went back inside and loaded my oversize purse with a flashlight, a notebook and pen, my camera, and the Mace my dad had forced on me when I started at the upper school. Considering my history with the building, I had to be prepared for the worst. If it was creepy during the daytime, I couldn't imagine what it would be like in the dark. A girl could never be too careful, even if she had a skinny, ginger-haired super-hero by her side.

By the time I ran through the garage door, Seth had pulled the minivan into my driveway. Even through the rain-streaked windows, I could see the huge smile on his face.

Crap. He was probably misinterpreting our little errand as a date. Oh, well, beggars can't be choosers, and this beggar needed a ride. I was just lucky he hadn't changed into his fancy clothes or something.

I climbed into the car and got to work thinking about the task that lay ahead.

"You okay?" Seth asked. "You're so quiet."

He was right. I was quiet and more than a little scared. I hadn't forgotten about the rock that had come sailing through the window on my last visit to the old building. Someone seemed to know my every move before I knew it myself, and they didn't appear to be thrilled about my investigation. I'd have to be careful.

"Yeah, yeah. Just a little nervous. Everyone says the Brown build-ings are haunted."

"Come on, you don't really believe in ghosts, do you?"

"I…well, I never did. But lately I've changed my mind," I said, thinking about Grace's emails and the girl in the plaid skirt.

"I think you've got bigger problems than ghosts, Kate." He flicked on his turn signal and turned left—hand over hand, of course.

"What do you mean?" I panicked, wondering if he'd figured everything out—if he knew all of the lies, all of the secrets I'd been hiding.

"I mean Liam Gilmour. What are you doing with him? He's dangerous."

I couldn't hold in my sigh of relief.

"Liam? Seriously, Seth? He's the least of my problems."

"I heard he's dangerous, Kate, unstable. You know what everyone says. It's true." Seth pulled into a parking spot in the student lot and put the van in park.

"Liam is a lot of things, but dangerous isn't one of them." Well, unless you counted him potentially breaking my heart. "You don't know him. People just like to gossip." I leaned my head against the window.

"He started a fire," Seth blurted out.

In an instant, the van filled with tension so thick I could barely breathe.

I whipped my head toward Seth. "What are you even talking about? What fire?"

"It happened before he started at PB. When I was working in the office last year, I had to refile his folder. The report slipped out."

I was reminded of Liam saying everyone had something to hide. Could that be what he was hiding? I shoved the thought away. It couldn't be true. If he had told me he'd caught Liam making out with Beefany I would have believed Seth, but there was no way that Liam was some kind of pyromaniac.

"Why can't you just be happy for me? A guy finally shows interest, and you just have to get jealous." The anger came out of nowhere and surprised even me. Each terrible word hung in the air, punctuated only by the sound of the swishing windshield wipers and Mrs. Allen's soft-rock radio station. I chewed on my nails, and Seth squirmed in the driver's seat.

"I'm sorry," Seth said. "I just don't want you to get hurt."

I replayed the words I'd spat at him. "I'm sorry I called you jealous," I said. "I've got a lot on my mind, and I don't really have time for lies about Liam."

Rain pounded down on the roof, trailing like tears down the windows surrounding us. Watching the raindrops' jagged paths helped me get over my anger. Just a little.

"Actually, I've been meaning to tell you," Seth said, changing the subject, "I figured out the meaning behind this." He lifted his bony butt off the seat and dug into his pocket, handing me a crumpled piece of paper.

"I printed it off one of my forums," Seth said, referring to one of the many online chats he participated in to discuss God only knew what. "It's the old Pemberly crest." He was very pleased with himself. "But the *S* here?" He pointed to the ornate letter. "That should be a *P*, you know, for Pemberly."

"Oh, right. Thanks," I said, glad our little spat was over but annoyed that Seth was telling me things I already knew about the damn crest.

The crest was clearly important, and I'd seen it in enough different places to know that the *S* wasn't a typo. Why did Naomi have the words carved into jewelry? Why had Ms. Cole warned me to be careful? And why was part of the crest on all of our invitations? Why, why, why? I felt like a freaking three-year-old.

"Look." I turned toward Seth. "Why don't you just wait in the car? I'll be right back. Plus there's only one umbrella." I needed answers, and if Seth came with me to the heart of Brown, there would only be millions of additional questions.

"Yeah, right. It's dark. You're not going on campus alone. What did you forget at the building? Why can't this wait until tomorrow? And I'm the one with the keys, remember?" Seth jangled his key chain in front of me. I took in the ridiculous, beaded key-chain monstrosity he'd probably made at sleep-away camp.

"Right," I said, snatching it from between his fingers. I threw my hood up and rearranged the bag on my shoulder. "Well, are you coming or not?"

Seth continued to ask different versions of his initial questions approximately one hundred times as we made our way across campus, huddled under the same umbrella. I wondered how long it would take before he gave up.

The campus spread out around us, an entirely different world at night. The trees that seemed magical during the day were foreboding in the dark. Streetlights dotted corners and cast light onto branches and blades of grass, making them look like shards of broken glass. A foggy haze hovered over Pemberly Brown Lake and spilled into the gardens.

As we came upon the pathway, a part of me wished that instead of the dim lights situated on each side of the path, huge stadium lights illuminated the entire space. The rain, the fog, the gardens—it was like something out of a bad horror movie. I tightened my grip around Seth's thin arm.

He finally gave up on all the questions, and we hurried along the path in silence. Unfortunately, silence really wasn't the blessing I'd thought it would be. When it's quiet, you can hear all sorts of other noises. Like rain pounding down on leaves, the sighing of the wind, and whispers from the ghosts I was sure I saw lurking in the dark.

A shadow crossed over the foggy path in front of us. My hand flew to my bag, my fingers curling around the Mace tucked inside.

"Did you see that?" Seth whispered.

"Yeah, it was probably just a deer or something."

"How many deer do you know that stand upright?"

"Ugh, come on." I pulled on the sleeve of Seth's jacket, guiding him in the direction of the old Brown campus.

As we exited the gardens, the campus opened up, making me feel a little more comfortable. There were fewer places to hide out in the open. The downside was that there were fewer places for *us* to hide.

Seeing in the pelting rain was difficult, but the familiar outline of the three Brown buildings in a row was unmistakable.

"I don't think you heard when I asked you before, but what did you leave here?" Make that one hundred and one questions. You had to give him credit for tenacity.

"I actually dropped one of my earrings, and they were my grandma's. My mom will kill me if I don't find it."

"Don't you think you might have been better off looking in the daylight?"

I wanted to ignore him but knew he'd never give up. "There's no way I'll be able to sleep tonight if I don't find them. Plus"—I reached into my bag and pulled out a flashlight—"I brought this."

"Hey, you could have brought that out a little earlier. We could have shined it on the upright deer."

"Don't get your panties in a bunch—we're here."

We stood huddled under the tiny umbrella, staring up at the old brick building.

"Well, what're you waiting for? Let's get out of the rain." Seth moved forward, and I threw the open umbrella into the corner of the entranceway.

I unlocked the door with Seth's keys, and as soon as we stepped foot inside, Seth began sneezing uncontrollably.

"Are you sure you don't want to just wait outside?" I asked, annoyed. If anyone was in the building, they'd have plenty of warning about our arrival, thanks to Seth.

"I'm"—*sneeze*—"fine"—*sneeze*—"just"—*sneeze*—"keep"—*sneeze*—"going." He sneezed again as if to punctuate his sentence, and I mumbled something about dead weight.

The beam of the flashlight created a path of light for us to follow, and I flicked it from wall to wall hoping to find whatever I was supposed to be looking for. I continued to walk forward slowly, pearls bumping my chest with each step. Something caught my eye, so I bent to take a closer look. At first I thought it was a thumbtack, but after I peered closer, I saw that it was a small pin bearing the lion and key, Brown's old crest. I wondered how long the pin had been there. Could this possibly be Grace's big clue?

"I think this is it. Right?" I whispered and lifted my head as if I expected Grace to answer.

"Kate!" Seth yelled. I practically jumped out of my skin and said a silent prayer that Seth hadn't heard me talking to myself.

"Jesus, Seth. This better be good."

He was kneeling in front of the brick staircase and holding a piece of paper.

"Check it out."

I bent next to Seth and shined the flashlight on the paper. It was an invitation identical to the invitation Cameron had sent me with Grace's name on it and the invitation Naomi had pulled from her glove compartment. But this invitation was a little different.

Not only was the piece of crest in the upper left-hand corner, but this invitation was addressed to me.

Chapter 31

Last Fall

I'm going to be sick." I grabbed my stomach and begged my dad to pull the car to the side of the road. As soon as we stopped rolling, I jumped out and vomited into the grass below. My body heaved with such force that I fell to my knees, pieces of gravel cutting into the thin skin. My mom rubbed my back and held my hair, saying nothing. She didn't tell me everything was going to be okay; she didn't tell me not to worry. She couldn't.

As soon as I'd finished, I climbed back into the car and pushed the Send button on my phone again. Instead of holding the phone to my ear, I watched the call timer tick through the seconds. I knew that when I got to thirty-one, I'd hear Grace's cheerful voice explaining that she was away from her phone and couldn't pick up.

As the phone rang, I stared at Grace's face on the screen. We had programmed pictures into our phones that popped up whenever we called each other. Grace was sticking her tongue out at me.

Twenty-nine. Thirty. Thirty-one

"Hi, this is Grace. I'd love to talk, but I can't. I'll call you back!"

I wanted to believe her—that she'd call me back—but a part of me knew she never would. I left another message, each one more desperate than the last, and went through the entire sequence over and over and over.

As soon as we pulled into the garage, I rushed upstairs to my bathroom to get sick again. I thought maybe it had to do with the smell of smoke on my body and in my hair, so I took a shower, violently scouring my scalp and body with soap. I scrubbed and scrubbed, taking a break only to call Grace, beads of water rolling down my arm and onto the screen of my phone.

Twenty-nine. Thirty. Thirty-one.

Twenty-nine. Thirty. Thirty-one.

Twenty-nine. Thirty. Thirty-one.

I must have fallen asleep with the phone in my hand, because in the morning, when I woke up, it was gone.

"Where is it?" I sat up in bed and screamed at the top of my lungs, searching the space around me wildly. "I need it!" I stumbled out of bed and into the hallway, falling into a heap at the top of the stairs. "I need it!" I cried now, pulling my legs into my chest, my body jerking with each sob.

"Shh," my mom whispered as she walked up the stairs. It was early in the morning, but she still wore the same clothes as the night before. I wondered if she'd ever gone to sleep. "Oh, Kate." My hair stuck to my tears, and she pushed it back from my face and sat next to me. Pulling me into her lap, she held me in her arms and rocked me back and forth like I was a baby instead of a teenager.

I looked up at her through bloodshot eyes and said the words I feared the most.

"She's gone, isn't she?"

"Oh, sweetie. They found a body…in the basement. They're not saying who it is yet, so we need to pray."

But I didn't have to pray. I already knew. It was Grace. She was gone.

Chapter 32

Present Day

We huddled under the green glow of an Applebee's lamp, our heads nearly touching. Seth held the invitation, his brow furrowed.

"I don't understand. What were you being invited to that night? And if you were invited, why weren't you there when the fire broke out?" Seth pointed at the flowery calligraphy on the invitation. We had placed the three invitations—Grace's, Naomi's, and now mine—together, the pictures forming three-quarters of the crest.

"And the Pemberly crest?" he asked picking up the crumpled page of Cameron's drawing. "It matches this?" Seth pointed to the incomplete crest and looked at me, confused. "And where's the last invitation? Who does it belong to?"

I had a choice to make. I could continue to play dumb and risk Seth's incessant questions and inevitable involvement, or I could tell him everything and get it over with. As scared as I was to break my promise to Grace, I needed help. Besides, he already knew way too much.

The upside to putting it all out there was the sheer volume of random information Seth housed in his brain. He was incredibly resourceful—if he didn't know the answer he almost always knew where to find it. And it would be kind of nice to have a sidekick.

"Let me start at the beginning," I whispered, feeling an invisible weight slide off my shoulders the second I began.

By the time I'd finished, the waitress had come by our table at least five times, annoyed that the bill book remained empty, and my story had been interrupted three times by Seth's cell phone. His mom wanted to know if we were having a good time.

"So...now what?" When Seth asked the question, I almost wanted to leap across the table and kiss him. It felt that good to have someone in on my secret. Someone who cared.

"I honestly don't know. Naomi's at tennis camp and Cameron ran away, and they're the only two people who know about the invitations who might be able to help."

Without saying a word, Seth picked up his phone and connected a call.

"Mom? I think we're gonna catch a movie," he said. "Yeah, a late one. I know it's a school night, but I did all my homework...I'm almost sixteen and a half." Seth paused and held the phone away from his ear, and I heard his mom's voice screaming into the air. "Okay, I'll call you when it's over." Seth snapped his phone shut and beamed at me.

"A movie? Are you kidding?..."

But Seth didn't let me finish. "So you think they've found Cameron yet?" he asked.

I smiled, understanding then, and stood up from the table. "Worth a shot."

• • •

As we pulled down Cameron's street, I honestly wasn't sure what to expect. There was a good chance that Cameron was already back. Students quietly left Pemberly Brown all the time, and based on his history, I couldn't imagine that the Thompsons would have been in any rush to put him back in school.

But when Seth carefully parked the minivan a few houses down from Cameron's, I barely registered the fact that his driveway was empty aside from a nondescript sedan. Instead my eyes locked on the house next to his. It wasn't one of the insane mansions that lined most of the streets in the area, just a modest colonial. It looked dark, almost vacant, but I knew better. Grace's parents were holed up inside somewhere, along with most of my childhood memories. I tried to hide the grief that overcame me, but Seth noticed. Of course.

"Are you all right?" he asked, looking down at his hands. "If you're cold, you can borrow my jacket." We both knew he was talking about so much more than being cold.

I shook my head, and he gave me a second more to swallow back the enormous lump I felt growing bigger in my throat the longer I stared at Grace's house. I pulled my eyes away and breathed deeply, switching gears.

"So exactly what is the plan?" Coming here had seemed like a good idea when Seth had suggested it at Applebee's, but now I wasn't so sure. I mean, we couldn't just ring the doorbell and ask the Thompsons if Cameron had given them any information about Grace's death and how it might connect to our headmaster's brother, who may or may not have been a rapist.

Luckily, lights were still on downstairs, and in spite of the rain, most of the windows were cracked an inch. The chances that we'd actually find anything were fairly slim, but I figured it couldn't hurt to take a look around Cameron's yard and maybe peek into the windows to see if there were any signs that Cameron had come back home.

"Come on. I've got an idea." Seth opened the car door and stepped into the wet street. I yanked the hood of my sweatshirt up over my ponytail, relieved to relinquish the lead.

Please be back. Please be back. Please be back. I chanted the mantra in my head the entire way through Cameron's soggy yard. For extra luck, I touched Grace's pearls, a reminder of the importance of our mission.

"Okay, let's just walk around the house. We'll look in the windows and see if he's home," Seth said.

"And if he's there?" I asked.

"I don't know. We try to talk to him, right? This could be our only chance." I hung on to the words "we" and "our." They had never sounded more beautiful. Even if they had been said by Seth, who simultaneously pulled a small plastic bag of pickles out of his pocket and began munching.

He must have seen the look of disgust on my face, because between bites he said, "What? I can't help it. I get hungry when I'm nervous—low blood sugar."

I shook my head and grabbed his arm. "Come on. It's now or never."

We started toward the side of the house. When we reached the low side windows, we saw a dark dining room but no sign of Cameron.

I motioned for Seth to be quiet as we crept along the perimeter of the Thompsons' home. As we approached the backyard, light reflected off the wet grass from the kitchen windows. They were placed higher on the house, so we were both able to stand undetected as long as we hugged the brick exterior.

"Seth," I whispered, "I hear someone." Seth ducked down and pulled me with him.

"Yes, I'm here. They still haven't found him." The voice from inside the house was muffled but still audible.

Well, I guess that was that. No Cameron. But the voice sounded eerily familiar, and I was almost positive it wasn't Cameron's dad. We heard the scraping of a chair and a soft thud as someone sat down.

"Who is it?" Seth whispered, his hot pickle breath rolling over my cheek. I shushed him and wrinkled my nose at the same time.

"No, I don't think they know anything, but we can't be too careful." The voice paused. "No, that won't be necessary. At least I don't think it will be. As far as I can tell, he didn't leave the evidence behind." The speaker lowered his voice, and I struggled to make out the words. "…Family…anything…sisterhood exposing…he's coming. I have to go."

A brief pause was followed by the sound of a chair scraping against the floor again. I looked over at Seth. His eyes were wide. Whoever this guy was, he clearly was worried about the evidence Cameron had gathered about Grace's death. The evidence that now belonged to me.

"Thanks again for stopping by." A new voice rang out in the still night air, and this time I was positive it was Cameron's dad.

"Of course." The voice trailed away as Mr. Thompson and the visitor moved toward the front door. "I hope the information… alternative schools…Cameron…support…" was all we could make out.

"Come on! They're moving to the front of the house." I grabbed Seth and started to take off for the front yard, but suddenly the entire backyard was flooded with blinding light. It must have been a motion sensor.

Two sets of footsteps pounded back toward the kitchen and the screen door screeched open.

Shit.

Chapter 33

I don't think I'd actually ever seen Seth run before. If we hadn't been in danger of being busted by Cameron's dad and his sketchy visitor, I'm sure I would have taken more time to appreciate the fact that Seth ran like a prepubescent girl, but I was too busy sprinting.

"Hey! You! Stop right there!" Cameron's dad had made it out of the house and was chasing after us.

Thankfully, he gave up about halfway through his massive front yard, and I didn't think he'd be close enough to see the license-plate number as Seth's minivan tore down Cameron's street. I tried to twist around to get a good look at the other man behind the voice, but he must have ducked back inside.

The car was completely silent except for our ragged breathing. I don't think either of us wanted to jinx our getaway until we knew for sure we were safe. When we made it to my driveway without the sound of sirens wailing behind us, I released the breath I'd been holding.

"Oh, thank God. I can't believe we made it." I grabbed Seth's arm, and he must have interpreted my fingers digging into his upper arm as "I'm so grateful—ravish me" instead of "I'm terrified and need to squeeze something, and your arm just happens to be in reach," because he placed his fingers on my chin and pulled my face to his.

"It's okay, Kate," he said softly, leaning forward.

"*Eww*, Seth!" I yelled, shoving at his chest. "Lay off!"

"What?" He held his hands in the air. "I thought maybe...oh forget it." He didn't even pretend to be hurt anymore; it was like he'd expected the reaction before I even had a chance to react. "And what the hell is that crap about sisters? Cameron doesn't have any sisters."

"What did you say?" I asked.

"Sisterhood. The headmaster said something about the sisterhood."

"The headmaster? What are you talking about?" I bumbled, my mind struggling to connect the pieces.

"I'd recognize his voice anywhere. I work in the office, remember?"

"You're sure?" I asked, trying to understand the significance of Headmaster Sinclair visiting the Thompsons. Maybe it was protocol? But his visit had to be so much more than that. My mind reeled back to Seth's other realization.

"Sisterhood," I repeated. "Why does that sound familiar?" I closed my eyes for a second, and then it hit me.

"Elisa, at the nursing home. She said something about sisters." I opened my eyes and suddenly felt an overwhelming urge to start clapping. "I thought she was being general, but now it makes sense. Abigail Moore's death and Grace's are connected somehow."

"By a group called the Sisterhood?" Seth asked breathlessly. I could almost hear him mentally composing his post for the conspiracy-theory boards he frequented.

"I think so. Ever heard of them?"

"Um, no? Wait…" Seth looked up at the ceiling as though he was scanning the file drawer of his brain that housed long-term memories. "Well, maybe. And I think I know exactly where to look."

Seth started backing the car out of my driveway. "Hey, what are you doing?"

"You're coming to my place." Seth deftly pulled up his own driveway and maneuvered the car into the garage.

"But why?"

"You'll see."

Seth sprinted through the door and yelled, "MomI'mhome Kate'shereandwe'vegottachecksomethingforschoolquick. Okay? Okay." He practically shoved me up the stairs to his room, leaving his mother downstairs asking about eight hundred questions that we could no longer hear.

"Okay, there's this guy who always posts on my blog…"

"Wait. You have a blog? Seriously?"

Seth looked offended. "Do you want me to help or not?"

"Yeah, yeah, I want you to help," I said guiltily.

"Okay, so like I was saying, there's this guy I know who specializes in regional secret societies." Seth typed furiously into his PC as he talked. "He's totally obsessed with a society that supposedly formed in the Midwest sometime after World War II, and guess what they're called?"

"The Sisterhood?"

"Yup."

"Here, take a look."

Sure enough, there was a quick paragraph about the Sisterhood. ConspiracyLuvR (and, yes, that was indeed his actual screen name—you can't make this stuff up) had never been able to find any definitive proof that the group existed. Just anecdotal mentions in old diaries and letters, but based on what he'd pulled together, the group had formed in the Cleveland area during the 1950s.

I looked up from the computer.

"And does…"—I could barely bring myself to say his name out loud—"ConspiracyMother think they're still active today?"

"It's ConspiracyLuvR, and, yeah, he's always trying to dig up proof, but they're too smart and they lie very low. None of that Skull and Bones crap for them. He thinks they're very active and expanding."

"Wow," I breathed, trying to make sense of all this. And then it occurred to me. The letter on the crest. "Are you thinking what I'm thinking?"

"Yeah, I'll ask my mom to bring up some snacks."

"No, I mean about the crest. The *S*. It's not supposed to be a *P*. It's supposed to stand for the Sisterhood."

As I said the words, I could practically hear the sound of a puzzle piece clicking into place. This was it: the truth that might set Grace free.

Chapter 34

B ack home, I stood under a scalding hot shower, letting the water run over me as the rain had just hours before. No matter how much I complained about Seth, I knew I never could have accomplished anything that night without him.

After I dressed, I sat down at my desk and pulled up my email to thank him. But before I could even begin to type, I noticed the bold words.

I had one new message.

To: KateLowry@pemberlybrown.edu
Sent: Tues 11:21 PM
From: GraceLee@pemberlybrown.edu
Subject: (no subject)

You are close.
Please don't stop.
Liam knows, be careful.

I read the words on the screen over and over again. What does Liam know? I hadn't told him anything.

And yet she said I was close. And Grace was right—I couldn't stop now. If I was being honest with myself, I knew deep down that something wasn't right with Liam. Seth would never make anything up just to hurt me. Liam was definitely hiding something, and I was willing to bet it went deeper than his dysfunctional relationship with Beefany.

Did he know about the Sisterhood? Or did he know what had really happened to Grace? Did he really have a history with fires? But why would he have wanted Grace dead? Why would the Sisterhood have wanted her dead? My mind spun with questions.

I felt like my head was going to explode, so I tried to pull the emergency brake on my overactive brain. First things first: the email said Liam knew something, so I needed to focus on that. The mysterious Brown pin, the missing invitation from that night, and the Sisterhood would all have to wait. For now.

As for Liam, it was time to go all *Law & Order* on his ass and find out the whole truth and nothing but the truth. And as much as I wanted to be surprised, I wasn't. I liked Liam. A lot. And yet I'd always known deep down that he was hiding something.

I wish I could say I'd never seen it coming. But all the signs were there. My heart just chose to ignore them.

Chapter 35

I cradled my head in my palm and pretended to listen to Beefany drone on about Homecoming weekend. But my thoughts alternated between a mental list of who might be a member of the Sisterhood and just how much Liam knew.

Clearly, the Sisterhood was meeting for some reason at the chapel the night of the Spiritus bonfire, but I still believed Naomi when she said that she and her "friends" had nothing to do with Grace's death. I was missing something, something big. And I couldn't ignore the feeling that I was running out of time.

"This dance is the single most important night this fall, and it's our job to make it more than perfect." Beefany had something red stuck between her front teeth, and I absentmindedly wondered if it was a piece of human flesh. "But before we can start making decorations, I'm going to reveal the theme of this year's Homecoming dance."

The room full of wannabes buzzed with excitement and looked expectantly at Queen Taylor, who sat behind Beefany, as usual.

"Okay, people, quiet down." Beefany rapped her gavel a few times. I noticed that it sort of sparkled. Unbelievable. The gavel was now bedazzled. I wondered if that was Beefany's or Taylor's handiwork. Maybe Beefany had applied the crystals when she had weekend custody. Taylor didn't seem like the bedazzling type.

"The theme is…" She raised her strong arms in the air like a preacher and paused as though waiting for a drum roll. "Mardi Gras!"

The room erupted in squeals. I looked around and watched as girls jumped up and gave each other hugs, the jocks shoved each other, wide-eyed at the possibility of such a scandalous theme, and one random chick in the corner power-punched into the air.

I wouldn't have been surprised if one of the girls had pulled up her shirt in hopes of getting assigned to work on centerpieces with Taylor. Who needed beads when you could vie for the queen's approval?

The loyal subjects began shouting out ideas associated with the theme, and Beefany wrote each on the board in her careful print. Taylor nodded her approval as the brainstorming continued. But then she motioned Beefany over and whispered in her ear.

Contrasting eyes settled on me—Beefany's dark brown and Taylor's bright blue. Finally Beefany straightened. "Kathy?" Her eyes narrowed in my direction. "Kathy, how about you? What's your contribution to our little think tank?"

"Well, it's Kate, and I think you have a pretty good list there," I said, annoyed.

"Cape?" she asked, feigning confusion.

"No, K-A-T-E," I practically shouted.

"Okay, Cape, do you have anything to add?"

Only that a Mardi Gras Homecoming theme might be the worst idea in the history of bad ideas, I thought, but I shook my head instead. Although I had to admit I wouldn't miss Homecoming night for the world. This was one train wreck I'd have to witness in person. Only one issue: I needed a date.

I mentally crossed Liam off the list of potential date candidates. Call me crazy, but it seemed in poor taste to go to Homecoming with a guy who was probably involved in your best friend's death.

When he poked his head into the classroom a moment later, I gasped. It was like he could read my mind or something. He signaled for me to join him in the hall, and for the first time since I'd started hanging out with him, a wave of nervousness washed over me. And not nervous in that butterflies-in-the-stomach-I'm-about-to-kiss-my-crush kind of way; I was veering more into heart-starts-racing-when-you're-alone-in-a-dark-parking-garage-at-night territory.

Although I had spent the bulk of the previous night developing my plan of attack, seeing Liam's face squelched my courage. I wasn't ready. But he didn't look like he was going to leave until he talked to me, so I snapped my fingers. Beefany insisted we snap our fingers to get her attention—something she and Taylor had learned at a Young Leaders of America conference.

"Cape? Do you need something?"

"Just the bathroom."

"Well, don't be long. We have lots to do, and we haven't even started designing the centerpieces."

She glanced at the door, but Liam had already ducked out.

"What's going on?" I asked Liam as soon as I'd shut the door behind me.

"I just thought maybe you'd want an excuse to get out of there."

"That's okay," I said, refusing to meet his eyes. "It's getting kind of…interesting." The lies were second nature now.

"All right." He looked kind of embarrassed that I'd turned him down. "Did you get my texts?" He lightly grazed my arm as he asked, and I flinched.

"I've just been super-busy," I said. "I should get back in there."

I grasped the door handle, but Liam continued talking.

"They're liars. You know that, right?" he asked, lowering his voice. "Don't get sucked in. You're too good for that."

I spun back around automatically. "It's funny that you're calling them liars. Are you ready to tell me exactly what happened between you and Bethany?"

Liam's entire face fell. "What are you talking about?"

"Don't play dumb. I'm not an idiot, Liam. You can't keep pretending that there's not something going on between you guys."

"It's not what you think." His eyes darted toward the door as though he was afraid she'd hear or something.

"Well, then, tell me, Liam. What happened?"

When it was obvious he wasn't going to answer me, I turned to leave, but he grabbed my arm and pulled me further into the hall. He wasn't holding me that hard, but when I wasn't able to free myself, I began to panic.

"What are you doing? Let me go!" I didn't realize I had shouted the words until the door to the classroom swung open and Alistair Reynolds came barreling out.

"Dude, lay off!" He pried Liam's hand off my arm and threw it down. "What's your problem?"

"Kate, I didn't mean…" Liam began, but Alistair's arm was already thrown around my shoulder, my head pulled close to his chest.

"Just leave me alone." Even as I said the words, I wanted to take them back.

Before Alistair guided me back into the safety of the classroom, I couldn't resist one last long, hard look at Liam. He was still gorgeous. No denying that. His longish hair was messy in a way that somehow ended up looking stylish. His khaki pants fit low on his hips, and he'd layered another one of his vintage tees beneath the required white-collared shirt. The thin material of the button-down gave way to words underneath. This one looked like it might be an old-school-band T-shirt.

And then it hit me.

Naomi had seen someone running from the chapel with longish hair and a Rolling Stones T-shirt.

"Come on, Kate. Let's get back inside," Alistair said.

"You go first," I said, distracted, waiting for the door to close behind him. I pointed at Liam's chest. "Is that…a Rolling Stones T-shirt?"

Liam looked at me like I was a little crazy. "Uh, yeah. Why?"

"Turn around," I practically shouted.

Sure enough, when he spun around, a faint pair of lips with a tongue hanging out could be seen through the white.

Without another word, I lunged for the door of the classroom and yanked it open, leaving Liam in the hallway staring after me. Liam was the missing piece of the puzzle. He was the one Naomi had seen running through the woods that night.

Chapter 36

As soon as I was free from the hell that was centerpiece planning, I sprinted through the empty halls to Station 3, marveling at how the station inscriptions shifted based on the kind of day you were having. *Faber est suae quisque fortunae.* "Every man is the artisan of his own fortune." Last time it had been doughnuts; today it was petty theft. Lucky for me, it was Tuesday, which meant Seth had afternoon duty at the office. My fortunes were looking up.

When I arrived at the office and peered through the glass walls, I found just who I was looking for. His red curls sprung out from behind a filing cabinet.

"Hey, Seth," I said, poking my head into the office.

He popped up like a little groundhog and smiled. If nothing else, Seth was always happy to see me. With everything that'd been going on in my life, I was grateful for that.

"What's up?" he asked in a voice that was about ten decibels too loud for my taste. Mrs. Newbury shot us a disapproving look, so I grabbed Seth's arm and yanked him into the hall. I scanned the hallway to see if any teachers were within earshot. The coast was clear.

"Can you pull a few files for me?" I asked quietly.

"You mean, like, student files?" he said, clearly shocked by the idea.

"Yeah, I need to know the deal with Liam, Bethany, and Taylor. I got another email from Grace, and she mentioned Liam's name. And something tells me that if there's a secret society at Pemberly Brown, Bethany and Taylor are in on it."

"Whoa, wait a second. You've had an actual conversation with Taylor Wright?"

I shook my head, annoyed. "Um, not exactly, but I had to join Concilium. It's a long story. But I need the files. Can you help?"

"Okay, okay. Sorry." Seth's eyes darted around skittishly. "I don't know…if we got caught…" Seth trailed off.

"Look, Seth, you spend all your time reading those crazy books about unsolved mysteries and conspiracies, and you're finally in a position to help me solve what might be an actual murder. But we can't do anything unless you're willing to take some risks."

I needed to know what had really happened between the two of them, but more than that, I needed to know exactly what Liam was capable of. If he really was some kind of pyro, maybe he had somehow played a role in what happened to Grace.

"Fine. I think I can do it. Mrs. Newbury always leaves early on Tuesdays for her bunco game."

"Great. I'll save you a seat on the late bus," I said, already starting to walk away. I wanted to get out of there before he changed his mind.

"Oh, and Seth." I turned back and gave him a quick kiss on the cheek. "Thank you!"

He turned bright red, and a huge smile practically split his face in half.

• • •

True to my word, I sat on the bus waiting for Seth. I had the entire bus to myself until Bradley and Alistair decided to climb on, draping their arms over the seat in front of me.

"Oh, hey, Kate. I didn't know you were on this bus." Alistair smiled lazily.

"Um, yeah. Most days, actually. I didn't know you guys even knew buses existed," I shot back. What the hell were they doing here? Seth was supposed to be here with the files any minute, and I didn't have time to deal with these jackholes.

"Yeah, we're not exactly bus people, but we were passing by and saw you sitting all by yourself and wanted to say hi." Bradley's smile was so bright, I had to look away.

There was a knock on the window next to the boys, and we all looked down to see Porter waiting outside, guitar and all.

"What're you doing, Al? Mom said you have to take me to guitar practice today. I'm not walking again," he called through the open window. I wasn't sure if it was the pathetic note in his voice or the news that Porter actually took lessons and was still *that* abysmal at guitar, but I found myself laughing.

"Well, duty calls." Alistair shrugged and stood up.

Bradley hung behind for a second, and his almost black eyes pierced mine. "Take care of yourself, Kate." What the hell was that supposed to mean?

I nodded and watched him jog off the bus and over to Alistair and Porter waiting outside. Alistair and Bradley shoved at Porter as they walked, and I heard Alistair make some snide comment about Seth's rolling backpack when he crossed their path.

Seth's geriatric bag caught along the edges of the seats as he pulled it down the aisle. It made my heart hurt a little that he seemed so unfazed by the bullying outside, but I was soon distracted by the three fat files he delicately lifted from his bag as he sat down.

"I got them," Seth said, looking around the bus like he was an undercover agent of some sort. "Not sure what you're looking for, but whatever it is, it's probably in here."

We started sifting through the files and found all sorts of interesting information.

Apparently, Taylor's father had donated a huge chunk of change to the school right before she was accepted. Guess she didn't have to fill out that tedious application to get into PB like the rest of us.

As interesting as it was to learn about Taylor behind the scenes, the information wasn't exactly what I was looking for. I thumbed through the pages in search of her guidance records. I knew from experience that the guidance counselors were forced to document every student visit by completing a form.

Taylor had a huge stack of guidance forms. Most of them were boring requests for more honors classes and petty complaints about teachers or students who had dared to defy Pemberly Brown's reigning queen bee.

But one form had been flagged with a sticky note that read, "Urgent." The entire page was filled with notes, and the counselor had stamped CONFIDENTIAL in huge, red block letters at the top of the sheet.

Taylor suffering from severe depression. Doctor has prescribed Zoloft to alleviate symptoms.

Taylor depressed? I felt like this must have gotten stuck in the wrong file. It was dated last November, so apparently she'd spent the last year stuffed with antidepressants too. This shouldn't have made me happy, but it sort of did. I wondered if she went to Dr. P. I'd love to see the look on her face if I caught her in the waiting room.

Bethany's file was completely useless. No trips to the guidance counselor, just a bunch of demerits for getting into fights throughout lower school. You'd think someone would have gotten this girl into anger-management counseling at some point.

But Liam's file was just as fat as Taylor's, although for a completely different reason. His guidance forms told a stereotypical bad-boy-with-issues story. One session from his middle-school years outlined feelings of loneliness after moving from school to school after his mom died. Detentions, suspensions, and one expulsion riddled the other forms, while another counselor marked notes about Liam's struggle to transition from public to private school.

I felt a twinge of guilt looking through all of his confidential information, but I reminded myself I was doing this for Grace. I flipped through every form in the file, but there was nothing about a fire. Was it just another rumor?

"I thought you said Liam had some kind of history with fire," I hissed at Seth.

"He did. The form should be in the back. Here, let me see."

Seth grabbed the folder from my hands as we rounded a corner.

"All right, it's got to be in here somewhere," Seth whispered. "But I don't see it. I know it was in here at the beginning of last year. I saw it when I was transferring files after the office was remodeled." He sounded confused.

"Are you sure? Like, really sure? Because if he didn't really do it…"

"Wait. What's this one say?" Seth asked and picked up another form flagged with a sticky note. The bus hit a bump, and the file's contents spread out on his lap. His forehead wrinkled as he read. "Something about community service."

"That could be for any of these little incidents. What does it say?"

"Replanting trees…picking up garbage…rebuilding a garage…"

I was starting to get bus sick reading over Seth's shoulder. I looked out the window to see how much longer we had and then glanced back at Seth. He was staring at the file, deep in thought. "They give an address. Maybe if we look it up we'll be able to find more info."

"Fine. I'll check it out tonight and see what else I can find."

The bus jerked to a stop, and our driver pulled the door open. I shoved the papers back into Liam's file and, with a heavy heart, stepped down into the fresh air.

The street was blanketed in red, yellow, and orange leaves that crunched beneath my feet as I headed home. Only yesterday, the leaves had been arranged neatly on branches, vibrant against the blue backdrop of the sky. Now they had all come tumbling down, edges curled, color faded, making the world look a whole lot less beautiful.

I regretted ever getting involved with Liam, regretted ever trusting him, letting him in, liking him. I used my finger to catch the tears before they fell, wiping them across my skirt.

Whoever said "The truth hurts" wasn't kidding.

Chapter 37

Google is a beautiful thing. When I plugged in the address, "2547 Longview Drive, New Albany, OH," all sorts of things popped up. First off, I could actually see the property, a gorgeous home set on a stately lawn (thank you, Google Earth), and one hit was a helpful news article—a blurb from the local newspaper's police blotter.

This particular blurb referenced the address in Liam's file. Apparently a minor had been charged with arson. A shed had burned down and a neighboring house damaged.

Liam.

It had to have been him, and I had to find out exactly what had happened that night. I spent the entire night planning my attack. I couldn't avoid him anymore. I'd have to pretend like everything was fine in order to infiltrate. Yes, I said "infiltrate." I was taking this investigation to a whole new level.

It also occurred to me that I was starting to sound like a spy from one of Seth's crazy-ass conspiracy theories. Obviously my new side-kick was wearing off on me.

Mental note: no matter how tempting it may seem, do not start hanging out in tree houses and reading books about how the moon landing took place in some studio on Hollywood Boulevard as opposed to the actual moon. The last thing I needed was more distractions.

. . .

I sat in the office sending as many brain waves as I could muster toward Mrs. Newbury. *Bunco, bunco, bunco.* Seth and I needed her to get the hell out of there so we could effectively launch Investigation Firestarter. Yes, that's a code name, and no, it definitely wasn't my idea.

Finally Mrs. Newbury leaned under the desk to grab her purse. "That about does it." She swung the bag over her shoulder. "I leave the office in good hands." She ruffled Seth's red curls, and I felt a little guilty about what we were going to do next.

We gave Mrs. Newbury exactly seven minutes and thirty-nine seconds to leave the building. A habitual woman, she stopped to visit with the same three people: Mrs. Laney in guidance; Mr. Stewart, one of the youngest male faculty members, who we were fairly sure she had a tiny crush on; and Bob, the nicest custodian on staff. If my calculations were correct, Liam would hold the door for Mrs. Newbury after he finished hanging out with his friends in the courtyard on his way in to grab books from his locker.

"Okay," I said, staring at the clock on my cell phone. "Now!"

Seth picked up the phone receiver and pressed the "All School Page" button. He lowered his voice approximately three octaves and said, "Liam Gilmour to the main office. Liam Gilmour to the main office." He sounded like a serial killer.

"It'll be a miracle if Liam or any remaining teachers in the building don't call the police after that page." I couldn't help myself.

"I didn't want him to recognize my voice," Seth replied, hurt.

I decided not to mention that Liam wouldn't have been able to pick his face out of a lineup, let alone his voice. "Okay, so you have your assignment. Hunter-green Jeep, zip windows, lower-left area of parking lot, license plate number EIO315."

"On it!" Seth scurried out of the office in the direction of the parking lot, and I waited to see whether Liam would actually show up after that bomb threat of a page to the office.

Sure enough, about four minutes after Seth made his exit, Liam casually pulled open the glass doors. When he saw me, his forehead wrinkled in confusion.

"Did you hear someone page me?" He set his book bag down inside the office. "I thought maybe Mrs. Newbury needed help. It sounded like an ax murderer."

"Oh…um…yeah, it was just a temp that they hired for after school, but…um…he had to step out." Wow. This was going well.

"So you've decided to talk to me again? I've tried calling and texting every day and nothing, but now you're waiting for me in the office?"

Really well.

"I've just been…busy, that's all. And I'm not waiting for you. Like I said, the…um…temp paged you."

"Well, do you know why the temp called me down here?" He looked amused. Clearly he could smell my bullshit from a mile away.

"Lost and Found," I said, realizing too late that my lame excuse sounded much better in my head. "I think they found something of yours."

"Ahh," he said, approaching the box and peering in. He lifted up a ratty-looking sweatshirt, one dirty sock, and a broken pair of sunglasses. "Wow, thank God they found my sock. I've been looking everywhere for it."

"I think they have the valuable stuff locked up or something," I finished lamely.

He glanced at the clock and then back at me. "Well, tell the temp I'll come back tomorrow. I've gotta run."

I thought of Seth probably just having found Liam's car and only about halfway through unzipping it. I couldn't let Liam leave. I had to stall him.

"Oh, wait!" I said, getting to my feet. "Did you…um…see the new fish they added to the tank?" I rushed over and patted the glass. "Mrs. Newbury said this big one ate all the smaller ones." Officially the worst stall attempt in history.

Liam again flashed me his amused semi-smile. I was failing. Miserably. He reached for the door. *Oh, God. Here goes nothing.*

I rushed to the door and threw my arms around Liam's middle. He stiffened as I touched him, and I realized all at once that I'd never hugged him before. We'd knocked shoulders or touched arms, but full-body contact with my fingers spread across his stomach? No. I tried not to think about the grooves I felt beneath his uniform shirt or how the back of him grazed the front of me. This was about figuring out how he was connected to Grace's death. Nothing more.

"I'm sorry. This is so stupid," I mumbled into his back. "I just…I needed a hug, and…I don't know, you're here." I loosened my grip around him, each second of silence adding to my humiliation. I wondered which was worse, having to pretend to need a hug from the guy I used to like but now suspected was a convicted arsonist— or having Seth get caught breaking and entering.

"I really have to go," he mumbled, and headed for the exit. I swore under my breath and slipped out the doors behind him.

Lucky for me, Liam stopped to talk to a few kids who were hanging out near the entrance of the school. I sprinted as fast as I could and made a big loop around the parking lot so he wouldn't see me. When I found Liam's car, I saw Seth had slung his body over the seat and was digging around in back. Without thinking, I slammed my fist on the side of the car to get his attention, and Seth fell headfirst into the back, grabbing at his heart.

"Geez, Kate, are you trying to give me a heart attack?" he yelled.

"Get out of there *now!*" He stared at me blankly, so I tried speaking a language he'd understand. "Code Red! Code Red! Abort! Abort!"

Seth dove up into the backseat, clutching a sheet of paper to his skinny chest, and slid out the unzipped plastic window. He shoved the paper at me, which I pushed down my uniform shirt, and we both scrambled to re-zip the window. We were casually leaning against Liam's Jeep when he walked to his car looking more confused than ever.

"Um…hi?" He looked from me to Seth and back.

Seth nodded his head, and I said a quick prayer that he'd let me do the talking. No. Such. Luck.

"Oh, hey, there, Liam. Kate was just showing me your sweet set of wheels here." Seth banged on the side of the car. "What type of gas mileage does this beauty get?"

Oh, my God. He sounded like a geriatric car enthusiast.

Something dark flashed in Liam's eyes as he looked closely at Seth and me. Was it jealousy or something else? I wasn't going to wait around to find out.

"Actually, Liam, we were just going." I dragged Seth by the sleeve of his shirt and didn't look back. "I'll, uh, see you tomorrow. Bye!"

Once we were settled into our usual seats on the late bus, I reached down into my uniform shirt to retrieve the paper and smoothed it on my thigh.

Audi, Vide, Tace was sketched across the page. But this had taken time—he had included shadows and shading, a level of detail only a true artist could apply.

"I knew I didn't trust that guy," Seth said, staring at the words. "He just had that look about him."

I wasn't in the mood for Seth's I-told-you-so's.

But as I flipped the sheet over, I noticed another set of words drawn in the same way. *Fortes Et Liber.* "Strong and Free." For a second I was hopeful.

"Maybe it's just a coincidence?" I showed Seth the back of the paper. "This is the motto on Brown's old crest. Maybe he was using them for a band poster or something."

Deep down I knew the truth, but I shook my head, not wanting to believe it. Despite the evidence stacked up against him—the conspiring with Beefany, the Rolling Stones T-shirt, the email, and now the Latin words—I wanted a different ending. One that didn't involve me asking the tough questions.

We had plenty of proof to confront him, but my stomach twisted at the thought. I remembered all too clearly the feeling of Cameron's fingers gripping my upper arm in his car or the way Liam had grabbed me in the hallway. So it was looking like we were going to have to go black ops for this one.

And, yes, I just made that up. I have no idea what "black ops" means, but I can tell you it most definitely doesn't involve confronting another suspect in or near a car. Been there, done that.

Chapter 38

When Seth and I finally made it home, the sun had just about set. We said a quick good-bye and headed back to our respective worlds. He ran home to have a nice, normal dinner with his family while I walked into a dark, empty house and found twenty dollars on the counter and a note to order takeout.

I called Geraci's and placed the order for my favorite pizza with pineapple. I briefly debated grabbing a pint of Chubby Hubby from the freezer to take the edge off but settled for catching up on some mindless reality television instead.

The soothing sounds of catfights must have lulled me to sleep, because when I jerked awake, the family room was almost pitch-black. Out of sorts, I glanced at the clock and wondered why the pizza guy hadn't come yet. The phone showed no missed calls, so I headed into the kitchen to grab a Diet Coke. And that's when I saw it.

A shadowed figure ran in front of our huge bay window.

I froze. I could hear the blood pumping in my ears. And then I heard something else.

Tap. Tap. Tap.

The glare of the TV made it impossible to see anything except the outline of a person.

The tapping turned to knocking, and the figure gestured at the front door. He wanted to be let in.

The TV flashed to a commercial break, and in the brief moment of darkness, I got a look at my visitor's face.

Liam.

I screamed. I couldn't help it. I knew he was somehow involved in whatever had happened to Grace, but I'd never expected him to show up at my house. I grabbed the phone to call the police, but when I started to dial he disappeared.

"Oh, thank God," I said to the empty room as I collapsed back onto the couch.

"Yeah, thank God," a voice said from behind me. It was Liam.

I jumped up from the couch and held the phone out like a weapon.

"How did you get in here? I'm calling the police!"

"I've been calling your cell for the past two hours, but you never picked up. And then I rang the bell a million times and no one answered." Liam walked toward me and reached out his hand. "When I heard you scream, I tried the door. It was open."

I jumped back to avoid his touch.

"Kate, what's going on? One second you're having coffee with me, and the next you're digging through my car with some seventh grader and screaming when you see me. Just tell me what's going on, and I'll leave you alone. I swear."

And in that moment he was the old Liam again. The charming

guy who'd given me a ride home and blushed when he'd asked me out the first time. The one who'd held my hand and made me laugh. And out of nowhere, I heard myself telling him the truth.

"I know you started that fire. I know you're somehow connected to the Sisterhood. Seth found the symbol in your car. Just tell me. What really happened that night? I promise I'll never tell anyone." The words tumbled out of my mouth. So much for black ops.

Liam stared at me as I held my hand behind my back and crossed my fingers. I wish I could say he looked murderous or even angry. Instead he looked defeated.

The doorbell rang, breaking our spell. I whirled around, standing on my tiptoes and stretching my neck to see who stood behind the door, but by the time I turned back around, Liam was gone.

I ran to the front door and yanked it open, not sure what to expect. Maybe the police had some new technology that could sense when someone was about to call 911? Or maybe Seth had seen Liam's car.

"Pizza's here," said a bored-looking guy. He held up a large pizza box.

I grabbed the twenty dollars off the counter and shoved it into his hand.

"Keep the change." What can I say? Pizza guys who practically save my life deserve a hefty tip.

I checked the lock on the front door eight times to be sure any additional unwanted guests would remain where they belonged. Over the past few years, I hadn't spent a lot of time wishing my parents would come home, but standing in our foyer with a huge box of pizza and a pounding head, I'd never been more lonely. Or less hungry.

I shoved the pizza into the fridge and flipped on every light in the house. Once I made it to my bedroom, I flopped onto my bed, hoping to clear the thoughts racing through my mind.

But I couldn't relax. My head throbbed in time with my heart, and I jumped down from my bed in search of either aspirin or a sleeping pill, whichever I could find first. The medicine cabinet was out of aspirin and didn't usually carry sleeping pills, so I headed down the stairs for Tylenol PM or even NyQuil.

As the steps creaked beneath my feet, I looked back over my shoulder a few times just to be sure no one was behind me. I could have sworn I heard footsteps following my own. Tree branches scratched across one of the living-room windows, but when I glanced across the street at my neighbor's trees, they were moving too. Wind.

Rhythmic creaking rang through the living room, forcing my eyes to the window. The porch swing was swaying. More than anything I wanted it to be from the wind, but then I saw her. Her face was tilted up at the dark sky, and she wore her school uniform, just like all the other times. She rocked the swing slowly, strands of her long hair lifted by the wind. I stopped on one of the middle stairs and rubbed my eyes in an effort to erase her image, to make her disappear.

It worked.

When I opened my eyes again, she was gone, and the swing rocked gently in her wake. I shot right back up the stairs and into my room, leaning against the closed door.

"Calm down. You're seeing things. You need to sleep." Honestly, I wasn't sure which was worse, the fact that I'd begun talking to myself or the fact that I was seeing ghosts. Neither bode well for my sanity.

As soon as I sat on the edge of my bed, I noticed that my computer screen was no longer black. Instead my inbox filled the screen. One new message had been delivered.

I ran to the desk hoping the message was from Grace. But the email in front of me wasn't from a ghost.

Chapter 39

To: KateLowry@pemberlybrown.edu
Sent: Fri 8:31 PM
From: LiamGilmour@pemberlybrown.edu
Subject: (no subject)

Kate,
You're still not answering your phone, and I didn't know how to explain all of this to you earlier. I don't know anything about the Sisterhood or if they set the fire, but I do know someone who's involved.

Call me.

Liam

I finished reading Liam's email, and instead of reading it again and again as I usually would have, I picked up the phone.

"Tell me," I said, my voice shaking.

"It's a long story," he said.

"Okay, I'm listening."

"First you need to hear about what happened before I—"

"I don't have time for this," I interrupted.

"Trust me."

The strangest thing happened in that moment. The bitterness I'd felt after seeing his T-shirt and snooping through his car released its grip on my heart. I hadn't even given him a chance. In spite of the email from Grace, and although I'd been seconds away from calling the police on his ass an hour ago, I decided to trust him one last time.

So Liam began his story and I listened.

Once upon a time, there were two brothers. They stuck together and protected each other, but the younger one could only do so much for the older one. The big brother made mistake after dangerous mistake, and soon his dad and stepmom gave the final warning. One more screw-up and he'd be shipped off to some military school.

But one day he came home messed up as usual and slumped against the shed for a cigarette. The shed caught fire. Once the flames broke out, the big brother sobered up pretty quickly. His younger brother came running, and when the fire department arrived, the younger brother, Liam, took the blame. If it got out that his big brother had done this, the younger brother would lose him forever.

"So I lied." At this point in the story Liam paused. We sat in silence for a second, listening to each other breathe.

"I'm sorry," I finally said. As I listened to the words leave my mouth, I knew they were all wrong.

"That's why my dad and stepmom decided to move, to get a fresh start. Only my brother and I know the truth. But it did force him to get his shit together." I could hear Liam breathing on the other end of the phone. "So I had to do some community service and help rebuild the shed, but it was worth it. Having it on my record is the worst part, but in a couple years when I turn eighteen, I won't have to worry about it anymore."

So I guess his dad wasn't an arms dealer after all. It was the first thought that popped into my head as I took in all of this new information, and it was immediately followed by about a million questions I wanted to ask. I settled on the most important one.

"But what about the Sisterhood's motto you sketched?" I hated myself for the apology I heard in my voice. I had a right to know the truth.

"I saw the chapel burning the night of the bonfire. I was walking in the woods when I saw the fire and grabbed my phone to call 911. But then I ran into Taylor, Bethany, and your friend Maddie. They looked scared shitless."

"Wait, what? You were just *walking* in the woods?" I narrowed my eyes even though he couldn't see them.

"Okay, fine. I was having a cigarette. Taylor, Bethany, and Maddie ran right into me, but Bethany did all the talking. She said it'd be a shame if someone found out I was there when the chapel burned. Especially since I was smoking.

"I know I should have told someone, but I'm still on probation for everything that happened in New Albany, and my parents swore they'd send me away if I even got a freaking detention." I could hear the guilt in his voice, the agony over being forced to hide the truth. "Those words were drawn in chalk on the walkway leading up to the chapel."

"The crest?" I asked.

"Yeah. With the Latin words on it."

"Hear, See, Be Silent," I whispered. "The motto of the Sisterhood." My mind worked frantically to connect the pieces.

"It meant something—I knew it. I drew the symbol and words as soon as I got home. I thought I could use it as proof that those girls were there that night, that they were involved. But when I showed it to Bethany, she laughed in my face. It was her word against mine."

"Okay, so Taylor, Bethany, and Maddie are involved in the Sisterhood." As I said the words, it explained so much. Maddie's betrayal, Taylor's and Bethany's bullying. "And Bethany is black-mailing you, so they're clearly hiding something." *Why, thank you, Captain Obvious.* "She sent the threats," I continued, more to myself than to him. "She was there and started the fire."

"I'm not sure it's that easy," Liam whispered. "I saw someone else there too." I held my breath while he paused. "Alistair Reynolds. He was running in the opposite direction, but I'm sure it was him."

Oh. My. God.

Chapter 40

Last Fall

Half-empty paint cans clattered to the floor in the garage as I yanked on the handlebars of my bike, attempting to release it from the jaws of junk. Instead of picking the cans up, I kicked them out of my way. It didn't matter. Nothing mattered. I just needed to see Maddie. To be with someone who understood.

After finally freeing my bike, I swung my leg over the seat and pedaled furiously, tears streaming down my cheeks. I pushed up Maddie's steep driveway and jumped down from the bike without bothering to stop. It fell to the concrete in a heap. The entire ride there, I'd imagined the front door opening before I even had a chance to ring the bell. I pictured Maddie throwing her arms around me so I could cry with someone who had lost as much as I had.

I did not expect Taylor Wright to open the door. Her long hair was damp and twisted on top of her head, and she wore a pair of Maddie's pajama pants rolled at the waist and paired with one of her lower-school T-shirts. Taylor's eyes were wide and skittish, and she shook her head slowly back and forth when she saw me.

"I'm so sorry." She opened her arms to hug me, and I awkwardly wrapped my arms around her. But it was all wrong, forced, uncomfortable, tense. "Everyone's inside."

The word "everyone" made me want to stop, and yet my body continued to move. When I saw the crowd of people in Maddie's kitchen—Bethany, dressed impeccably with a full face of makeup; Maddie's younger sister and a few of her friends; and even Alistair—I knew it had been a mistake to come.

The news was muted on the TV, and Mr. Greene sat on the couch with his head in his hands. Maddie was distraught, seated at the kitchen table next to her mom, who gripped her hand, their knuckles so white I imagined it must have hurt. As soon as Mrs. Greene saw me, she jumped up from her seat and pulled me into a hug.

"Kate, sweetie, Maddie said you couldn't come." She rocked me back and forth, resurrecting that shard-of-glass feeling in my throat as I swallowed. Tears slipped out the corners of my eyes and soaked Mrs. Greene's shoulders. I didn't want to think about why Maddie had lied to her mom; this was about Grace. Mrs. Greene pulled away, grabbed my hand, and led me to Maddie. But Taylor had already taken the seat next to my best friend, her arms wrapped around her, pulling her close.

Just like that, I had been replaced.

I elbowed my way past the lower-school kids, Bethany, Taylor, and even Alistair, who put his hand on the small of my back.

"Kate, if you need to talk, I'm here," he said so softly that I could barely hear. "I lost my cousin when we were kids. We were like brothers."

Anger seethed through me. Even though he was trying to be understanding, trying to show that he cared, I resented his empathy. He had no idea what I was going through. No one had any idea. I had come because I thought maybe Maddie would, and now I wasn't even sure of that. His hand still rested on my lower back, and when I jerked away from him, his arm fell to his side. I elbowed my way in to face the only friend I had left.

"Do you want to get out of here for a while? Maybe go on a walk or something?" I asked, my voice edging on desperate.

Maddie continued to sob, more so when I tried to sit down near her. Worse, Taylor stood up, almost blocking Maddie from my view. I didn't care that Taylor Wright was the most popular girl in school; I wanted to claw her empty blue eyes right out of their sockets and talk to my friend.

I ignored Taylor and tried to reach Maddie. "I just really need to talk to you. I miss her so much." Maddie raised her bloodshot eyes and looked at Taylor, who offered an almost imperceptible shake of the head.

"Why don't you sit down, and we can all talk," Taylor said, loud enough for Mrs. Greene to hear. "We're all missing Grace."

"*Maddie.*" My eyes pleaded as I said her name. I heard the desperation in my voice, the tears lurking just beneath the words. "Please?"

But Maddie just kept crying, unwilling or unable to respond.

Mrs. Greene pulled me aside. "She's having a really hard time with this, Kate. Don't give up on her, okay? She needs you, and sooner or later she'll be ready to talk."

I nodded my head. There was no way any words would be able to make it past the huge lump in my throat.

I took one last look at Maddie and her newly formed entourage of grievers and walked back out the Greenes' front door.

Another best friend lost without even a good-bye.

Chapter 41

Present Day

The next morning, I walked through Seth's garage door without knocking. Mrs. Allen insisted I come through the garage as opposed to the front door, which was for her "formal guests."

"Hi, Mr. and Mrs. Allen." I awkwardly glanced from person to person. "Seth."

They were seated at the kitchen table eating a fairly extensive-looking breakfast together—eggs Benedict, potatoes, some pancakes. I didn't think families ate breakfast together anymore—well, maybe the occasional bowl of cereal, but nothing like this. It looked like they were filming an orange-juice commercial or something.

"Oh, Kate, you're just in time," Mrs. Allen sang. "Come eat. I'll get you a plate."

Mr. Allen beamed at me as I pulled out a chair to sit down. His appearance offered a very accurate window into Seth's future. His hair was flaming-red despite his age, and he barely pushed five feet, seven inches. I looked back and forth between Seth and his dad as his mom placed a heaping plate in front of me.

I hadn't realized how hungry I was. I never did get to eat any of that pizza the night before, and an Allen breakfast was just what the doctor ordered. It was kind of nice to spend some time with a normal family.

"Now, Kate, Cindy Woodrow down the street says you've taken a break from tennis," Mrs. Allen said. "What about States, dear?"

I take that back. Maybe normal wasn't always nice.

"I was having a hard time deciding between tennis and the Concilium," I lied. "My coach is holding my spot if I change my mind."

"Taylor Wright heads up the Concilium, is that right?" Mrs. Allen asked. I rolled my eyes in Seth's direction. "I've always encouraged Seth to join, but he insists on helping in the office." She frowned toward Seth.

"That's enough, Rebecca," Mr. Allen stepped in. "Kate, how are your parents?"

"They're fine, Mr. Allen. Thanks," I said.

"Here, Kate, have a few more pancakes. You're too skinny!" Mrs. Allen heaped three more pancakes on my plate.

I think Seth's mom secretly kept tabs on the Lowry household, which probably included counting the number of times she saw the pizza-delivery guy at our house each week. As a result, she was constantly trying to shovel home-cooked food down my throat on account of my deprived upbringing.

Seth mopped up extra hollandaise sauce with his toast. He was heaving food into his mouth at an incredible speed. It was obvious he couldn't wait to talk privately—and not for the usual reasons a guy wanted to get a girl alone. At least I didn't think so. He cleared his plate and lifted mine before I even had a chance to tuck into the additional pancakes.

"Oh, um…thanks." I almost choked on a hash brown. "Breakfast was delicious!"

"Seth, honey, she wasn't even finished. Kate, I'll make you a to-go container," Mrs. Allen said, jumping up from her chair. She threw some pancakes into a plastic container and even added a little side of syrup.

I grabbed them and followed Seth up to his room. I mean, who was I to turn down homemade pancakes? As soon as I entered the room, Seth slammed the door behind me.

"I know something you don't know," he taunted. "Check this out."

Seth practically shoved me onto his neatly made bottom bunk. When I was little, I used to be really jealous that Seth had bunk beds. Come to think of it, I was really jealous Seth had a tree house as well. Funny how quickly jealousy turned into cringing embarrassment.

Seth sat next to me with his laptop and brought up an email from his good buddy, ConspiracyLuvR. He turned the computer so I could read it.

Over the years, the definition of the term "secret society" has been debated. Some believe that to be a true secret society, members must deny any involvement and knowledge of the society. While others believe the integration of rites and rituals forbidden to outsiders grants a society the label "secret." Whatever the definition, secret societies are very much a reality, and some may even

be linked to your own community—although finding them is
the true challenge.

I looked up at Seth.

"So? Can you believe it?" he asked, excitedly.

"Which part? That you're still talking to ConspiracyLuvR or that
secret societies exist?"

"Geez, you're a slow reader!"

He pointed at a paragraph in the middle of the next page, so I
read it aloud.

My recent research on the Sisterhood leads me to believe that
they might be made up exclusively of females...

"Um...duh. It's called the Sisterhood, jackass."

"Keep reading!"

There is another secret society active within the area known as
the Brotherhood. In the early '50s, many of the area's most elite
private schools went coed, and I think this might have forced
small, militant sections of the faculty and student body of many
area schools underground. These two societies have been warring
since their inception in the early '50s...

"B is for Brotherhood," I said, putting the pieces together.
"So clearly the invitation was for some kind of initiation at the
chapel." I didn't even stop to think about the fact that I had been

invited to join on the night of Spiritus. "But why was Alistair there? Doesn't sound like the Brotherhood and the Sisterhood get along too well."

Seth wrinkled his forehead. "What're you talking about?"

I held my hand up in front of Seth's face. I couldn't focus on his question right now; I was trying to work through some of my own. "This makes perfect sense. Taylor, Bethany, Maddie, Grace, Alistair—they are all involved. Sisterhood, Brotherhood, whatever. They were there. They had a hand in this. I still don't get why they all would have been there together, though."

"Wait. How do you know Taylor, Bethany, Maddie, and Alistair are involved?"

I told him the entire story about Liam. Seth's mouth hung open as the words tumbled out of my mouth.

"Are you sure we can trust him? If he's telling us the truth, that means he was there the night of Grace's death too."

"That's exactly what Bethany said. It was her word against his, and who would believe the guy who had charges of arson on his permanent record? Plus they all saw him smoking. But I trust him, and I think he can help us."

Seth looked like a child forced to share his favorite toy.

"He's telling the truth," I continued. "And he actually has some good ideas. He thinks that Taylor and Alistair are at war. And your friend ConspiracyLuvR just backed him up. Whatever happened to Grace, she was caught in the crossfire somehow. All we need is proof, and Liam says he can help us find it…" I let my voice trail off and gave Seth my most pleading look.

"Oh, no. Not again. We are not going back to those abandoned buildings. We'll get caught for sure."

"Come on, you know we'll be fine as long as we go at night. And he didn't go into much detail over the phone. He was worried about the line being tapped."

The expression on Seth's face was priceless. He looked half scared shitless and half excited out of his mind at the prospect of tapped phone lines.

"I was kidding about the tapped-line thing." His face fell and I felt bad for bursting his bubble, but it was just *so* easy. "But serious about the break-in. Maybe tomorrow night?"

"Okay," Seth finally agreed. I guess the potential for discovering the truth about the secret societies of Pemberly Brown was too much for him to resist.

When I got home, I had a full belly, my to-go container of pancakes, and what appeared to be a flawless plan. I slept the afternoon away. A perfect, dreamless sleep. When I woke up, I needed a second to place how I was feeling, and it finally occurred to me that I was excited. I was one step closer to justice, and it felt good.

Chapter 42

I woke up early on Monday morning and splashed cold water over my face, pushing the sleep away. When I heard the door creak, I opened my eyes and tried to focus as droplets of water hung from my lashes.

She stood behind me, staring at me, still wearing her school uniform, inky hair spilling over her shoulders. A scream stuck in my throat as I rubbed at my tired eyes. But when I opened them again, she was gone. I looked at myself in the mirror, wondering if I was crazy, and noticed my computer was no longer idle.

I swiped my face with a towel and rushed to my desk, clicking on the message before I even sat down.

To: KateLowry@pemberlybrown.edu
Sent: Mon 5:33 AM
From: GraceLee@pemberlybrown.edu
Subject: (no subject)

Time is almost up.

Go back to the beginning.

The truth is underground.

Talk about a case of the Mondays.

And it didn't get much better from there.

"Kate, do you have anything to add?" Mr. Erikson, my Physics teacher, stared me down while tapping his wing-tipped foot.

My page of notes consisted of my random thoughts about tombs and their connection to an underground truth. Not much to add there.

"Um, no…I was gonna say what Anthony said." Across the room, Anthony nodded at me and licked his lips. Eww.

Mr. Erikson walked over to my desk, and even though I tried to lay my arm across the page, it was clear I hadn't been following the discussion. He tapped his pen on my desk. I had the sinking feeling that he wasn't going to stop until I looked up at him. So I did. He held my eyes for a second and then walked back up to the front of the room.

"Okay, class, go ahead and pass up your notes. I'm going to count them toward participation points this week." Mr. Erikson stared at me while he said it. I flushed at feeling singled out. What had I ever done to him?

I looked down at my mess of doodles in relation to Grace's latest email. Words like "tombs," "graves," and "catacombs" filled the page and *The truth is underground* was underlined three times. I couldn't exactly submit this to a teacher. Instead I flipped back a few weeks and tore out an old page of notes so I'd at least have something to hand in.

"Mr. E.?" Bradley called from the back of the room. "My water bottle smeared my notes. Can I recopy them tonight and give them to you first thing tomorrow?"

Mr. Erikson shuffled the papers in his hands and chuckled.

"Not a problem, but don't forget or it's a zero."

I guess after earning one too many demerits, I'd lost my touch. I looked back at Bradley, and he shrugged his shoulders and threw me a half smile as if to say he totally knew how I felt. And I suppose he should, since he was taking this class for the second time. Mrs. Garrety had failed him the year before.

The bell finally put an end to my miserable day, and I rushed out to the arches, our designated meeting spot to prepare for the evening's investigation. I was the first to arrive and was alone in the gardens as the late afternoon sun sank behind the trees. I sat down on Grace's bench to think about our next logical step. We had planned on going back to the heart of Brown, but now I wasn't so sure. Grace's email seemed to be leading us in a different direction. Belowground. Honestly, I wasn't sure about anything anymore.

A gust of wind blew in from behind me, and I smelled the distinct smell of burning wood. I jumped up from the bench, my senses heightened. The smell of smoke triggered a response in me I couldn't quite explain. Dr. P. claimed it was a sensory association. That the smell of wood burning would always force the trauma of losing Grace back up to the surface, but I preferred to think of it as a fight-or-flight response. Six months earlier I would have been running as far as I could from that smell, but things had changed. And I was sick of running away.

I pushed my way through the brush until I made it into the forest surrounding the gardens. The smell was stronger now, and I could hear the crackling of burning leaves.

And then I saw it.

A small fire had been lit in the clearing up ahead. A circle of stones kept the blaze contained, so theoretically there was nothing to be afraid of. But "theoretically" was not a word my instincts were familiar with. The smell, the woods—this was all too familiar.

Tiny hairs on the back of my neck pricked up as I felt a pair of eyes fixed on me through the trees. I spun in a circle, but the person watching me was hidden well, tucked in the cover of the trees. And that's when I noticed it. Something was there in front of the fire. A card with my name on it leaning against a rock.

I picked it up, and my fingertips identified the creamy paper immediately. The fire blazed below me, and the sense of déjà vu was overwhelming. But this time when I read the card, there was no invitation to meet at the chapel. No beautiful calligraphy. Just a simple warning penned in bloodred ink.

Liar, liar

I heard a branch snap behind me, and some soft laughter rang through the leaves. Without thinking, I began to run in the direction of the laughter. If I could find the person behind the threats, the person who had the most to lose, I'd find myself one step closer to the truth.

I followed the sound of pounding feet through the woods, blood rushing through my ears, my throat burning. I would not stop until I got answers. The second I burst back out into the clearing of the gardens, it was obvious that I'd lost the person. The students milling around campus were giggling, flirting, and whispering, not gasping for air. Whoever had been in those woods had either taken another way out or had already blended into the crowd.

I sank down onto Grace's bench, struggling to catch my breath. The sky closed in on me, and my vision blurred, darkness creeping in along the edges. Familiar with the sensations, I shoved my head between my knees, hating every second of the panic attack, because it meant they had won.

"Hey, you okay?"

It was Liam. Thank God.

In an instant he was next to me on the bench, one arm rubbing my back and the other gripping one of my hands. Slowly my breathing returned to normal, and I cautiously lifted my head out from between my knees only to find my mouth inches from his.

Dizziness threatened to overtake me again, but this time for entirely different reasons. I hovered near the ground, mostly because I liked the way his breath felt on the delicate skin surrounding my lips, and I knew that standing would break the spell.

"You look…"

"Ready for the big mission? We're meeting here at ten, right?" Seth interrupted Liam with a breathy whisper inches away from both of our faces. I felt the urge to yank each and every red hair right out of his head.

"Uh, yeah. I was just catching my breath." I untangled myself from Liam and stood up. "Change of plans, though," I said, still searching the crowd. "We'll meet at the chapel, *where it all began*, and we'll need shovels. I think we might have to do a little digging. But first we've got a fire to put out."

Chapter 43

R emind me what we're doing here again." Seth flicked his flashlight beam around like a third-grader at sleep-away camp.

"We're starting at the beginning," I hissed. "This is where it all began." I stepped over ragged police tape that had long since fallen and nearly tripped over a charred wooden beam that had been dragged to the perimeter of the property. "There has to be something there in the basement."

"But isn't that where…" Seth looked anxious.

"Don't even think about it, okay? The Sisterhood and Brotherhood were clearly up to something that night, so there must be some clue here that will help us figure out what really happened." My voice had taken on a slightly hysterical edge, and I felt Liam's hand on my shoulder.

We continued walking until we came to the chapel's remains. Most of the large debris had been cleared away, but the intense smell of burnt wood remained. My foot hit something solid. When I shined my flashlight on the object, I realized it was the bronze plaque that used to mark the chapel as Station 11. It was now charred and warped. I ran my fingers over the blackened Latin phrase *Ad vitam aeternam*, "to eternal life," and thought of Grace. If only everyone's definition of eternal life was the same. The discrepancy pissed me off.

We walked to the edge of the foundation and peered down into what used to be the basement, where Grace's body had been discovered. I was always surprised to see that the lower level looked to have escaped most of the damage, and I had to remind myself that the smoke, not the flames, had killed my best friend.

"Look, there's a set of stairs over there." Liam pointed to the back of the building. "If you really want to do this, I think we can go down."

I nodded and breathed in deeply. Seth let out a little squeak but followed us with his flashlight.

Sure enough, the stairs were still intact. I looked at my two knights in tarnished armor and raised an eyebrow. "Well?"

"Yeah, all right. Let's just get this over with." To my surprise, Seth began the descent first.

It got darker and darker with each step into the basement. Even though much of the basement was exposed to the night sky, the moon didn't offer much light. With each step, my legs shook, barely supporting the weight of my body. I tried to remain calm, but my emotions ran wild.

Here I was, at the place where my best friend had lost her life, dragging the only two friends I had left down with me, and I had no idea what to look for. I felt like giving up, but when my foot hit the solid surface of the basement floor, I felt a new resolve. Grace had died here. Alone. She deserved justice.

We began walking the perimeter of the basement. Our flashlights illuminated stacks of charred wood, but otherwise the basement appeared to be empty. I got down on my hands and knees and crawled, shining my flashlight over every inch of the floor. Nothing. If something had been down here that night, it was gone now.

But my stream of light landed on a new texture tucked close to the far wall. The light shook as I rushed over and found what looked like a trapdoor made of solid wood, flush with the floor of the basement. I tried to pull at the edges with my fingers, but it wouldn't budge.

"Hey, guys, check this out."

Seth and Liam immediately joined me by the small door.

"I thought the underground Grace was referring to was the basement. But maybe there's something underneath this place?"

"No way; it doesn't even move. They probably had to cut into it for a pipe repair or something," Seth replied.

"I don't know," Liam said, his forehead crinkled in thought. "Listen."

He pounded on the floor, and it made an echoing sound. There was definitely a hole underneath the square. It had to be a hatch or a door of some sort.

"There's got to be a way to get it open. Move for a second." Liam struggled with the door, trying to pry it open with one of the shovels, a flashlight, and even a stick (yeah, I wasn't impressed either), but the door wouldn't budge.

Annoyed, I wondered if we should call it a night; the dark basement and narrow streams of light were giving me a head-ache. Just as I was about to get to my feet, I heard muffled voices coming from down below.

"Shhh," I whispered to the boys. "Listen."

All three of us put our ears to the dank floor and held our breath.

"Are you sure we can't take the library route? This freaks me out," a voice from below said.

"Not with Big D. on duty. We'd never make it out of the stacks," was the muffled reply.

The footsteps underground seemed to be coming closer to where we lay. Seth and I froze, and Liam had to drag us into the dark recesses of the basement to hide behind a stack of charred wood. The three of us managed to squeeze behind the pile, but it was a tight fit. All at once, the door we had just been kneeling in front of swung open, and two heads emerged. The gaping cracks between the stacked wood left me feeling completely vulnerable. I held my breath, sure they'd spot us instantly.

"Be careful. You know it's not safe anymore." It was Bradley Farrow.

"Whatever. You're just being paranoid." I could see through one of our many peepholes that the second voice belonged to Alistair.

And just like that, pieces to a puzzle much more complicated than I ever imagined began to fall into place. The Brotherhood really did exist. Alistair and Bradley were members, and the secret doorway underneath the chapel must lead…somewhere.

Whatever they had been up to that night, Bradley must have been in on it. Guess it wasn't a coincidence that he'd decided to ask me to go on a walk at the exact same time I was supposed to be meeting with the Sisterhood.

Did he know there was going to be a fire? Is that why they wanted me out of the way? But why had they decided to keep me away? Why not Grace? What was I missing?

There was the muted thud of the trapdoor slamming shut and the sound of footsteps heading up the stairs and out into the night. They were gone.

I exhaled, and someone's warm breath caressed my cheek. I looked up and found Liam's face about an inch from my own. My entire body pressed up against his. In the darkness of the basement, in spite of the fear and confusion and guilt and grief that snaked through me, I wanted to kiss him. Bad. I leaned back a little more and turned my face up to his. His hands gripped my arms, but in a good way, making me feel like he was just as desperate to kiss me as I was to kiss him.

"Ahem." Seth cleared his throat and shuffled awkwardly right next to us.

I flushed and moved away from both of them, walking back over to what I now knew was a trapdoor.

"Well, that was a little close," Liam whispered, catching my eye. For a second, I wondered what he was referring to.

"Yeah, thanks, Captain Obvious," Seth said as he stepped out from behind the pile of wood. Great, now Seth was stealing my lines. Clearly we were spending too much time together.

"So there's definitely a door, but where does it lead?" Liam asked.

"The underground. Maybe that's what Grace was trying to tell us, er...you, Kate. Maybe they live underground or something," Seth answered. And then after a second he added, "Like the mole people."

"I think you've watched one too many reruns of that conspiracy theory show." I rolled my eyes and tried to push my fingers under the edges of the trapdoor to no avail. There must have been a latch on the inside or something. As I knelt beside the trapdoor, I pushed away the thought of Grace doing the same on the night of the fire.

"Come on, it's getting late. We'll figure this out tomorrow." Liam grabbed my hand, and I let him lead me away. It felt nice to be led by an actual living, breathing person for once. Following a ghost hadn't really gotten me all that far lately.

The three of us made our way back out into the cool October night. We might not have found everything we were looking for, but we had caught a quick glimpse of the Brotherhood. And based on what I'd seen, I was beginning to worry that if they had played a role in Grace's death, the truth might be lost forever.

Chapter 44

I'd like to believe that if secret tunnels really ran beneath the school, they'd be documented on the school's original blueprints. Unfortunately all of the books about Pemberly Brown at the library had those particular pages removed, and the rest of the books were out of print. Secret societies were very thorough.

There was only one person I trusted enough to ask. I cornered Dorothy at the library after school. She was in her usual spot by the entrance, keeping an eye on things.

"Hi, there, Kate. Don't usually see you around here during normal hours," she said with a smile.

"Ha. Ha. For your information, I'm actually here to see *you.*"

"Are you, now? What could you possibly want with an ancient security guard?" she asked, amused.

"I'm actually writing a paper on the history of Pemberly Brown, and rumor has it you were a History teacher way back when."

Dorothy's smile disappeared. "I just remembered that I have to check on something over in the main building."

"No worries. I'll walk with you."

We walked out into the October sunshine and followed the brick path back to the main building.

"So…you used to be a History teacher? When did you decide to change jobs?"

"Well, that's complicated."

Okay, this was harder than I'd thought it would be. Considering that my current objective was to get information out of Dorothy, I thought of Seth, the Great Inquisitor himself and considered, "What would Seth do?" The answer was simple. Seth would ask more questions. Better yet, he'd ask the same question in a different way until he got the information he was after. I gave it another shot.

"So you were fired?"

Her eyes darted around the campus, like she was checking to make sure someone wasn't listening to our entire conversation.

"No, definitely not fired. I still work here, don't I?"

"No offense, but isn't security guard sort of a demotion?"

"Well, that all depends on how you look at it," she replied.

Okay, clearly this wasn't going well. I mean, the woman was sealed tighter than the CIA's files. Time to play hardball.

"Huh, well, from my perspective I'm sort of wondering if you were kicked out by some crazy misogynistic secret society called the Brotherhood." I forced a laugh, just in case she had no idea what I was talking about so I could play it off as a joke.

The color almost completely drained from her face. And she did that thing again where she looked all around, making me feel like I was in a James Bond movie or something.

"I have no idea what you're talking about, Kate." She said it like a sniper gun was trained on her.

"I understand. Maybe you could at least tell me where I might be able to find blueprints for the school? I tried all of the libraries, but there's nothing. I'm interested in finding out if there might be tunnels—"

"Sorry, no. Can't help you there either," she said, cutting me off.

By now we'd made our way into the history building and were stopped right in front of Alumni Hall, Station 6. *Respice, adspice, prospice.* "Look to the past, the present, the future."

Dorothy stopped in front of all the alumni pictures and put her hands on my shoulders.

"I'm sorry I can't help, Kate, but you need to leave this alone." And then, so quickly I thought I might have imagined it, she winked. "Now I've got to be going. Take care of yourself. Things will *turn around.*"

Well, that's just great. Real helpful, Dorothy. And thanks a lot, Grace, for leading me on some kind of wild-goose chase. I mean what exactly was I doing here? Yeah, these societies might exist, but even if they played a role in Grace's death, it wasn't like I'd ever be able to prove it. And who the hell was going to believe me when I started ranting and raving about all this stuff anyway? I'd sound like some crazy, old conspiracy theorist. Or pretty much exactly like Seth in sixty years.

I turned around to look at the pictures that lined the walls of the Academy, students from years past. And there it was, right in front of me.

A picture of Josephine Reynolds and a plaque underneath iden-tifying her as the lead architect behind the combined campuses of Pemberly and Brown. I remembered the book then and its description of Josephine's accomplishments. I ran my finger over the letters of her name and continued on to the dedication plaque beneath. There, listed in script, were two names: Alistair and Porter Reynolds. Her grandsons.

Guess that explains the wink.

Of course Alistair probably wouldn't be all that helpful, given that he was in the Brotherhood and somehow entangled in this whole mess. But I thought back to Porter whining for his brother to take him to guitar practice. Something told me he might be a totally different story.

Thank you, Dorothy. And hello, Porter.

Chapter 45

Lucky for us, we didn't have to search hard to find good old Porter during lunch. As usual, he was sitting underneath one of the massive oaks in the courtyard. His shaggy hair hung in his face as he picked out the notes to John Lennon's "Imagine" on his guitar. Based on the warbled tune carrying across the courtyard, those lessons really weren't paying off.

Fortunately Porter's small but devoted fan club of first-years didn't seem to mind as they sat fanned out in a semicircle around the tree, sighing and nodding along to the music. To their credit, so far the girls had suppressed the urge to join arms and sway.

"John Lennon's got to be rolling in his grave right now," Liam whispered.

"Nah, he's probably happy that people still get action after playing his songs," I replied.

"True. It's Yoko that Porter should be watching out for. She'd kick his ass."

The song finally wrapped up, and Porter graced his fans with a cheesy smile and told them that was it for the day. The girls mock, pouted and giggled, promising they'd be back for more tomorrow.

Seth puffed out his chest. "Okay, I'll give it a shot." The look on his face was sheer determination. He had insisted on approaching Porter first, since he was tutoring him in Calculus.

Liam and I watched as Seth marched over to PB's resident singing sensation and began talking and making grand gestures with his arms. Porter looked confused, then annoyed, and finally dismissive.

Seth walked back to where Liam and I were waiting on the bench outside the main building and shrugged, kicking grass with the toe of his Puma.

"I tried, but he says he doesn't know anything about his grandma. Can't help."

I remembered the moment between Grace and Porter in the lake at Nativitas and realized there were two very good reasons that Seth wasn't equipped to handle the situation as well as I was. I unbuttoned the top buttons on the shirt of my uniform, adjusted the "girls" to achieve maximum attention, released my hair from its ponytail, and licked my lips. I looked over at Liam and Seth. "I'm going in."

Seth stared at me, mouth hanging wide open like some kind of redheaded fish, while Liam watched me with a wry smile. "Knock 'em dead," he said with a laugh.

I strode over to where Porter was snapping his guitar case shut and cleared my throat.

As he stood, I noticed his eyes travel up my legs, pause at my chest, and finally meet my eyes.

"Well, hello again, Kate," he said, his eyes already flirting. "I was wondering when you'd come around."

"Yeah, well after hearing your completely unique take on 'Imagine,' how could I resist?" I punched him lightly on the shoulder and wanted to kick myself for the awkward gesture. Totally embarrassing, even though I was only dealing with a second-rate Casanova.

He grabbed my hand and lifted it to his lips.

"That's got to be the nicest thing I've heard all day."

"Don't get too excited. I didn't say I liked it. Besides, it was just a song." I batted my eyelashes, hoping he liked it when girls played hard to get.

"It's never *just* a song," he replied and licked his lips. Eww. Maybe this was working too well.

"Yeah, anyway, I was just wondering...I'm doing a project for school on the history of PB, and I think your grandmother designed the building."

"Sure did, but unfortunately she's dead, so no interviews unless you're up for a séance." He grabbed his guitar case and began walking toward the main building. I followed.

"I'm so sorry."

"Don't be. She was a crazy old woman, completely paranoid about everyone and everything. She scared the shit out of me as a kid, and between you and me, I wasn't all that broken up about her dying when I was seven."

We walked past Liam and Seth, who were sitting on the bench like a couple of rejects. I could feel Liam's eyes on me and knew he was shooting daggers at Porter. It was amazing that Porter didn't notice, but I guess when your dad's income rivaled Steve Jobs's, you didn't much care about people staring you down.

Porter held the door for me as we walked into the school.

"Listen, I can't find any of the information I need at the library. I want to understand the history of all the buildings on campus and how they were renovated at the time of the merger. Do you have some of her old blueprints? Anything that might help?"

Porter stopped and looked at me—or, rather, looked at the "girls" again.

"Actually, I think we might have some of her old crap in our attic. Why don't you swing by after school to check it out?"

"Really? That would be so great. Thank you so much."

"Consider it a date, Kate," he said with a wink.

"Great. I'll be there by four."

I turned to run back outside to tell the guys the good news and ran right into both of them.

"Er…hi, great news—"

"We heard. It's a date, right?" Liam sounded annoyed.

"Yeah, it's a date, Kate," Seth echoed.

"Whatever. There could be some valuable clues in his grandma's old junk. I'm sure she was part of the"—I looked around to see if anyone was listening—"Sisterhood."

"Fine, but we're coming with you." Liam crossed his arms across his chest.

"Yeah. No way you're going to be alone with that hustler in an attic." Seth copied Liam's gesture and crossed his arms as well.

Why was I suddenly feeling so outnumbered?

But if I was being honest with myself, I'd take the dramatic arm-crossing and protective gestures any day if it meant I didn't have to do this alone. Something about my knights in not-so-shining armor made me happy to play their damsel in semi-distress.

Chapter 46

The Reynolds family lived in one of those gorgeous historical mansions previously occupied by families like the Rockefellers and the Mittals. As Liam maneuvered his Jeep up the stone driveway, I began to get a little nervous. After all, Alistair was Porter's older brother and a member of the secret society potentially responsible for killing my friend. If he was home, there was no way I'd make it an inch past the doorstep.

But I knew Liam would call the whole thing off if he sensed the slightest hesitation from me, so I forced myself to paste on a bright smile.

"Ready?" I asked.

"I guess. Don't you want to button up your shirt?" Liam asked.

"It's fine."

"Yeah, it's fine…" Seth echoed in a faraway voice.

"Okay, *eww*. I'm buttoning. I'm buttoning."

The three of us marched up to the front entrance and into another time. Four Roman-style pillars towered around us, and a pair of carved marble lions guarded the entry. An ornate iron *R* hung from the massive double door, and even the doorbell looked intricate and historic. The surveillance monitors hanging above antique-looking sconces were the only vestige of the twenty-first century.

"We're being watched," I whispered, nodding to the cameras while reaching to ring the bell. I hoped Alistair wasn't around to see. Moments later, the large door creaked open and there stood Porter.

He looked confused. "Kate?"

"Hi! Hope you don't mind that I brought my friends. They're, er…in my group for the project. This is Liam and Seth. Gorgeous house, by the way."

There were a few rounds of boy nods, and Porter reluctantly let us into his house.

The inside of the house was even more magnificent than the outside. Whoever had designed the interior had preserved the history of each room, making it feel as though we were literally stepping back in time as we walked through the door. Granted, motion sensors were installed in every corner and surveillance cameras followed our every move, but it really was pretty incredible.

"You didn't mention that this was a group project," Porter whispered loudly as he led us down a hallway decorated with paintings that looked like they should have been hanging in a museum.

"Oops, sorry. It must have slipped my mind," I responded, trying to stop my jaw from hitting the floor as I admired the art. I elbowed Liam, who was just as impressed as me, and he shook his head in awe.

Porter guided us around to what would have originally been used as the servants' quarters. "Whatever. These stairs lead up to the attic."

A staircase not nearly as grand as the one we'd passed on our way in led up to the third floor. "All my grandma's old stuff is up there. Just don't touch the jewelry, okay? My mom would flip her shit."

We slowly climbed the rickety stairs to the attic. It smelled of wood and mold, and as we neared the top, we broke through into a layer of moist heat despite the cool October afternoon.

I knelt down and surveyed the attic. It was full of random junk. Old hatboxes, broken furniture, and discarded clothing lined the walls of the cramped space.

"Where do we even begin?" Seth asked, pulling a packet of fruit snacks from his pocket.

"I don't know, but we'd better get started," Liam said, grabbing a box out of the corner and wrinkling his nose as he opened it and pulled out a crusty-looking wedding bouquet.

We went through box after box of junk. I found love letters, old gloves, a kimono, and loads of old photographs, but nothing about Pemberly Brown.

"What about this?" Liam asked, pulling an old campus map out of one of the boxes. "Someone marked on it."

Seth and I carefully walked across the beams to where Liam sat. I traced my finger across the page.

"This must be from before Brown merged with Pemberly. She must have used it to map out the new campus," I said.

Seth lost interest and returned to the trunk he'd been rummaging through. I gave Liam a pat on the shoulder.

"Maybe next time," I joked. He rolled his eyes at me.

"Hey, look, guys," Seth called. "Coconuts!"

Seth strapped on a coconut bra and tied a grass skirt around his narrow waist. When he started doing the hula, I reached into the box nearest me and threw a deflated soccer ball at him. He ducked and the ball hit a shelf, knocking over even more random crap.

"Watch it, Lowry," Seth squeaked.

"Everything okay up there?" Porter's voice traveled through the rafters.

"Um, yeah, sorry!" I called back.

Seth bent to pick up yet another one of my messes but instead became distracted by a random piece of crap that I'd knocked over with the ball.

"I think I've got something," he yelled.

He carefully stepped over to us with a long white tube in his hands.

"Check this out," he said and pointed the end of the tube in our direction so we could see.

The Sisterhood crest.

"Nice," Liam said with a smile.

"Open it, open it!" I cried.

Seth yanked off the cap and slid out huge papers. Blueprints.

"Oh, my God, this is it," he breathed. "This is everything! It's the plans for the whole campus. That's the new main building right there, and look, there's the lower school."

"What do all these lines mean?" Liam asked. He pointed to tubes that ran throughout the upper school.

"Hmm…let me see, I can't really tell. Maybe ductwork or something?" Seth squinted at the documents and flipped them around trying to figure out what the lines could mean.

"And what are all those pictures of the crest?" I asked. The crest was positioned on top of the clean lines of the blueprints at seemingly random spots.

"What do you mean?" Seth asked, still distracted by the mysterious tubes running throughout the blueprints.

"Like that, right there by the clock tower," I pointed. "And there's another one by…what's that? The auditorium. And see right there, that one's marking the chapel."

"It's the stations. They're marking the stations," Liam said.

He was right. Each of the Twelve Stations was marked, but then a larger version of the Pemberly crest was right in the center of campus.

"If they're marking stations, then what's that?" I asked pointing to the large symbol.

"I don't know…maybe that one's just decoration or something," he replied.

"Tunnels!" Seth's voice rang out in triumph. "You guys, these lines are the tunnels!"

I grabbed the blueprints from him to get a closer look.

"If those are tunnels, they're all leading to the same place, the large symbol." I thought about it a minute, and then it came to me. "The stations must be…um…entryways or something…to get into the tunnels." I stopped for a second to catch my thoughts. "And that large crest in the middle…it's got to stand for something. It's at the center of everything for a reason."

The three of us stared back and forth at each other, digesting everything I'd just said. And as though we'd rehearsed it, we all whispered at the same time.

"Headquarters."

Well, Liam and I whispered it. Seth whispered the word "nest" instead. Liam and I both screwed up our faces.

"Did you just say, 'nest'?" Liam asked, shaking his head.

"What? You know, the nest of the crest? I bet that's what they call it. The Bird's Crest Nest. Or something like that." Seth shrugged his shoulders.

I started laughing but was interrupted by footsteps pounding up the attic stairs. Porter poked his head into the cramped room.

"Quick, guys! It's my mom. You need to get out of here. She'll kill me if she knows I let you go through all this old junk."

Seth rolled up the blueprints to put them back in the tube as a smaller piece of paper floated to the ground. Without hesitation, I grabbed the paper and stuffed it into my pocket.

"Porter? Alistair? I'm home! Boys? Where are you?" We heard a tinny voice call from downstairs.

"Come on, guys. You need to hurry. Just leave that stuff." Porter practically pushed us down the old flight of stairs and shoved us all into his bedroom.

"Porter? Where are—Oh, hi, I didn't know you had friends over." Mrs. Reynolds popped her head into his room and gave us a broad smile.

"Yeah, just a study group, Mom."

"Oh, how nice. Ana's making dinner. Would you three like to join us?"

"No, thanks. We really need to get going. Right, guys?" I looked at Seth and Liam, who were already nodding in response to my question.

"Well, thanks for all of your help, Porter. See you around." I couldn't stop myself from giving him a quick wink. It was just too easy.

Liam must have caught my little gesture too, because he grabbed my upper arm and dragged me to the door, rolling his eyes.

"Easy, tiger. Time to get home."

Chapter 47

As soon as I was in the safety of my bedroom, I pulled the crumpled paper from my skirt pocket. Carefully smoothing it out on my desk, I flipped on my desk lamp and sat down to take a closer look. It listed thirteen stations and their original Latin inscriptions.

I wondered if we were right about the headquarters, if there really was a Station 13 beneath Pemberly Brown. I shook my head back and forth at the possibility. Just the thought of an underground room full of secrets made me feel as though I'd landed in the script of some crazy movie. This was the stuff Hollywood was made of, not Pemberly Brown. But as I ran my fingers over number thirteen on the list, I began to wonder.

If there really was a headquarters, did the stations actually lead down under the school? And what about the Brotherhood? We had seen boys coming out of the tunnels yesterday. Did that mean the two societies shared the tunnels? If so, maybe they weren't really at war. Or maybe the Brothers were the ones in control at this point. Based on what ConspiracyLuvR said, it sounded like the power was always changing hands.

The buzzing of my phone interrupted my thoughts. Right on time, I had mail.

To: KateLowry@pemberlybrown.edu
Sent: Thurs 6:15 PM
From: GraceLee@pemberlybrown.edu
Subject: (no subject)

Station 13 is the place to be.
Each Latin word holds the key.

Was it weird that I was sort of getting used to the ghostly missives? They didn't even give me the chills anymore. Maybe it was a sign that Grace really wasn't a ghost after all.

I pushed the thought from my mind. That was absolutely ridiculous; besides, I had to focus on the task at hand. There was a Station 13, a headquarters, the place all the tunnels led to, the heart of the societies.

Each Latin word holds the key.

And yet I had to find some sort of key to get inside. Like a password. I was close, yet so, so far away.

But I had to start somewhere, and at least this time around I'd have Seth and Liam to help. I held the yellowed paper between my fingers and let my eyes fall to my favorite station, the clock tower.

Tempus edax rerum. "Time, devourer of all things." I stared at the ancient words, trying to find what was hidden, trying to find the key. But all I saw was a dead language.

This was going to be interesting.

• • •

After school the next day, the three of us sat huddled on the first level of the clock tower practically twiddling our thumbs.

"Well, we might as well go down to the basement. I'm thinking if there is a door, it will be down there," I said, already starting down the stairs.

Seth rushed down past me and, as soon as he made it to the bottom, began groping the entire length of the old brick walls like some type of redheaded spider.

"What exactly are you looking for, Seth?" I asked.

"There's got to be some kind of button we can push to reveal a hidden staircase." His hands were everywhere, and he almost knocked one of the Time Keepers' pictures off the wall.

The Time Keepers, or *Vicis Custodis*, were yet another PB tradition. Each year, one fourth-year student was selected to be the Time Keeper. In the old days before the clock tower had been remodeled, the Time Keeper would actually climb to the top of the tower and set the clock at the start of each school year. But now it was just one of those random honors that came with a college scholarship and a picture on the interior walls, the words *Ab Aeterno*, "From the Eternal," engraved into the ornate frame.

When we were in lower school, Grace, Maddie, and I used to come down here to admire the rows of upper-school students, all grown up and official-looking. They were mostly boys, hot boys from where we were standing. We'd make up stories about who was going out with who and who was most likely to become a *Vico*

Custodio during our fourth year. It might have made me sad to remember the three of us, but I was too distracted to reflect.

"Grace's email said the Latin words hold the key. There's got to be some sort of hidden key box around here. It probably has Latin words engraved on it," I suggested. "You know, like the ones they put in gardens and stuff." I got down on my hands and knees and began feeling around, searching for the hidden box.

"I don't think they'd make it that easy," Liam responded, his eyes locked on the rows of pictures. "I mean if there was a box down here with a key in it, anyone could find it, you know?"

He smiled, but I still felt stupid for being so literal. Then when he whispered, "Maybe next time," with a raised eyebrow, I felt a blush creep into my cheeks. I brushed my knees off and punched him lightly on the shoulder.

Suddenly Liam was on his feet. He moved so quickly that it made me jump a little.

"What is it? Is someone coming?" Seth sounded panicked.

Without saying a word, Liam began lifting pictures off the walls and setting them gently on the ground. He ran his fingers over the brick, pressing every so often.

"The Latin words hold the key, right?" he asked, still lifting pictures. "The Latin at the bottom of the frames. This has got to be it."

I rushed to the wall and began lifting frames as well. Once we had examined the space beneath each and every Time Keeper, we were no closer to Station 13 than we had been when we started. There was nothing but brick and mortar beneath the frames—no keys, no passwords, no answers. After replacing the final picture,

I slapped at the bronze plaque marking the clock tower as Station 2. Not for good luck, but more out of frustration.

Think, Kate. "The Latin holds the key." What did that mean? I ran my fingers over the raised bronze letters as Liam knocked on the floor with his ear to the ground and Seth attempted to pull bricks from the wall with his fingers. And then it hit me. The phrase *Tempus, edax, rerum* was made up of letters. Lots of them.

If I rearranged the letters, I could form words, or passwords. I pushed the *T* in "*Tempus,*" and sure enough, the letter clicked into the plaque like a key on an old typewriter. Only it stayed indented. I tried to pick it back out with my nonexistent nails, but the *T* was stuck.

I stepped back, frustrated that I'd probably just destroyed our chances at getting in because I jumped the gun on the button pushing when, just as suddenly, the letter popped back out again. It was clearing itself! It might take a few seconds, but whatever controlled the access to the tunnels would reset, waiting patiently for the correct series of letters.

"You guys!" I shouted, stepping back and narrowing my eyes at the Latin words. "I think I know how to get us in."

Seth and Liam rushed to each side of me, eager for an explanation.

"The letters can be pressed, and if they're pressed in the right order, a door or something will open, granting us access."

"So what? You just have to guess at what order to press the buttons?" Seth asked, stretching out his fingers in preparation for all the pressing.

"No, I think we have to form new words using the letters. 'The

Latin holds the key'," I repeated, more to myself than anyone. "At least, I think that's what it means. It's worth a try, I guess."

"Murder, era, set, seat, and dare." All this time, Liam hadn't said a thing, and now he was listing random words hidden inside the Latin phrase like he'd been doing it all his life. Seth and I watched, mouths hanging open. "What? I'm kind of good with puzzles."

I punched in each letter, forming Liam's words, but nothing. The letters all stuck in and all popped out without as much as a hint to where the trapdoor could be. We were missing something. I just hoped the code called for an English word. I was good at Latin, but not that good.

Time, time, I repeated in my head, thinking of the clock tower. The code would probably have to do with time. And then, as though the letters were lit up from behind, I saw them, one by one. M-E-A-S-U-R-E. Time was the eternal measurement—that had to be it!

Each letter clicked into place, and as I pressed the second letter *e*, our final chance, I heard the dull pop of a door right next to Seth's bright white Puma. A second ago it had blended in with the stone floor, and now out of nowhere came a door. I couldn't believe it. All of us fell to the floor and pulled at the edges, peering down into the depths below. I clicked on my flashlight, took a few deep breaths, and hoped for the best.

We were going down.

As we descended the stairs, I was overwhelmed by our surroundings. Antique-looking sconces lit our way. The heels of my riding boots echoed softly on the well-worn stones that made up the stairs. The air felt damp and somehow ancient. It was like a totally different world.

"Guys," I whispered. "Can you believe this?"

Seth ran his hand along the rust-colored brick that surrounded us.

"No," they said at once.

The cobblestones beneath our feet glimmered, flecks of crystallized rock set off by the dim light of the sconces. I could tell that the tunnel branched off a few feet from us, and I found myself wishing we could have taken the blueprints as well.

"Which way are we going to go?" I asked.

"I don't know. I'm totally turned around," Liam answered, stopping for a second and trying to get his bearings.

"I think we should keep going straight," Seth said.

"That's funny, because I was gonna say we should turn right," I said. "But I'm always wrong with directions. Let's go straight."

As we continued walking through the arched tunnel, I felt a pit form in my stomach. Here we were, walking beneath the school without any sense of direction and no way to defend ourselves if we got caught. We were confined by brick, and no one would hear our screams or even find our bodies, if it came to that. Grace had lost her life underground—could we? The brick walls seemed to cave in on me. I was trapped.

"I have to go back," I said, nearly choking. "Turn around."

I grabbed at the brick wall with one of my hands and began to breathe deeply. At that second, I wished I was anywhere but there. I'd even have taken the uncomfortable wooden chair that made my butt fall asleep at Prozac's office over the tunnel. I took off in the direction we had come from and felt completely turned around when I made it back to the branch in the tunnel.

"Kate, wait!" The boys tried to whisper-shout, but I couldn't stop. I turned left, stretching my neck to see if I could see light or anything at the end of the tunnel. But there were only stairs that led down, and I knew we hadn't climbed up any stairs on the way there. I'd chosen the wrong branch. My horrific sense of direction had impeccable timing. I sat at the top of the stairs and put my head between my knees.

Liam and Seth ran to either side of me and rough-armed each other to see who could get a better hold. Liam won.

"It's okay. It's just a little claustrophobic down here," he said. He gathered my hair away from my face and swirled circles on my back with his palm.

I looked up and over at him, just to make sure Liam was doing the touching, and noticed that Seth wasn't next to me anymore.

"You guys!" Seth called from the bottom of the steps without even looking up at us. "It's the nest...or the headquarters or whatever."

Liam helped me to my feet, and we headed down the stairs. Portraits of women hung on both sides of the wall for as far as I could see down the hallway. The ones nearest us were the oldest photographs, so I assumed they got more recent the farther you walked down the hall. Each of the girls wore white along with a pendant around her neck. The same charm Cameron had found and the one in Naomi's locker.

"Check it out," Liam said, pointing to one of the girl's necklaces. "That's what was sketched with chalk the night..." He trailed off. I think we must have all noticed it at the same time. As we continued down the narrow hallway, we could see that the glass on the most recent pictures had been smashed.

"Why do you think they did this to the pictures?" I asked. It was weird, because they had clearly been hung with care. Not a single picture was crooked, and yet they had been systematically destroyed.

As soon as we got to the bottom of the stairs, we stood with Seth before a heavy wooden door. An intricate crown was carved into the grain and sat atop a Gothic-looking letter *S*. The crest. The door was a real, live version of the Pemberly crest, the Sisterhood's symbol.

A bronze plaque hung below the *S*, the words *Audi, Vide, Tace* raised along it. But the beautiful door had been destroyed by a huge letter *B* someone had painted down the center.

"I don't think we're in Sisterhood territory anymore..." I ventured.

"No, it looks like there's been a takeover. A hostile one." Seth agreed.

"Well, that explains why Alistair was coming out of the tunnels." Liam ran his fingers over the red paint of the letter. "Guess they haven't patched things up after all."

"The Latin holds the key," I reminded the boys, but mainly Liam. Seth and I stood back as he began working his magic, sizing up the bronze letters.

But when we heard the muffled thump of a hatch shutting, we whipped our heads in the direction of the sound.

"Let's get out of here!" I bolted up the stairs and sprinted down the long hallway, praying that this time I could lead the team out.

Lines of light from the sconces filled my peripheral vision as I ran, and I remembered a song I'd heard in Liam's car about light guiding a person home.

The end of the tunnel loomed before us. We rushed up a set of stairs and met a door, this time with a handle. As my fingers wrapped around the heavy iron, I said a quick prayer that the door was unlocked and pushed. Never in all my life had I felt such relief at the give of a door. The door thumped as it hit the ground above, and I stole a quick glance back before letting the daylight wash over me. We were safe. For now.

Chapter 48

Sleep was hard to come by again that night. The memory of the tunnels and the secrets behind the carved door haunted me. I felt like all the pieces were laid out in front of me, but I still couldn't quite put them together. I knew that once I figured out how the big picture looked, I'd be able to see the truth about Grace and the secret of the fire. And if I could just figure out the truth, there might finally be justice.

I scooted up against my headboard and adjusted the pillow behind my back. And there she was. Moonlight shone through the window, illuminating her silhouette as she sat on my window seat. As usual, her back was to me. She had her legs curled beneath the familiar Pemberly Brown plaid skirt. Her straight, dark hair hung to the middle of her back. Surprisingly, I wasn't scared of her this time, just curious. Maybe I was too tired to be afraid.

Barely breathing, I pulled back the duvet covering my legs and lowered them to the floor, trying not to make a sound. I walked toward her slowly, my arm outstretched. I wanted to touch her. To feel her. To finally figure out if she was real or just some figment of my imagination. Just as my fingers were about to graze her shoulder, I opened my eyes.

I wasn't near the window at all, but in my bed. I must have fallen asleep. Turning to my side, I pulled my hand up under my cheek and stared out the window. She was gone. Or maybe she was never there in the first place.

My room had brightened, the moonlight mixing with the glow from my computer screen. I pulled the covers down, for real this time, and tiptoed to my desk. I had another new message.

To: KateLowry@pemberlybrown.edu

Sent: Fri 1:30 AM

From: GraceLee@pemberlybrown.edu

Subject: (no subject)

You found the 13th.

But we're out of time.

Come back the night of the dance.

Alone.

I'll be waiting.

I read the last line a few times and felt a wave of butterflies. I tried to remind myself I was seeking justice, not an impossible resurrection. But no matter how hard I tried, a tiny spark of hope remained. A spark that lived in whatever lobe of my brain was run completely by emotion. And sometimes I'd even fanned the spark a little and started a small fire, convincing myself that everyone was wrong, that the funeral was fake and that Grace was alive, hidden away and waiting for me to find her.

I had no idea what would be waiting for me inside the head-quarters, and I wasn't even sure if I'd be able to get in. But I'd find a way. I'd find a way because she'd asked me to. And I'd go alone because that's what Grace wanted.

Chapter 49

I f I was a normal girl, I would have spent hours picking out the perfect dress and coordinating accessories for Homecoming. If I was a normal girl, I would have booked an appointment to get my hair done with friends and then headed over to someone's house to jockey for a spot at the mirror and giggle over eyeliner and body glitter. If I was a normal girl, I'd have had butterflies in my stomach as I waited and wondered what type of corsage my date would bring and whether or not he'd kiss me good night.

But I was not a normal girl.

I spent the Saturday of the Homecoming dance rearranging the letters in the words *Audi, Vide, Tace* in an attempt to create a comprehensive list of possible passwords. I couldn't ask Liam for help, because Grace had specifically said to come alone. Besides, this was something I had to do on my own. Feeling fairly confident about my list, I folded it into my clutch and decided to focus on my next problem. Finding something to wear.

I pulled on a pink strapless dress from our Sadie Hawkins dance two years earlier. Not only did it clash with my hair, but apparently

I had grown, because it barely covered my butt. I tried rearranging Grace's pearls a few times in an effort to bring the eyes up. Not happening. The slutty look worked well for Hollywood starlets and girls hanging out on street corners, but I decided it might be best to attempt a slightly more subtle fashion statement for my first Homecoming dance.

After yanking the pink dress off, I dug into the back of my closet for the dress I'd worn to the New Year's Eve gala my parents had forced me to attend the year before. I bent over, pleased that my butt was still covered, and sat on my bed waiting for two dates instead of just one.

I had butterflies in my stomach. But not because I was worried about which date I'd kiss. I was a little more focused on figuring out the password into the underground lair of a secret society to meet my dead best friend.

Yeah, I was definitely not a normal girl.

When I finally heard the doorbell ring, I ran downstairs as fast as my fabulous gold heels would take me and found Liam and Seth squirming on my front porch. Technically, we had decided to go as a group to monitor any potential Brotherhood-Sisterhood activities, but I had to admit this whole threesome thing was getting a little tired.

"You look…" Seth began but appeared to be at a loss for words.

"Hot. I think the word you're looking for is *hot*," Liam finished for him.

I swear I'm not one of the "oh, this old thing?" type of girls. It's just that my old dress happened to be a slinky black number. And

Grace's pearls spilled down the center of the V-shaped neckline, setting off the cut of the thin material. Guess sometimes that whole effortless beauty thing actually worked out. Good to know.

After a painfully awkward photo session with my parents and the Allens (Mrs. Allen couldn't stop crying and blowing her nose), the three of us piled into Liam's Jeep, an unlikely trio as we bounced down the road toward Pemberly Brown.

Seth's suit was approximately ten sizes too big (is it just me, or can you hear his mom saying, "We want it a little big, honey, so you'll have something nice to wear to all those college interviews. I'm sure that a growth spurt is just around the corner…"), and his red curls had been tamed by some serious man-product. Liam, on the other hand, wore a fitted, three-button corduroy blazer and dark jeans. He looked like he was going to a hip club opening in New York City instead of a school dance.

But when Seth opened the door for me and Liam held my hand to help me down, I smiled. I couldn't help but stand a little straighter and hold my head a little higher as I walked with the two of them at my side. Seth was like the brother I'd never had. Well, aside from the fact that he was constantly asking me out.

And Liam, as guilty as it sometimes made me feel, reminded me how to be happy. He gave me chills when he touched me and filled me up with that I-need-to-kiss-this-boy-or-I-will-die type of feeling. Which was dramatic, yes, but also the best feeling in the world.

Pausing before the double doors that opened to the gym, I looked down at Seth and up at Liam and looped an arm through each of theirs. We had arrived.

The dance was in full swing as we pushed through the doors. Girls wore barely there dresses that probably required a few rolls of double-sided tape to keep things PG-13. Their necks were adorned with their dates' discarded ties. The boys were already starting to sweat through their button-down shirts, their blazers carelessly strewn about the floor.

When you mix a Mardi-Gras-themed dance with teenage hormones, the result is a combination of girls who look largely like underage prostitutes and oversexed boys who dangle copious amounts of beads in hopes of finding a girl drunk enough (or slutty enough) to flash them. There were plenty of both. In short, it was every parent's worst nightmare. Something the school administrators might want to consider next time they blindly approve one of Beefany's or Taylor's dance themes.

The three of us found seats on the bleachers, which had been decorated to look like a huge Mardi Gras float, and watched the chaos of Homecoming unfold from the sidelines.

"Any society sightings?" Seth asked between sips of punch, an anxious look on his face.

"No, I don't think the future queen and king have made their entrance just yet." I guess it goes without saying that Taylor and Alistair had been elected third-year Homecoming attendants this year. I, for one, was really looking forward to seeing them dance together. I was almost 100 percent positive they hated each other. Almost.

"Oh, they're here," Liam said. "Over there by the Bourbon Street sign."

I followed Liam's line of vision and surveyed Taylor and her groupies. They all wore the same dress in different colors. Taylor's was a pale baby pink. With her white-blond hair in a low bun, she reminded me of a ballerina. Beefany couldn't have contrasted more. She towered over Taylor in a bright turquoise version of the dress, which set off her olive skin and dark features.

Maddie stood hunched over in bright red, crossing her arms over her chest and looking like she wanted to melt into the floor and disappear. The rest of the girls wore orange, yellow, and purple. They looked like a flock of exotic birds. Of course, knowing these birds, it was only a matter of time before they went all Alfred Hitchcock on the place.

At that moment, Taylor looked directly at me. It was as though she could read my mind.

"Bradley and Alistair are here." Liam nodded toward the double doors. Sure enough, the boys had arrived in style. They each had two first-year dates, one for each arm, and they looked very pleased with themselves.

I watched Naomi nudge Taylor and point at her brother. Taylor gave them a quick look and began moving across the dance floor. Beefany and three others quickly flew after her. Guess even high-school birds tended to move in flocks.

"Come on guys. Let's take a lap." I dragged my dates up off the bleachers, and we began to wind our way around Bourbon Street. I wanted to get a better view of whatever was about to go down on the court.

I was so focused on Taylor's purposeful strides toward Alistair that I didn't see Headmaster Sinclair until I literally ran right into him.

"Oh! Sorry." I felt the color drain from my cheeks as I met his sharp eyes.

"Lovely to see you tonight, Ms. Lowry. I was just heading to the refreshment table. Care to join me?" His smile made me edgy.

I exchanged quick looks with Liam and Seth, but I didn't really have a choice.

"Uh, sure. Of course." I nervously wrapped Grace's pearls around my finger, unwound and rewrapped them, thinking of Elisa Moore and her poor sister, Abigail. The headmaster's brother had been cleared of the charges, but I didn't know what to believe anymore. I was beginning to wonder if I'd ever be able to uncover the truth buried beneath all these years of lies.

I followed him as he walked toward the abandoned refreshment table, trying to figure out exactly how to play this.

"Well, Ms. Lowry, I have to admit I've been a little concerned about you lately."

I did not like where this was heading.

"Really? Um, why?" It was a dangerous question to ask, and I could practically taste the bitterness of regret on my tongue after the words left my mouth.

He poured himself a glass of punch. "I hear you paid a visit to one of our alumni, Elisa Moore, poor woman. She lost her mind when her sister took her own life years ago."

"I, um…I should really get back to my date…"

"Don't be nervous. We're among friends." He nodded toward

Liam and Seth waiting across the dance floor. "I'm just worried about you. I think you might be in over your head."

"Well, you know what they say: *Veritas Vos Liberabit.* The truth shall set you free." I forced myself to smile brightly.

"Please just be careful, Kate. You might not believe this, but I don't want to see any other students get hurt." He offered a smile, but it never reached his eyes.

Elisa's thin form flashed to the front of my mind, and I thought of his brother, the all-American track star conveniently cleared of all the charges against him. Not to mention Headmaster Sinclair's own name painted on the walls of Brown. No doubt the Brotherhood had a hand in everything. It was all connected.

"You know, Headmaster, thanks to my experiences here at Pemberly Brown, I really feel like I've learned how to take care of myself. But I appreciate your concern."

I wasn't bluffing. I felt strong. I knew that I'd be able to do what I had to do to uncover the truth, to finally save Grace. But as I walked back across the dance floor, back to the safety of Liam and Seth, I was happy I didn't have to do it alone.

Chapter 50

"Well, that was awkward," I said, trying to keep my voice steady in front of my faithful sidekicks. Liam shook his head back and forth, and Seth looked like he might poop his pants.

"He's scary," Seth said, eyes wide.

"Not scary. Scared." Liam grabbed my hand. "This is the first time more than one person has been a threat to them. It's easy to silence one guy but not so easy to shut three people up."

I looked at him and smiled.

"They haven't seen anything yet." *Just wait until I find proof that the Brotherhood is involved.*

Liam smiled at me. "Hey, you want to…"

"Oh, my God," I said, cutting him off, "is that…" I pointed at the entrance to the dance.

"Cameron," Liam finished for me. Under normal circumstances I would have been worried we were turning into one of those annoying couples who finished each other's sentences, but that night I was grateful he'd said the name I couldn't.

"What the hell is he doing here?" Seth asked. "And where has he been?"

"I don't know, but we need to find out," I said, standing up.

We made our way through the sea of people and tried to keep up with Cameron. He was on a mission, and the crowd appeared to sense his determination, because they parted like the Red Sea to let him through. He came to an abrupt halt right next to Taylor, grabbed her arm, and twirled her around to face him. Her pink dress floated prettily around her thighs.

We hid behind a few fake streetlights and watched the scene unfold.

"We need to talk," Cameron said, eyes darting left and right wildly.

Beefany planted herself between them, protecting her queen. "Oh, Cameron. You're back." She cocked her head and sighed dramatically. "Sorry, but you'll have to catch up with Taylor later. We're right in the middle of something. Not a good time."

Cameron grabbed Beefany by the arm and pulled so that her face was mere inches from his own.

"We need to talk. Now," he repeated.

"Fine. Go ahead," Beefany said as if she were bored by the whole tiresome situation.

"In private."

"No, whatever you have to say, you can say it here. In front of everyone. Taylor isn't going anywhere with you alone." Beefany nodded to their audience.

"That's how you want to play it? Fine. I'm done with your lies, your threats. I know the three of you were there that night. I saw you when I was leaving," he said. Maddie took a step away from the crowd, crumpling into herself like a discarded piece of paper.

I wasn't sure how many people in the room knew what night he was talking about, but I felt a collective gasp.

"I have no idea what you're talking about, Cameron," Taylor said softly.

Beefany took over again, her voice loud and sharp. "Are you sure you're okay? Maybe I should call a teacher over here. I think all those drugs are really starting to take their toll."

Cameron grabbed Taylor by the arms, and I could already see two angry red welts forming around his fingers. He swore, a droplet of saliva backlit by the strobe lights spinning above us.

"I want to know what happened in that chapel. I saw her invitation."

Taylor's icy eyes widened for a split second, revealing fear and maybe even a little weakness.

Beefany swooped into action. "Maddie!" she cried. "Get Headmaster Sinclair over here right now. Cameron is clearly high, and he needs help."

Maddie stood frozen to her spot, probably torn between obeying her leader and disappearing into the crowd. Before she could make up her mind, Headmaster Sinclair came running.

"Cameron, you shouldn't be here." He pried Cameron's fingers off Taylor's arms. "We have a lot to discuss, son. Why don't we take this conversation some place more private?"

"Get him out of here," Taylor said with quiet authority.

"That's enough, Ms. Wright. I'll take care of this." The headmaster dragged Cameron out of the dance as a crowd gathered. The two moved past me, and I heard the headmaster hiss, "I thought I made myself clear to your parents. This school is no longer the best place for you, Cameron."

I turned to Seth. "Did you hear that?"

Seth nodded his head. "I was right. He was at Cameron's house."

Suddenly Cameron shook himself free from the headmaster's grip and came rushing back at me.

"Don't let them get away with it." His voice was thick with emotion.

I stood frozen as the headmaster whipped back around, grabbed Cameron by the arm, and escorted him toward the exit once again. Cameron was almost completely hunched over as he walked, as if to protect himself from the looks of pity and disgust from both his friends and enemies.

I felt tears prick my eyes. In a way we were both in this together. We both wanted the same thing. The truth. And revenge.

I managed to break away from Liam and Seth and ran after Cameron and the headmaster. By the time I'd caught up, they were walking into the school office.

"I've tried so hard to protect you. I know this might be hard for someone like you to understand, but there are traditions of honor within this school that simply can't be broken. Tragic mistakes were made that night, but there's no undoing them, and no good will come from the truth getting out." Headmaster Sinclair maintained a tight grip on Cameron's arm.

I hung on to his use of the word "honor." It was such a simple word, but it said so much about his involvement with the Brotherhood. He may not have had anything to do with the fire, but he had been covering for the Brotherhood, hiding their secrets all this time.

"You don't understand what happened that night. It was them... they..." Cameron's face was twisted with desperation. I wanted to run over to him, but I kept myself hidden around the corner of lockers. "I tried to tell you. I even tried telling the police. I was supposed to meet Grace in the chapel that night."

"I know all about what happened that night, Cameron. You are the one who doesn't understand. This situation is far more complex than it might seem." Headmaster Sinclair's voice was fading as they moved deeper into his office. "You are no longer a student here. It's over."

I stood there paralyzed, unable to find the courage to storm the office and smart enough to know it wouldn't make any difference if I did. Besides, I had a date with a ghost.

Chapter 51

Liam and Seth came running toward the office as I rushed away. "What are you doing? You shouldn't be out here alone, Kate. You're practically a walking target." Liam grabbed my hand and guided me back into the safety of the dance.

"Calm down. Nothing happened. She's fine." Seth eyed Liam's hand, clearly debating whether or not he should step in.

I untangled my fingers and put some space between me and Liam. "I'm fine. Seriously. I just needed to hear Cameron's side of things, that's all."

"And…" Liam raised his eyebrows.

"And nothing. Cameron has been manipulated like the rest of us, but he doesn't know any specifics about that night either… I don't know…this whole thing is just so messed up. Obviously Headmaster Sinclair is still involved with the Brotherhood."

"Ya think?" I was actually impressed with Seth's sarcasm.

We walked back into the gym, and I felt the panic well up inside of me. I'm not sure if it was the heat generated by all those dancing bodies or maybe the garish decorations that felt like they were closing in on me, but I was close to losing it, and it was only 8:30.

Liam must have noticed the panic on my face, because he grabbed my hand.

"Come on, dance with me."

I hesitated, imagining the investigation crumbling around me. And then I glanced at Seth. "I don't know…" Not only did everything feel like it was exploding at my feet, but I felt bad leaving him out.

"No, no, it's fine. It's Homecoming. You should dance." Seth offered us a weak smile. "Besides, I've had my fair share of dances with you. Remember junior high?"

"How could I forget?" Seth had always made it a point to ask me to slow dance during the most excruciatingly long songs. I looked at Liam and then back at Seth. "Okay, one dance. But only if you dance with me next, okay?"

Seth smiled, and my worries about Headmaster Sinclair, the Sisterhood, the Brotherhood, and even the damn tunnels seemed a little farther away.

For the next hour or so we danced and danced. It wasn't exactly how I'd envisioned myself at Homecoming when I was younger, but it was close enough. And better than that, it was fun.

I kept my eye on Beefany, Taylor, Maddie, and the Sisters, and Alistair, Bradley, and the Brothers, but no one seemed to be making any move to leave.

The band went on break, and I saw the Homecoming court preparing for the big crowning ceremony. A quick glance at my phone confirmed that it was already 10:30. Almost time for me to make my exit.

And then I saw her—the now familiar flash of plaid skirt and black hair. The girl slipped out a side door, escaping into the cool night air. I looked around at the rest of the people in the room, wondering if anyone else had seen my ghost, and my eyes fell on Maddie. She faced the double doors and, as though she could feel my eyes on her, turned and looked directly at me.

I cocked my head and offered a smile, but she just nodded slowly and turned away. Guess the girl in the plaid skirt had two people on her list to haunt.

When my phone buzzed in the pocket of my dress, I whipped it out, expecting another email. But this time it was a text from a private number.

You're running out of time.

I clenched my stomach muscles as I read the words. I whipped my head around the crowded gym searching for anyone who could have sent it. But it was no use. People danced and laughed and gossiped. Like normal.

Liam must have been studying me closely as I read the text. "What's up?" he asked, shaking a strand of hair from over his eyes.

"Uh, nothing." My mind flashed back to the night of the bonfire and sitting on the bench with Bradley while the chapel burned. I couldn't make the same mistake again. I had to get out of here. I had to go to her.

I felt bad about keeping Seth and Liam in the dark about my rendezvous with Grace that night, but this was something I had to do alone. That's the way Grace wanted it. And I knew if I told them the truth, they'd never let me go.

But I needed a safety net, just in case. I typed, "At headquarters. Come looking for me in twenty minutes if I'm not back yet. Need to do this alone," and saved the message as a draft. I knew Liam would never wait the full twenty minutes, so I would send it after I cracked the code to the headquarters. Just in case I needed backup. A wave of guilt washed over me as I considered what came next, but it couldn't be helped.

"I'm going to the bathroom," I told Seth and Liam. As they both prepared to protest, I played the ultimate trump card. "It's all just too much for me. Grace should be here tonight, and she's not. I just need some time to process." I should have felt guilty using Grace as an excuse, but something told me she'd understand and probably even approve.

Seth's face fell, and Liam looked concerned.

"You want to talk about it?"

"I can't. I just need a minute, okay?" They both mumbled something about taking my time, and I walked away, praying that I'd made the right decision in leaving them behind.

The second I made it outside the school doors, I took off my heels and ran as fast as I could for the clock tower. I felt a surge of courage as the cool air whipped through my hair and my bare feet pounded the brick path to the tower. Whatever was waiting for me beneath Pemberly Brown, I was ready for it.

Chapter 52

I navigated through the secret clock-tower door and down into the maze of tunnels like an expert. I didn't have time to think about how scared I was about meeting Grace's ghost or whoever else might be waiting for me at the headquarters. I just wanted to get there, figure out the damn code word, put all the pieces together, and take down the Sisterhood, Brotherhood, whoeverhood.

When I finally stopped in front of the carved door, my skin glistened with sweat and my breathing was ragged. My hair had fallen and lay in a frizzy heap down my back. I had ditched my fabulous gold heels somewhere along the brick path to the clock tower, and my feet were sore and dirty. But all of that barely registered as I stood in front of the symbol of the Sisterhood on the door. The Brotherhood's calling card still screamed across the wood in blood-red paint, and I again wondered if I was making a mistake. But I didn't have time for regrets.

Audi, Vide, Tace. "Hear, See, Be Silent." Reaching into my clutch with a shaking hand, I pulled out the scrap of paper I'd used to brainstorm possible passwords. I tried "divide" first, taking care with each letter. After three seconds, the letters popped back out at me. My heart sank a little, because that was the best word I'd come up with.

Next I tried "cat" (see?), "ace," and "die." The letters stuck and then popped. Again, again, again. Scrambling, I punched in the last few words on my list and even tried some nonsensical ones. Still. Nothing. I sent a silent plea upward for clarity. I just needed to get in there, to finish this.

And that's when I noticed. A few of the letters were dull and more worn than the rest. The *a* from *Audi*; the *v*, *e*, and *d* from *Vide*; the *e* from *Tace*. A-V-E-D-E. Nothing. I tried a few more combinations, felt my eyes well up with tears of frustration, kicked the door twice, and all of the sudden I saw it. E-V-A-D-E. The perfect secret code word. To escape, to elude, to avoid. All the things the Sisterhood stood for. I punched the letters with my finger and heard the dull pop of the lock.

My arms burned as I pushed open the heavy doors and entered into a wall of darkness. Pulling my phone from my clutch, I navigated to my draft, keyed in the password Liam and Seth would need to get in, and hit Send. If nothing else, they'd know where to search for my body. A chill ran down my spine at the thought of it, but I was ready. I had come this far. I hesitated before releasing the heavy door and snuffing out the light, but there was no way I could feel for the switch and hold the door at the same time.

As the door thudded shut behind me, I used my phone as a flashlight and groped around for a light switch. When my fingers finally made contact with the wall plate, I flicked one of the switches and half expected to hear "Surprise!" or something. But no one was there.

"Grace?" I called out. "Grace, it's me."

Silence. Despite the fact that I was alone, my cheeks burned with embarrassment. How could I have been so stupid? Did I really think she'd be waiting for me after all this time? After the articles in the paper, the funeral, the endless trips to Dr. P., did I really not grasp that Grace was gone, dead, buried?

I squeezed my eyes shut and rubbed my temples, attempting to ward off the headache I could feel creeping from the center of my forehead out. I could leave now and head back to the dance, move on. But where did that leave Grace? And what about the next girl? I'd made it this far. I needed to finish what I'd started.

I slowly opened my eyes, and the room settled back into focus. The ceilings were taller than I would have expected, giving the space an airy feeling in spite of the fact that we were more than twenty feet underground. The hardwood floors gleamed. Cherry wood paneling covered all the walls except to the left, which instead contained built-in filing cabinets. Overstuffed couches and a huge flat-screen TV made it feel more like a well-appointed basement in a friend's house than a secret society's underground lair.

Okay, I was here, but now what? I wasn't sure if I should start digging through the filing cabinets looking for information, or if I should sit there and wait for whoever or whatever was going to meet me.

A few seconds passed with my bare feet shaking on the cold wooden floors. Who was I kidding? There was no way I could sit on the couch and wait without doing something. Instead I began doing what I had learned to do best—snoop.

The cabinets were a treasure trove of information. I found answers to all the most recent tests we'd had in school and answers to tests dated four months from now. I found a list of all the alumni who had attended Ivy League schools and their contact information. There were five or six different versions of the SAT and ACT, plus AP tests for every subject.

In one drawer I found a bunch of copies of Calvin Markwell's book, and when I flipped to the pages about the stations, everything was intact. The next drawer contained an incredibly heavy and worn-looking encyclopedia-type book. Page after page listed information about rituals, ceremonies, traditions, secret handshakes, maps, code words, oaths.

And then there were the student files. Folders were labeled by graduating class and went back as far as 1950, the year Pemberly merged with Brown. Every student who had ever attended Pemberly Brown was listed, along with biographical information, locker combinations, and, in the more recent files, Pemberly Brown email account information and passwords, our PB social website user names and passwords, and even the passwords to access cell-phone voice mails and texts.

One drawer contained files full of incriminating pictures. Girls were lined up in nothing more than their bras and underwear, faces turned toward the ground. They looked absolutely humiliated, and I wondered how anyone could think being in the Sisterhood was worth the mortification of being photographed half naked.

But then I remembered. This was Brotherhood territory. No wonder the societies were at war. The secrets in these files went much deeper than just pop-quiz answers.

And then I stumbled across a file for Abigail Moore, the girl who had died mysteriously so many years ago. I delicately lifted the yellowed paper from the folder and squinted as I tried to decipher the loopy handwriting.

It looked like minutes from a meeting back in 1971, pages of handwritten notes about Elisa, Abigail's sister, knowing information that could destroy the Brotherhood. And even some mention of her poor sister, Abigail, who had dared to accuse one of the brothers of assault. They had harassed her to the point of death, though it was unclear whether she had taken her own life or it had been taken from her. It was probably a little bit of both, I thought, a shiver running up and down my arms and legs.

As I fought back my anger, my eyes fell on the rest of the file drawers. There were so many of them—an entire wall full. How many files with girls' names on them were locked in this room? How many of the names matched those on the stones in the Memorial Garden? And more importantly, where was the file for Grace?

A noise at the door made me stop reading. I heard the dull padding of somebody running. After sliding the file back into the cabinet, I stretched my neck toward the entryway. The footsteps came closer, stopped for a few seconds, and were replaced with the pop of a lock.

The heavy door creaked open, and the hem of her pink dress came into view first. Then I saw Taylor (crown and all) standing on her tiptoes in the entryway holding both of her shoes. Her eyes locked on mine. Instead of looking surprised to see me, she looked like this was the most natural place in the world for us to meet.

"You made it, Kate," she said matter-of-factly. "You actually made it."

Chapter 53

S omething about her words sounded different to me, and then I realized it was the first time she'd spoken to me since I'd seen her at Maddie's the day after Spiritus. Ever since that day, Beefany had been the one doing the talking.

"You'd better sit down, because I don't know how much time we have," Taylor said, moving toward the couch.

"Wait, how did you know I was going to be here?" I asked, confused. "Did you get an email from Grace too?"

"Not exactly." Taylor glanced nervously between the door and my face. "I don't know how else to tell you this, so I'm just going to say it. There were no emails from Grace."

Before I could even make sense of what she said, the door to the headquarters swung open.

"Kate! Thank God I got here in time." It was Alistair Reynolds.

"What? I mean, what's going on?" I was beyond confused.

Taylor's face darkened. "What are you trying to pull, Alistair?"

He rushed to me and grabbed one of my hands. "I'm trying to save her from you. She knows too much, isn't that right, Taylor?

Were you planning another fire for tonight?" Alistair asked, as he dragged me toward the door and pulled the handle, his voice spiked with anger. I shook my head, even more confused, and turned back to Taylor.

"He's lying, Kate. You can't believe him." Taylor eyes bugged out. She looked panicked.

The word *lying* echoed in my brain. How could you ever really know the truth?

"Oh, really, Taylor? So you've told her all about the emails then?" Alistair sneered.

"What about the emails?" I finally asked, pulling my hand from Alistair's and walking back to Taylor.

"Yeah, Taylor, what about the emails?" Alistair repeated.

She looked down at her freshly polished nails. "I sent them," she whispered.

"Speak up, T. I don't think she heard you," Alistair snapped.

"I sent them." She spoke slowly, lifting her eyes to meet mine. "I had to. I mean, I needed someone to figure out the truth, but I couldn't risk coming forward myself. The Sisterhood would have been compromised, and everyone would have disowned me. What happened that night…it's been eating me alive. And I guess I thought you might be able to save us, to take back what is rightfully ours."

She glared at Alistair. "I was wrong." When she turned back to me, I saw that something had changed in her eyes. The ice queen was back.

"You see, Kate," Alistair began, spelling it out for me as though I were a child, "this is all Taylor's fault. She lied to you, pretended she was your dead best friend. And all along she was in charge of the Sisterhood's new pledges that night. She lit the candles that set the entire chapel on fire, and she's the one who sent Grace to the basement to die. Come on; let's get out of here while we still can. There's no telling what she's capable of."

"You liar!" Taylor threw her hands in the air and screamed at the top of her lungs, slowly unraveling. "I didn't set the fire, and I don't know why Grace was even in the basement. She was late like everyone else. And you weren't there! How could you possibly know?" She began to cry.

"The chapel is completely sealed. The only way in or out is through the tunnels. And there was so much smoke." She choked on the words. "We could barely find the way out."

Adrenaline coursed through my veins, igniting each of my senses. My heart pounded in my ears, my feet burned, and my stomach heaved as Taylor's perfume clashed with Alistair's cologne. Something didn't feel right.

You weren't there! How could you possibly know? I repeated the words in my head. She was wrong. Alistair had been there that night. Liam had seen him.

"She started the fire. She saved herself, and she forgot all about Grace," Alistair said, straightening. "Something tells me *you* wouldn't have forgotten her, Kate." He turned to the door. "Are you coming or what?"

At this point, the room began to spin. It was all too much. Nobody was supposed to get hurt, yet Taylor had left my best friend in the basement to die? Alistair wasn't there that night, but Liam had seen him running through the woods? Taylor was hysterical now, practically choking on air as Alistair stood at the door, impatient and self-assured.

I didn't want to believe either of them. I almost wished I didn't know anything. An accident was so much easier to swallow. Setting a fire and leaving someone to die? I couldn't wrap my head around it. But worse than that, Alistair was right. There's no doubt that if I had been there on time, I never would have left without Grace. A wave of guilt washed over me for the millionth time since she died. This was my fault too.

"I didn't do it, Kate," Taylor cried. "I didn't start the fire. I don't know how it started, but what I do know is that somehow the Brotherhood got access to the tunnels that night. Someone let them in."

Wiping at her eyes, she pointed at Alistair. "Someone died, but all you and your Brothers cared about was this." She opened her arms and gestured to the space around us, hiccupping a little.

I tried to imagine Grace's last moments, to fill in the pieces and finally see the truth. And that's when I remembered. Cameron. How did he fit into the puzzle? He was supposed to meet Grace. To meet Grace in the basement. And when the fire began, instead of following the others, she must have been searching for him through the smoke. Only he wasn't there.

Alistair was lying.

"You're lying," I whispered. "Taylor didn't put Grace in the basement. Grace was trying to find Cameron." Taylor looked over at me, her blue eyes round and red from crying.

Alistair laughed. "You're going to believe that druggie loser over me?"

"Actually, yeah, and…" Before I could accuse him of being in the woods that night, the click of a lock interrupted me. All of our heads turned to the door.

And in walked Maddie.

She didn't look surprised to see any of us, and I was starting to wonder just how many people had access to Grace's email account. And mine. Guess that explained why Taylor felt the need to write her emails in riddles.

Alistair went a little pale when he saw her. "What are you doing here? Are you here to save Kate from Taylor too?" He gave her a look that begged her to play along.

"I came to tell the truth," Maddie said quietly. "This has gone on for way too long."

Alistair's face froze.

Taylor sniffled. "What are you talking about, Maddie? What could you possibly know? You were only there for initiation."

The fourth invitation. It was Maddie's. I imagined how the creamy paper would finally complete the mysterious crest.

"Don't do this, Maddie. You know this is all Taylor's fault. I've spent the last year trying to protect you." Panic rose in Alistair's voice.

Maddie stood by the door, wavering. Her tiny body looked spent, broken.

"Maddie?" I asked, my voice small.

"It was my fault Grace died," she said, staring at her feet. "The Brotherhood found the pledge list, and Alistair approached me before I even got the invitation to initiation." Her eyes flicked over to him as she said his name but just as quickly turned back to the ground.

"He told me all I had to do was tell him where they were holding the initiation. I don't even know why I agreed to it. I guess part of me thought that if I could get Alistair to like me, it would transform me or something." She shook her head, still staring at her feet. "All I know is that if I hadn't helped him, Grace would still be alive." Tears streamed over the hollows of her cheeks.

Alistair swore at Maddie and began pacing the room.

She stared straight ahead, tears continuing to fall, and turned to look at me. "Taylor was there that night, but she's innocent. Alistair started the fire outside of the chapel. It was supposed to be controlled, just enough of a distraction to force us out of the chapel so he could see how we accessed the tunnels.

"His plan worked perfectly until the chapel went up in flames. But he still figured out how to break into the headquarters. And I lost Grace." The tears continued to slip from her eyes, falling long and hard and darkening the fabric of her dress, some gathering into a puddle on the shiny wood below.

"She wasn't even supposed to be there. He said she wouldn't be there. Other Brothers were supposed to keep you guys busy. Away from…everything. But by the time I made it back to the bonfire, people were screaming and…and she was gone. I wanted to come forward, to tell the truth." She hiccupped the words. "But he said he'd expose me. He took my invitation and said it was proof that I was there, that I killed her. I was scared. I had to do what he said."

Taylor's face twisted. "It was you. You let them in. We lost *everything*, because of you." Taylor said the words in a hushed voice that gave me goose bumps.

"I'm so sorry," Maddie whispered. "I'm not scared anymore. I don't care what happens to me. I just want everyone to know the truth."

"You think saying sorry is going to change anything? And the truth? *What* truth?" Taylor jumped up from the couch and lunged toward Maddie. Alistair stepped between them.

"Not so fast. Now that everything's out in the open, I think it's time for all of us to sit down and talk." Alistair grabbed Taylor's arm, separating her from Maddie. She sank back down into the couch, all the fight drained out of her, while Alistair paced.

"It doesn't matter what you *think* happened. When are you girls ever going to realize that nothing you say matters?" Beads of sweat dripped down his face. He sounded confident, but he looked nervous as hell.

"So here's how this is going to work. We're all going to leave this room and head back to the dance, and no one is ever going to discuss any of this again. Maddie, Taylor, I think you both know the deal. Sure, you can come clean and tell everyone you were there that night and that I set the fire. But it's my word against yours. And I think we all know who the police and Headmaster Sinclair will side with."

"They ruled it arson, you know," Taylor chimed in. "We have our sources at the police department too, Alistair. They know the fire was set on purpose. You can't bury this forever."

"And aren't you forgetting someone? What about me? Why should I keep quiet after you killed my best friend?" I asked. I knew it was stupid. I knew I should have kept my mouth shut, but I was done with silence. Done with the secrets and lies. Besides, I'd spent the past month gathering clues against the Brotherhood. I had Elisa, the headmaster, Liam. My slam book was full of evidence.

"I have to say, Kate, you surprised me. All those threats, and you still didn't give up. And the ghostly emails. Did you really think they were from Grace? Taylor can be convincing, but not *that* convincing." My face grew hot with shame, and Taylor lowered her head, probably feeling the same way.

"And even Bethany played right into my hands, blackmailing Gilmour to keep his mouth shut and stepping in to keep the Sisterhood's secrets after Taylor had failed. It made my job so much easier. But none of that matters now." I thought of Bethany and Liam, how deep the lies ran.

He reached into his blazer pocket and pulled out a card. Written in calligraphy was my name. It was the invitation Seth and I had found in the heart of Brown. I narrowed my eyes in confusion. How could he have that? We'd just found it.

"Look familiar? Tell your parents they should really invest in a better security system. Found some sparkle book too. Is that your little detective diary?" The slam book, the evidence. They had broken into my house and stolen everything. Heat rushed to my cheeks.

"It will never work. Headmaster Sinclair might defend you, but the police will have to listen. It's three against one."

Alistair laughed now, wiping his arm against his forehead.

"Nice try. Unfortunately for you, Bradley will go on record saying he saw you at the chapel at seven fifteen, before the fire broke out. You didn't think he actually liked you, did you, Kate? We just needed you out of the way like everyone else."

I thought of Naomi, who said she'd been late to the meeting just like me. They had probably distracted her too. Maddie and Taylor were the only ones they needed. I wondered who was supposed to stall Grace. Cameron had seen her talking with someone, but it didn't surprise me that she couldn't be stopped. She never would have ditched Cameron. As impulsive as she could sometimes be, Grace always kept her word.

I opened my mouth to respond but couldn't find any words. Alistair didn't seem to have the same problem.

"So try me, Kate. I have no problem twisting the story to make it so you were the one who sent Grace into the basement."

I looked at Maddie, whose frail body was still as a statue's, and then at Taylor, who had collapsed next to me in defeat. It was over.

But then I heard something. *Click, click, click, click, click. Pop.* I stopped and turned to the door. Thank God I'd sent the text. Sure enough, Liam and Seth came storming into the headquarters.

My knights had arrived at last.

Chapter 54

Alistair reacted instantaneously. I guess all those two-a-days during lacrosse season had paid off, because he was shoving past them and into the tunnels before anyone else had moved an inch.

Liam looked at me. "You okay?"

"I'm fine."

"Good. Don't move." And with that Liam sprinted out the door after Alistair.

I sat on the couch for a beat and then stood up. There was no way I was going to just sit around while Liam and Alistair fought in the tunnels. I was going in.

I made a dash for the door, but Seth moved to block me.

"Kate, it's not safe." He put his hand up like a misguided crossing guard.

"No, but it's better than sitting around and waiting. He has everything. All the evidence I've gathered. I have to get it back." My voice was shrill, desperate almost. Now that everything had finally clicked into place, I couldn't let Alistair get away.

"Fine. I'll come with you." Seth put on his best tough-guy face, and in that moment I knew he'd always do his best to help me slay whatever dragons might come my way.

"You've got to stay here with them. Please? For me?" I asked. He looked over at Maddie and Taylor. "I have to do this, Seth." My hands were already positioned on the door.

He shook his head back and forth. "Fine, but be careful and take this." He grabbed one of the swords positioned next to the entryway.

I had to laugh. Something about me running through underground tunnels with a sword was beyond funny, but I took it with me anyway. A girl could never be too careful. Besides, I was ready to start slaying my own damn dragons.

I could hear the guys ahead, so I took off in the direction of the noise, hoping I'd get there in time to save Liam and get my invitation back from Alistair. The sconces guided my way, with my bare feet padding against the stone floor, but the voices drifted away the more I ran. I must have taken a wrong turn. I heard footsteps again and picked up my pace, but as I broke into a sprint, I realized the footsteps weren't ahead of me—they were behind me. I was being chased.

"Kate, I know you're out here." Alistair's voice echoed through the narrow halls, igniting a scream deep in my throat. I managed to swallow it back and instead flew around a corner and stopped, pressing my body against the damp brick. I could barely hear his footsteps over the sound of my pounding heart.

"No use hiding. I know every inch of these tunnels."

The footsteps came closer to where I stood. Sucking air deep into my lungs and digging for courage I didn't even know I had, I jumped out, pointing a shaking sword at Alistair.

"Shit," he hissed, holding his hands up. "Calm down, Kate. Don't do anything you'll regret."

I lowered the sword an inch, but he dodged at the base of it, trying to rip it from my fingers. Trying to protect myself, I sliced the sword through the air and felt the blade hit something soft. Alistair's hand shot to his bicep and he dropped the invitation. It floated to my feet and, still training the sword on Alistair, I bent to retrieve it.

Swearing at me, he lifted his fingers to examine the damage the sword had caused. His hand was red with blood, and a long line of maroon tore down his arm where he'd been cut. He crouched to the ground and sucked air through his teeth, clearly hurt.

"You tell the truth, or I'm going to," I said, standing over him but lowering the sword. Witnessing his pain, I let my guard down. Big mistake. He lunged for my midsection, tackling me to the ground like a rag doll. The sword flew from my grasp, clinking against the brick wall a few feet from our bodies.

"Just stop fighting and listen to me for a second. You're going to ruin everything," he hissed.

"Stop. Hurting. Me…" I struggled to form words with the full weight of him on top of me. "It's not going to get you anywhere." My lungs felt as though they were crushed.

"Get off her." Maddie's voice rang in my ears. It sounded strong and confident, so much different from the way she looked.

All at once, I felt his weight slide away and I was able to breathe again. I scrambled backward and into the brick wall, trying to put as much distance as possible between us.

Maddie held the other sword out in front of her. It shook in her hands.

"Trying to redeem yourself?" Alistair asked, walking straight for her. "Once a traitor, always a traitor, isn't that right, Maddie?" He charged at her, easily knocking the sword from her weak grip and pinning her thin form against the brick wall with his body.

"I'm not about to lose everything because of *you*," he hissed. His voice was laced with both hatred and fear at the same time.

I couldn't take another second. I searched the ground around me for some sort of weapon besides the sword. I had cut him once by accident; I knew I didn't have it in me to cut him on purpose. My eyes were drawn upward, and I saw the portraits hanging on the wall. Acting quickly, I managed to lift one of the heavy frames off the hook and drag it toward Alistair, his fingers digging into Maddie's thin arms.

Her eyes widened as she saw me coming. Screwing up my features, I struggled to raise the frame above my head. Maddie squeezed her eyes shut and turned her face toward the wall as I slammed the substantial frame over his head. He didn't fall as quickly as I'd envisioned, and I wondered if one hit wasn't enough. But then, with his head lolling to the side, he fell to the cobblestone floor with a thump.

Maddie rubbed at her arms where he had held her, and I dropped the frame to the ground. Both of us looked at Alistair's body lying in a heap and took off down the tunnel without another word. As we rounded the corner, I saw Liam slumped against the ground near one of the trapdoors. I knelt down next to him.

"Liam"—I shook his shoulders—"Liam! Wake up."

When I heard him moan, I let the air out of my lungs. "Oh, thank God."

He rolled onto his back, and the instant I looked at his face, I noticed the black bruise already forming around his left eye.

"Your eye." He grabbed my hand, and I helped him sit up. "Does it hurt?" I placed my fingers on his cheek, barely touching his skin.

"I'm fine. It's fine," he said, reaching his hand up to touch my fingers.

I glanced back at Maddie, who stood awkwardly behind us, not knowing where to look. "I'm going to help you up, okay?" I said. "We have to get out of here. Alistair's out for now, and we need to call the police to tell them where to find him."

I pushed myself up and helped Liam stand as well.

"What about Taylor?" Liam mumbled groggily.

"I saw her take the stairs out to the clock tower," Maddie replied, gesturing for us to follow her.

"You just let her go?" Liam asked, shaking his head to try to clear it.

"I'll explain later. Let's just get out of here." I grabbed his hand, and we followed Maddie as she expertly navigated the tunnels until we came to another door. "Alumni Hall," she said, nodding at it. Liam climbed the stairs first, looking back when he didn't hear additional footsteps.

"I'll be up in a minute," I said. When he still didn't move, I continued. "It's okay. I just need a second." Slowly, he continued the rest of the way up without us. I turned back to Maddie. As soon as she met my eyes, hers filled with tears again. I clenched my hands into fists and found the courage to say what I needed to say.

"Grace is really gone, isn't she?" I asked, my voice cracking.

Maddie cried then. Huge, silent tears. "Yes." Somehow she looked even smaller than when I'd first met her all those years ago. I didn't know if she'd hug me back, but I wrapped my arms around her anyway. We stood together like that, crying for everything we'd lost, including each other.

"You have to get help, Maddie," I said, referring to more than just her obvious eating disorder. "Promise me you'll get help." She nodded into my shoulder and wiped beneath her eyes as she pulled away. "And we have to go to the police." I looked at her, praying the girl I once knew was still in there somewhere. That she was still able to see what was right.

"I already called them. It's over," Maddie said quietly.

I peered around her, taking in the narrow tunnels one last time, and wiped beneath my own eyes. There were more hurdles ahead, possibly even more challenging than the ones we'd just jumped, and I had to be strong. My invitation to the Sisterhood was crumpled in my hands. I had to finish what I had started.

After we climbed the steep flight of stairs, Liam reached down to grab my hand. His strong grip was comforting, my struggle with Alistair already drifting into the recesses of my memory.

We rushed down Alumni Hall, and I gave the plaque at Station 6 a habitual slap. *Respice, adspice, prospice.* I had just looked at the past, and we were off to the present. I'd worry about the future tomorrow.

Chapter 55

The next morning, my parents and I were called to the police station to give an official statement to the officer in charge of Grace's case.

Detective Livingston's office was overloaded with files and loose papers, but I noticed a Pemberly Brown bumper sticker pinned to his bulletin board.

"Please, everyone, have a seat. Can I get anyone something to drink?"

My dad rubbed at his eyes and asked for a cup of coffee.

"No, I'm okay. Is that evidence?" I asked pointing at the bumper sticker.

He smiled.

"No, 'fraid not. I graduated in the class of '97." Detective Livingston shuffled some papers on his desk. "So let me review why we've gathered today."

"We were under the impression that Kate was here to give an official statement," my mom said, transitioning seamlessly from mom to lawyer.

I reviewed the events of the previous night in my mind: me

cracking the code to get into the headquarters, Alistair threatening all of us, me slicing into his arm by accident, finally handing the invitation I'd received last year to a police officer. Never in a million years did I think I was the kind of girl who would get involved in a sword fight for evidence in a criminal investigation. But I also didn't think I was the kind of girl who would give an official statement to a police officer, either. I guess I didn't really know who I was, exactly.

"Kate." Detective Livingston met my eyes. "You need to know that Alistair Reynolds is pressing charges against you."

I was floored, speechless, literally unable to respond to the news. My palms began to sweat, and a dull ache pulsed at each temple. This was not happening. There had to be a mistake.

"Hold on just a second." My dad sat up straighter and put the coffee cup down on the detective's metal desk with a clink. "What exactly are you accusing my daughter of?"

"I know this might come as a shock to you, Mr. and Mrs. Lowry"—the detective looked at me as he said this—"but Alistair was treated at University Hospital last night for a knife wound. He claims Kate stabbed him."

"What's this all about, Kate?" my dad asked, wrinkles threatening to overtake his entire face.

"Kate, what exactly happened last night?" my mom asked, narrowing her eyes. I could feel their support waver. My mom scooted uncomfortably in her chair, moving a little closer to my dad and farther away from me.

"He attacked me! I was protecting myself," I yelled defensively. "Did Alistair mention that he started the fire that killed my best friend?" I stood up as I said the words, and my dad guided me back down into the seat.

"Kate, let's not say anything we'll regret," Detective Livingston said, referring back to his papers.

"I won't regret anything I say. What about the Brotherhood and the Sisterhood? What about their role in Grace Lee's death? They killed her."

"Kate, I'm going to have to ask you to calm down. Detective Sanchez took down all of your information about these so-called societies last night at the school, and frankly we've been unable to find any evidence of these types of groups at Pemberly Brown."

"Dad," I said, beginning to get desperate. "I showed him where the tunnels lead…I gave him my evidence, the invitation, their crests, everything."

The detective looked at my parents. "Mr. and Mrs. Lowry, we've investigated all of Kate's claims. The clues lead nowhere, and Headmaster Sinclair assures us that the only thing beneath Pemberly Brown are some old sewers."

"Of course he said that! He's one of them." And then I remembered Alistair's comment about the police. *The Brotherhood runs deep.* "You're one of them too, aren't you? Is that what this is about? Protecting your stupid secret society?"

"Kate, that's enough." My dad placed his hand on my forearm. "You've said plenty."

"I think we're done here. Without additional proof, it's Kate's word against Alistair's, and frankly after she assaulted him last night, her word doesn't carry much weight."

"But what about Maddie and Taylor?" I didn't bother looking at the detective; I asked the question of my parents. "They'll tell the same story." I was more desperate than ever now. I couldn't believe this was happening, and worse still, I couldn't believe he was right.

I had no evidence. Nothing. The past few weeks had been a huge waste. The only information I had left implicated me and the Sisterhood. The police even had the invitation I'd managed to get back from Alistair, and they'd probably already burned it.

"Honey, Maddie is very sick," my mom began. "I spoke with Mrs. Greene. They're sending her to a facility to get help. She's not a reliable witness."

Detective Livingston gave me a long, hard look and, to my shock, reached out across his desk and grabbed my hand.

"Kate, I know you're missing your friend and that you want her death to be something more than a horrible accident, but that's exactly what it was: an accident."

I pulled my hand away from his and looked back at my parents. They were nodding their heads in agreement. All the blood rushed out of my face. I was back at square one.

"Thank you for understanding, detective. We appreciate how much you've done already. What do we have to do to fix this?" my dad asked.

"The Reynoldses were hesitant to press charges in the first place, so I think with some reassurance they'd be willing to rescind. But I'll need Kate's word that she'll stop spreading all this nonsense about secret societies. It's dangerous."

I sat in silence.

"Kate?" my mom asked. "Did you hear what Detective Livingston said?"

I remained silent, but my mom didn't ask again.

"Detective," my dad said, standing, "please tell the Reynolds family we'll take care of all the medical expenses associated with this situation." He reached out to shake the detective's hand, and my mom stood as well.

"So if we don't hear from you, we'll assume the charges have been dropped?" my mom asked.

"Yes. I'll contact you if anything changes," the detective responded.

We left the police station in silence. I could see the questions forming on my parents' lips, but no sound ever left their mouths. I couldn't believe that after everything, it had come to this.

I'd played the game and solved the puzzle, but somehow I'd still lost.

Chapter 56

I rode home in a fog of depression. It felt familiar. Comforting. Like slipping back into my favorite pair of perfectly broken-in jeans. I'd get home, return Grace's pearls to my memory box, and shove them to the back of my closet. I had failed her; I didn't deserve her necklace.

But I wasn't the same girl I had been a year ago. I had been through hell and back, and if there's one thing I'd learned on the journey, it's that I wasn't going down without a fight. Another one. The fog began to lift.

After suffering through an almost hour-long lecture from my parents about letting go once and for all and having them threaten me with twice-a-week Dr. P. sessions, I was ready to take their advice and move on. Since no one believed me, it was time to take matters into my own hands and find real evidence. Again.

I gave my parents another hour to cool down and then grabbed my book bag, headed downstairs, and put my phone to my ear to begin a faux phone conversation with Seth. I wrapped Grace's pearls around my fingers like a telephone cord. My dad took one look at me and raised an eyebrow.

"Hang on a second. Let me ask." I covered my phone with my palm. "Dad, can I go to the library with Seth?"

He sighed and shook his head. "Tell Seth you'll call him back."

Not the answer I was expecting. I pretended to hang up with Seth and dropped my book bag, slumping into the chair next to my dad.

"Kate, just this morning I was listening to how my daughter was involved in some sort of knife fight, and now you want to go the library with Seth?"

I blinked long and hard.

"I want to trust you. I want you to go to the library and do all the normal things kids your age are doing. But how can I?"

I forced myself to look into his eyes. I wanted to tell him the truth, had tried to tell them the truth, but there was no point. No one would ever believe me.

"I'm ready to move on, Dad. I want to be normal too." The lie tasted bitter on my tongue.

"Then call Seth back," he said, putting his hand on top of my own.

I kissed him on the cheek and connected to my second fake call of the day.

It took some convincing, but I insisted on walking instead of being driven by my dad. I had quite a hike in front of me, but I needed the fresh air. The wind bit at my face and hands, reminding me that even colder weather would arrive like an icy sucker punch in a few weeks. The sky was crystal blue, and the bare branches looked as though they'd been etched into the clouds.

As I made my way across the greenish-brown expanse of lawn in front of Pemberly Brown's main building, I knew without looking that my cheeks were flushed from the cold. I was ready to take a break from the cool air…well, if I could get in.

I pounded down the stairs to the basement of the clock tower. I might have lost all my evidence against the societies, but it didn't matter. I would just have to start all over again. Grace was worth it. I punched in the word M-E-A-S-U-R-E, waiting for the satisfying pop of the secret door. But the only thing that popped were the letters, one by one, marking my failure. I tried again and again and again. Fail, fail, fail.

I walked over to the door that led to the tunnels, but there was nothing but smooth stone. Access to the tunnels had either been removed or had disappeared. It was like the door had never existed in the first place.

I struggled to catch my breath. Could I really have made all of this up? The police had to keep records. Maybe I could somehow convince them to give me back all the evidence I'd turned over to them. The other entrances couldn't be sealed. I knew all of the stations; surely I could figure out a way back into one of them. As I gasped for air, I could almost feel Alistair's body pressing into my chest again. I could see the triumph in his eyes.

My fingers found the brick wall surrounding me, and I used it for support as I lowered my body to the ground. This was yet another opportunity for me to use Dr. Prozac's infamous time-out approach, and I was all over it. I closed my eyes, shutting out memories one by one until the world disappeared and a calmness washed over me. It actually worked. Who knew?

Once my pulse had slowed and my breathing was under control, I began to walk up the stairs from the basement of the tower. I heard heavy footsteps closing in behind me, but I refused to look back until the sunshine had embraced me once again. At the top, when I finally turned back around, no one was there.

I rushed out of the clock tower and around the corner, and this time I did run into someone. But not who I expected.

Ms. D.

"Kate! Are you okay? I heard all about the incident in the tunnels last night." Her face was lined with concern, her lips drawn in a tight line.

"I'm fine. I just…" I don't know where they came from, but the tears of frustration finally began to fall. "I lost, Dorothy. I was so close…I almost had them. But I lost."

Her solid arms wrapped me up in a huge bear hug. "It's okay, darlin'. They don't fight fair—never have, never will. But that doesn't mean we stop trying. I fought long and hard, and I lost too." She gestured at her security badge. "But I'm still fighting. Every day, Kate."

I nodded and dried my tears. She was right. This was far from over. For me, the fight had only just begun.

Chapter 57

I sat on the swing hanging from our front porch for so long that my thighs ached against the hard wood. When I saw the Jeep pull into my driveway, I tried to smile. Tried to be happy to see him, to be normal.

Lucky for me, Liam made it easy. When he hopped out of the car carrying a bouquet of bright pink Gerbera daisies, my fake smile transformed into a genuine one.

"I thought you might need some cheering up," he said, handing me the flowers. The bruise around his eye was still a brilliant purple. I'd never be able to forget the sight of him lying collapsed in the tunnels after his fight with Alistair.

I inhaled the daisies' fresh smell in an attempt to forget.

"Thank you. They're perfect. They're my favorites. How'd you know?"

"I didn't. They just sort of looked like you. Plus they were the only ones at the grocery store."

"Come on, sit down," I said and slid over.

Liam flung his arm around me, and I laid my head on his shoulder, inhaling the scent of him. "So…how are you holding up?"

"I just can't believe it, you know? How could this have happened? Can the police really get away with ignoring the testimony of three different people?" I felt tears of frustration prick my eyes again. How could I have failed Grace like this?

"I don't know, but I do know that these societies have connections, so it's possible."

"They need to pay." I rolled Grace's pearls between my fingers.

"You need to stay out of this now, Kate. They're dangerous." He looked directly at me, and I knew in an instant that he was really seeing me—not just my eyes, my crazy pink hair, or even the almost invisible line of freckles that was scattered over the bridge of my nose, but me. "I just don't want you to get hurt."

"I went back there to the clock tower." I avoided Liam's eyes.

"Are you insane? How could you go there alone? You've got to be kidding me, Kate. Do you want to get yourself killed?" His face was bright red, and he threw my hand down like it was on fire.

"I tried to get into the tunnels, but they've sealed the entrance. It was like the tunnels never existed."

He froze and looked at me, the anger replaced with shock.

"Seriously?"

"Seriously. It's sealed. And now I have no idea how to get back in. I even tried the other words, every word I could find. Nothing."

"You need to promise me something." He stood up from the swing and stared directly in my eyes.

"Promise me you'll stay away from them." He didn't need to say their names. We both knew exactly who he was talking about.

"I just don't know if…I mean, I can't just…" I thought of Ms. D.

and how hard she'd probably fought over the years. But Liam gave me a hard stare, and I knew that if I didn't agree, he'd leave me and never look back. It wasn't that he didn't care about me. I think he probably cared too much.

"Okay, okay. I promise. For now." For a second I thought Liam was going to protest, but he just nodded his head and looked away.

I walked toward him then, pressing my body to his as he wrapped his arms around my back. My head fit perfectly against his chest, and I tried to memorize the feel of his chin resting on top. He smelled like soap and peppermint, and when I felt his fingers graze my own, I knew that this was it. I was finally going to kiss Liam Gilmour.

He lifted his chin and looked down at me, and we stood frozen for a moment. I studied the zipper of his fleece jacket before raising my eyes to his. And that's all it took. He leaned close enough for our lips to meet, and as they did, I felt a part of the sadness of the past year slip away, if only for a moment.

His lips were gentle but insistent as they moved against mine, and I realized that this was the moment I'd been waiting for over the past few weeks. Justice had eluded me, but this was something.

"Hey, guys, what's up?"

Oh, God, please tell me this isn't happening. I knew that voice, and I knew that the second I opened my eyes, I'd be assaulted with a mass of frizzy red curls and a huge smile.

"Oh, hey, Seth." Liam smiled down at me.

"Why isn't anyone talking about the Sisterhood or the Brotherhood? Did they cover it up somehow? I remember this one time when the Skull and Bones was being investigated and..."

Seth gestured to the porch swing and sat down where Liam had been sitting. I could tell he was gearing up to tell some big story, and I could not have this conversation right now. Not after what I'd just promised Liam.

I put my hand up in an attempt to silence him. "I just can't talk about this right now, okay? It feels like I lost her all over again." I hated that my voice cracked on the words. "I just need some time to think."

And as I said the words out loud, I realized they were true. This wasn't over. Not by a long shot. But I wasn't ready to think about what part of the fight came next. Not yet. I needed to grieve for Grace, to let her go.

"Oh, yeah, sure. Sorry." Seth looked uncomfortable, and I felt awful. He'd been my friend when no one else would give me the time of day. I had to be more patient with him.

"No, I'm sorry, Seth. It's not your fault…" I trailed off.

"Actually, we were just going to go grab some coffee. Want to come?" Liam shot me a questioning look, but I didn't blame him for asking Seth along. At least I'd gotten one kiss.

"Uh…thanks, but I'll let you guys head out on your own. I mean, I don't want to be like the third wheel or something and…"

"Come on, you're not the third wheel. Besides, we're totally planning on ditching you later." Liam grinned at me, and my heart flip-flopped.

My mouth formed into the type of smile that traveled all the way up my cheeks and crinkled my eyes. It was a huge dorky smile; it had been a long time since my face muscles had been exercised. I was surprised they still worked.

I thought back to the photograph of me, Grace, and Maddie. In the picture and for most of that summer, I had worn that same smile. I couldn't stop the tears from welling in my eyes. Even though I tried to push them back, tears gathered, resting on my eyelashes. I tried to raise my chin to fight gravity so the tears would stay put. But it was no use. They spilled over and found their way to the corners of my mouth.

When the tears wouldn't stop, I was thankful that Liam and Seth turned toward the street, talking quietly and giving me a chance to cry for Grace. At that moment, it was clear how much I had lost. And yet it was also obvious how much I had found. Liam and Seth were the kind of friends a girl can depend on. The kind that last forever.

Chapter 58

I walked into Dr. Prozac's office weighed down with even more issues than when I'd begun counseling the previous year. But for some reason, I felt lighter.

Prozac: You're looking well, Kate.

Me: Thanks.

Prozac: So life's good? (Dr. P. cocked his head and seemed shocked to have asked such a question.)

Me: Sort of. (I'd been attacked in secret underground tunnels, the police destroyed evidence I'd worked for weeks to collect, and the secret societies I knew existed had magically disappeared. But I was here.)

Prozac: Well, not many people are one-hundred percent good. (He tapped his pen on the desk twice as though to punctuate his point.)

Me: Yeah, I'm starting to realize that.

Prozac: So the reality is that "sort of good" is actually pretty great.

Me: Um, sure. (And, though it killed me to think it, he was right. I had managed to find a couple of real, live friends, maybe even a boyfriend. Life really was kind of great.)

Prozac: And what about Grace? Your parents filled me in on the most recent incident. It was an accident, Kate. You can't live your life looking for someone to blame.

Me: I know. (Besides, I had already discovered where to place the blame. Now I just had to figure out how to bring them down. An accident was never really just an accident.)

Prozac: I'm proud of you, Kate. You've really come a long way.

Me: You have no idea.

Chapter 59

I had a love-hate relationship with my computer.

After everything that had happened, I kind of hated it again. But I managed to brush aside my hard feelings and flipped it open to check my mail.

A few new messages had appeared in my inbox, but there was only one I cared to read.

> To: KateLowry@pemberlybrown.edu
> Sent: Sun 2:43 PM
> From: GraceLee@pemberlybrown.edu
> Subject: (no subject)
>
> Thank you.

Warm tears trailed down my cheeks, and I marveled that I still had any left. After everything that had happened, after investigating each of Taylor's clues and hoping to get my best friend back, after picking up the pieces of my broken heart again and again, I sat and I cried.

I cried for Grace, and I cried for me. I even cried for Maddie. And when the tears finally stopped, I was able to read the email again.

On some level, I knew the words had to be Taylor's. But an image of the girl in the plaid skirt who had guided me over the past few weeks flashed in my mind. And just like that, the words became Grace's. One last message from the friend I'd lost forever.

I grabbed my favorite picture of Maddie, Grace, and me, tucked the frame into the inside pocket of my parka, and pulled the coat over my shoulders. Despite the thin layer of snow on the ground, I yanked my bike from inside the garage. I didn't feel like asking anyone for a ride, so I'd just have to hope the streets were clear enough to ride.

As I rode, the wind bit at my ears and made my eyes water. Luckily, I didn't have far to go. My wheels slid a little as I made my turn and even more when I went to brake, but at least I made it without falling down. I leaned my bike against one of the huge oak trees and walked through the fresh snow to Grace's grave.

In loving memory of Grace Elizabeth Lee, beloved daughter and friend. "Blessed are the pure in heart for they shall see God."

I ran my fingers over Grace's name and reached into my pocket for the frame. I set it down near fresh flowers and looked at the girl I used to be.

"I miss you, Grace. I'll always miss you." I whispered the words, for once not feeling stupid for talking to a ghost. After I'd wiped away most of my tears, I straightened and turned to leave.

But there stood Taylor. Her head was bent to give me privacy, and she tugged at the fingers of her gloves.

"Hey." My voice cracked coming out, and I realized that aside from crying, I hadn't said much of anything that day.

Taylor lifted her head and dropped her hands to her sides. "I told them the truth, you know." She clenched and unclenched her gloved fingers. "Detective Livingston, I mean. I told him about Alistair, the fire, everything. He wrote it all down and then thanked me and said sometimes accidents happen. That we have no control over some things. And he let me go home. That was it."

"What about Maddie?" I asked.

Taylor wiped beneath her nose.

"I heard they let her go too."

We stood for a second without much more to say, so I nodded my head and walked back to my bike.

"Um, Kate?" Taylor's voice shook a little bit. "I also wanted to give you this." She held out a creamy white envelope and turned around to go. When I pulled out the card inside, I saw the crest that had become all too familiar. The symbol for shared secrets, unity, maybe even second chances.

The artist had used maroon-colored wax to carefully etch the crest of the Sisterhood on the creamy card stock. I ran my fingers over the image. It was smooth. Perfect.

On the back, Taylor had printed "Better late than never."

"Wait," I called out. Taylor stopped but didn't turn around. "Thanks for the offer, but I'm not interested in pledging. Right now I need to figure things out on my own." I placed the card back in her gloved hand and walked back to my bike, still leaning against the tree where I had left it.

"Kate," she called. I turned around and met Taylor's clear eyes once again. They were glassy with unshed tears. "I'm sorry. About Grace, I mean." She adjusted the sleeves of her jacket. "It was never supposed to happen that way."

I stared down at the frozen ground, trying to steady my voice. "Yeah, I'm starting to understand that."

Taylor turned and walked toward the cemetery gate.

Life was never going to be the same without Grace. I stole one last glance at the three laughing girls in the photo and realized I would never be that girl again.

But I think I was finally ready to give this new Kate a chance. She deserved it.

Acknowledgments

When we set out to write books together we had no idea what we were getting into. Publishing is a tough business. But luckily it comes complete with some of the most amazing people we've (n)ever met.

To our incredible agent, Catherine Drayton, you saw promise in our work and never lost faith in us or in Kate. Thank you for telling us our original title was "wet," talking us off ledges, making us laugh, and cheering us on.

To our editors—Dan Ehrenhaft for giving us a chance, Kelly Barrales-Saylor and Leah Hultenschmidt for pushing us to make this book the best it can be. To Kristin Zelazko, production editor extraordinaire, who helped us walk the fine line between bad grammar and voice. To Mallory Kaster for contributing to hundreds of covers and finally finding one that is so totally Kate. Thank you to the entire team at Sourcebooks for believing in our work and putting up with our crazy ideas (we're looking at you, Paul Samuelson).

To all of our amazing writer friends—Loretta Nyhan, there is absolutely no way we could do this without you. Not only are you the original beta ninja, but you are an incredible friend. To Elana Johnson for reading our first draft and including us in all of your grand schemes. To Scott Tracey and Beth Revis for ripping into our millionth revision and pushing us even further. To Joanna Stampfel-Volpe for being one of the nicest, most supportive people in publishing and hooking us up with an incredible network of writers. To Katie Anderson, Sarah-Frances Hardy, and Jeanette Schneider for clicking onto our blog and into our lives. To all of our amazing blog readers, thank you for coming back every day and reading our randomness. Your comments are the highlight of our day. To the Hopefuls, the WriteOnCon team, the Elevensies, the Bookinistas, and our YA book club for helping us find our place in the writing community. And to Kiri for fixing our bastardized Latin. Apparently free online translators don't work. Good to know.

To Dianne Caywood, Tara McKendry, Sarah Berg, and Zack and Casie Markwell for reading our first doomed manuscript and "loving it." To Rick and Sarah Jackson and Erik Vaughan for being willing readers. And Alex, Emma, and Rachel, our first readers of the YA variety. To our grandma, Josephine Trinetti, for reading our blog every single day and saying enough novenas to land us a book deal. And Liz Stropki, our one-woman publicity team who never leaves home without our business card. To all of our friends and family, thank you for supporting our double lives as writers.

To our dad, Mike Roecker, for pushing us to write strong, female characters and to our mom, Joni "the Regulator" Roecker, for reading more book blogs than we do and keeping us abreast on all things publishing. To the third Roecker, Stacey Vaughan, for choosing to read our book, for acting as our personal graphic design slave, and for her unwavering love and support. To Ken and John for giving us the chance to live our dream. We're still not sure we'd be that supportive of one of your "hobbies." And finally, to Jack, Mia, Ben, and Lydia for not calling child services when we neglect you to write and for saying things like, "I want to write a pink book when I get older."

About the Authors

Photo courtesy of Michael Roecker

Lisa and Laura Roecker are sisters-turned-writing-partners with a love of all things Young Adult. Some call it arrested development, but the sisters claim it keeps them young. Plus, it's cheaper than Botox. Lisa and Laura live in Cleveland, Ohio, in separate residences. Their husbands wouldn't agree to a duplex. *The Liar Society* is their first novel. To learn more, check out www.lisaandlauraroecker.com.